W9-BUF-167

m Bre
Brett, Simon, author.
The strangling on the
stage

FEB 1 0 2014

THE STRANGLING ON THE STAGE

THE STRANGLING ON THE STAGE

A Fethering Mystery

Simon Brett

CRÈME de la CRIME

This first world edition published 2013
in Great Britain and 2014 in the USA by
Crème de la Crime, an imprint of
SEVERN HOUSE PUBLISHERS LTD of
19 Cedar Road, Sutton, Surrey, England, SM2 5DA.
Trade paperback edition first published
in Great Britain and the USA 2014 by
SEVERN HOUSE PUBLISHERS LTD

British Library Cataloguing in Publication Data

Brett, Simon author.
  The Strangling on the Stage. – (A Fethering mystery; 15)
  1. Seddon, Carole (Fictitious character)–Fiction. 2. Jude
  (Fictitious character : Brett)–Fiction. 3. Fethering
  (England: Imaginary place)–Fiction. 4. Women private
  investigators–England–Fiction. 5. Murder–
  Investigation–Fiction. 6. Shaw, Bernard, 1856-1950
  Devil's disciple–Fiction. 7. Hanging–Fiction.
  8. Detective and mystery stories.
  I. Title II. Series
  823.9'2-dc23

ISBN-13: 978-1-78029-056-0 (cased)
ISBN-13: 978-1-78029-542-8 (trade paper)

All Severn House titles are printed on acid-free paper.

Severn House Publishers support the Forest Stewardship Council™ [FSC™],
the leading international forest certification organisation. All our titles that
are printed on FSC certified paper carry the FSC logo.

MIX
Paper from
responsible sources
FSC
www.fsc.org   FSC® C013056

Typeset by Palimpsest Book Production Ltd.,
Falkirk, Stirlingshire, Scotland.
Printed and bound in Great Britain by
TJ International, Padstow, Cornwall.

To
Michael Green
(Author of *The Art of Coarse Acting*),
with admiration

ONE

'And the trouble is,' said Storm Lavelle, 'it's just total murder.'

'What is?' asked Jude.

'My life. Everything.'

Storm Lavelle was stretched out on the treatment table in the front room of Woodside Cottage in the seaside village of Fethering. It was February, cold outside, but snug with the open fire in Jude's front room. The scent of aromatic candles on the mantelpiece mingled with the smell of burning wood.

Storm had in theory come for a healing session, though Jude knew by experience she was basically there to unload the latest aggravations of her life. Which was fair enough. Jude also knew that listening was frequently as effective as any other form of healing.

The irony was that Storm Lavelle also practised as a healer, and she was the ultimate example of where the 'healer, heal thyself' principle broke down. Though very good with her clients, impressing them with her calm and stability, Storm was actually as mad as several container-loads of frogs. Her volatile personality ensured that she skittered from one alternative therapeutic cure-all to another. It was remarkable that she'd stuck with the healing, though it was now only as a practitioner rather than a patient. Storm had long since decided that healing was inadequate to her own needs, and embarked on courses of reflexology, kinesiology, homeopathy, naturopathy and any other 'ologies' or 'opathies' that came to her attention.

She had also dabbled in a wide range of leisure activities. Many of these were fitness-related. Within the previous couple of years Storm had, to Jude's knowledge, tried Aerobics, Aqua Aerobics, Padel Tennis, Pilates and Zumba. She had also taken up macramé, bird watching and bridge, and joined a choir.

None of this worried Jude or stood in the way of the two

women's friendship. Her attitude to her fellow human beings reflected a line that had once been quoted to her, the view of someone called Joe Ancis that 'the only normal people are the ones you don't know very well'. And beneath all Storm's traumas and dramas, Jude could recognize an honest, caring person whose only fault – if indeed it was a fault – was to get both too deeply and too shallowly involved with everything.

This applied particularly to Storm Lavelle's love life. As with alternative therapies, she also skittered from relationship to relationship. And in each one she made the same error, believing wholeheartedly that at last, after all of her past failures, she had found the perfect man on whom to lavish all of her affection. Invariably the men, frightened by the intensity of this passion, soon wanted to disengage. And Storm's heart would be broken once again.

It wasn't that she was unattractive, far from it. She was in her forties, some ten years younger than Jude, but unlike her friend, didn't carry a spare ounce of weight anywhere. This was partly due to the cocktail of diets and health fads that she followed, but the traumas of her frequent break-ups also played their part. She had innocent, pained blue eyes and was a natural blonde, though that original colour was very rarely in evidence. Storm was as fickle with new hairstyles as she was with everything else in her life.

That day her hair was cropped short and coloured a striking aubergine. She was dressed in black leggings and a sloppy yellow T-shirt. The precision of her make-up made her look almost like a geisha girl.

Jude sometimes wondered where her friend's name had come from. Surely no parents would actually christen a child 'Storm'? She wouldn't have been surprised to find out that in her younger years Storm had tried out as many names as she had other elements in her life. But she'd stayed with Storm Lavelle for the duration of their friendship.

Jude was giving her a basic relaxing massage, while the more important therapy of Storm unburdening herself continued. Storm would sometimes do a massage for Jude, so in these sessions no money ever changed hands. And whichever one was client or healer, it was still Storm who did most of the talking.

'I told you I'd split up with Paul, didn't I?'

'You didn't actually, but I'd kind of pieced it together from your manner.'

'What is it with men? One moment they're all over you like a rash, then suddenly they go all cold and start mumbling about "needing their own space".'

'Yes.' Jude paused, then decided to say it anyway. It wouldn't be the first time she'd raised the point. 'You don't think, do you, Storm, that it might be because you always go at relationships so full-on, you know, with all guns blazing? Maybe if you started a bit more casually . . .?'

'I can't be casual about love. I have to follow my heart. I knew when I met Paul that he was absolutely the one for me. And he said the same – he said he'd never met anyone like me.'

Jude reckoned that was probably true, but she didn't voice the thought.

'So how can someone be madly in love with you, saying he's having the best sex with you he's ever had, and then within a couple of weeks say he "needs his own space"?'

'If women knew the answer to that question, Storm, the relationship between the sexes might be considerably easier.'

'Yes. Do you think men are just differently wired from women?'

'If I did, I wouldn't be the first to have expressed that opinion. But I think there are more similarities than differences between the genders. Everyone, male or female, is afraid of having their personality swamped by another person.'

'And are you saying that's what I do, Jude? Swamp people's personalities?'

'I'm just saying that if you took a more gradual, a slower approach into relationships . . .'

'But I'm not a gradual person, I'm not a slow person. I have to obey my instincts.'

'Even if those instincts keep pushing you in the wrong direction?'

'What do you mean – "pushing me in the wrong direction"?'

'Well, look, Paul isn't the first man with whom your relationship has ended in much the same way.'

'How can you say that, Jude?'

'From simple observation. Do you want me to name names? Carl, George, Nick, Harry—'

'Those relationships were nothing like what I had with Paul. I knew from the start that Paul was the real thing.'

'I heard you say the same when you first met Carl . . . and George . . . and Nick . . . and—'

'No, I'm sure I never said that with them.'

It wasn't worth arguing the point, though Jude's recollections of Storm's announcement of each new man in her life were extremely accurate.

'Anyway,' Storm announced, as she had so many times before, 'I'm giving up men.'

'In favour of what?'

'Other things. I've wasted so much of my life agonizing over them, it's time I got on with the things that really interest me.'

'And what might they be?' asked Jude, wondering what new fad was about to be revealed.

'Acting,' Storm replied. 'I'm really going to concentrate on my acting.'

Now this was not as foolish an answer as Jude had been expecting. Storm Lavelle was actually rather good at acting. Perhaps the wide variety in her own emotional life had enabled her to see inside the characters of others. Or, then again, like many with a shaky sense of their own identity, maybe she found a security in playing a role, in being a different person.

Jude had been dragged along as support to a selection of West Sussex's church halls where her friend had been appearing with one or other of the local amateur dramatic societies. And though a few of the productions had been a bit ropey, Storm Lavelle had always shone in the not very glittering company. Acting was also a fad that she had stuck with. Whatever else was going on in her life, she was usually involved in rehearsal for some play or other. Jude, whose earlier career as a model had led to a year or two of acting, recognized genuine talent and was sure that her friend had it. Whether Storm also had the temperament and tenacity to pursue the theatre as a full-time career Jude was less certain.

Which prompted her next question. 'Do you mean concentrate on it exclusively? Make it your profession?'

'I wouldn't rule that out,' replied Storm, with a new confidence in her voice. 'I'm certainly going to take it more seriously, concentrate on getting better as an actor.' Jude was amused that the politically correct fashion of not using the word 'actress' had permeated the amateur section of the business.

'My quality is beginning to be recognized,' Storm went on. 'I'm being given better parts. I've just got a really good one with SADOS.'

She pronounced the acronym 'Say-doss', but Jude had to confess that the word meant nothing to her.

'SADOS,' said Storm, 'is the "Smalting Amateur Dramatic and Operatic Society".'

'Ah.'

'They've just held auditions for *The Devil's Disciple* and I've got the part of Judith Anderson.'

Jude had once again to admit ignorance. 'I've heard the title vaguely somewhere, but I'm afraid I don't know anything about it.'

Storm had clearly done her homework. 'It's one of George Bernard Shaw's earliest plays. Set during the American War of Independence. And it's about this bad American guy called Dick Dudgeon who's going to be hanged by the British because he's been mistaken for the good American pastor called Anthony Anderson . . .'

'Sounds a bit like *A Tale of Two Cities.*'

'I don't know that play, I'm afraid. But, anyway, Judith is Anthony Anderson's wife and she's really conflicted, because she hates Dick Dudgeon, but at the same time she's very drawn to him.' It didn't sound as if this summary was Storm's own, more as if she were quoting someone. 'And the play's also an attack on puritanism, and reiterates the common theme in Shaw of how people should stand up against convention if they think that convention's wrong. At least,' she concluded, 'that's what Neville thinks.'

'Who's Neville?'

'Neville Prideaux. He's playing General Burgoyne in *The Devil's Disciple*. He's actually quite important in SADOS. Particularly on the Play Selection Committee. He says Shaw's out of fashion, but he doesn't deserve to be. And he thinks that SADOS ought to do more challenging work, not just their usual safe diet of light comedies, Agatha Christies and episodes from television series.'

'Sorry? What do you mean – "episodes from television series"?'

'Oh, it's quite a popular thing now with amdrams. An evening of three episodes of something like *Fawlty Towers* or *Dad's Army*.'

'Yowch!' said Jude, as the ghastly image of local thespians doing their impressions of John Cleese and Arthur Lowe encroached on her imagination.

'Well, Neville says doing them is retrogressive.'

'I would agree with Neville on that.'

'But they are very popular with audiences.'

'Presumably because said audiences know every word of the script off by heart.'

'I think that could be part of it, yes. Anyway, Neville says that SADOS should make a stand against putting on that sort of stuff. He even thought last year's production of *Calendar Girls* was too lightweight. And that's a play about cancer.'

No, it's not, thought Jude. It's a play about women taking their tops off. She was constantly amazed by the British prurient attitude to nudity, which explained the disproportionate success of shows like *Calendar Girls*. It seemed that members of every amateur dramatic society in the country couldn't wait to get their wizened tits out.

But Storm was still continuing her encomium of Neville Prideaux. 'He says there's a wonderful archive of great plays which deserve revival much more than any trivial TV sitcom.'

The devoutness with which Storm was quoting the great Neville Prideaux made Jude wonder if, with Paul out of the way, he was about to be the next recipient of her all-embracing adoration.

She reached for a bottle on her mantelpiece. 'Just finish off the massage with some lavender essential oil. You happy with that?'

'Great,' said Storm, as Jude, with oil rubbed on to her hands, started kneading her friend's shoulders.

'And it's because of Neville's views that you're doing *The Devil's Disciple* – is that right?'

'Exactly. Neville says it would do the people of Smalting good to have their brains engaged by something they see in the theatre.'

'I'm sure it would.'

'Anyway, as I say, I'm delighted to have got the part of Judith Anderson. Though I say it myself, I knew I was the best person in the Society to play it, but I was still very nervous about the audition.'

'Why was that?'

Storm gave a conspiratorial wink. 'Oh, wheels within wheels. There's a lot of politics in SADOS. You see, there's this kind of diva called Elizaveta Dalrymple, who's the widow of Freddie Dalrymple, who's the guy who started the Society, and she's very much its social hub. Holds these little parties on Saturdays that she calls her "drinkies things" and if you're invited to one of those you really know you've arrived in SADOS. Anyway, Elizaveta is kind of used to getting all the major parts in the shows – even ones that she's far too old for. And she's very in with Davina Vere Smith, who's actually directing *The Devil's Disciple*, and with quite a lot of the older members. So I thought there was a real danger that Judith Anderson, who's meant to be – what, thirty? – well, that the part would go to Elizaveta Dalrymple, who's got to be seventy – and that's being generous.'

'But instead you triumphed?'

'Yes. Well, as I said, I was definitely the best person for the part.' In spite of the vagaries and vulnerabilities in other areas of her life, Storm Lavelle was very assured about her acting skills. And indeed it was when witnessing one of her performances that Jude had seen her friend at her most confident. Maybe getting into the professional theatre would be the resolution of Storm's personality problems. Not of course that getting into the professional theatre was an easy thing to be achieved by a woman in her forties.

'And have you actually started rehearsals for the play yet?'

'Read-through on Sunday. Open on the twelfth of May.'

'Wow! Three months' rehearsal. A lot of professional theatres would kill for that amount of time.'

'Maybe, but you forget that we aren't doing it full-time. Most of the cast have day jobs.'

'Yes, of course. I wasn't thinking.'

'So we rehearse Tuesday and Thursday evenings and Sunday afternoons.'

'And how many performances do you do?'

'Just the four. The twelfth of May's a Wednesday, and we go through to the Saturday. SADOS used to open on Tuesdays and throw in a Saturday matinee as well, but they can't get the audiences for that many performances now.'

'Ah.' Jude removed her hands from Storm's body and rubbed the oil off them with a towel. 'That's you done,' she said. 'Unknotted a few of the knots, I hope?'

'Great, as ever. Thank you, Jude.'

'My pleasure. I'm sure I'll soon be asking you to do the same for me. Anyway, good luck with the read-through on Sunday.'

'Yes, I'm a bit nervous about it. Excited too, but at the moment mainly nervous.'

'I'm sure you'll be fine.'

'Oh, I will . . . once the read-through actually starts. But, you see, the thing is . . . Ritchie Good's playing Dick Dudgeon.'

'Is he?' said Jude, though neither of the names meant anything to her. 'Should I know him?'

'Ritchie Good? Surely you've heard of him?'

'No.'

'Oh, he's a terrific actor. Everyone says he should have done it professionally. He's played star parts with lots of local groups – the Fedborough Thespians, the Clincham Players, the Worthing Rustics – Ritchie's acted with all of them. He even played Hamlet for the Rustington Barnstormers.'

'Did he?' said Jude, trying to sound appropriately impressed.

'He's really good. Somebody must have pulled out all the stops to get him for the SADOS. I suppose it might have been Davina, though I'd be surprised if she had the clout to persuade someone like Ritchie Good.'

'Davina?'

'Davina Vere Smith. She's the director. I said.'

'Yes, I'm sorry.'

'He's incredibly good-looking, Ritchie. Got quite a following in the amdram world.'

Jude wondered for a moment whether it would be this new paragon, Ritchie Good, rather than Neville Prideaux who was about to be the recipient of Storm Lavelle's full-on adoration.

Her friend was on the way to the door when she stopped and said, 'Ooh, one thing, Jude . . .'

'Yes.'

Storm looked around the cluttered room, whose furniture was all covered with rugs and throws. 'I just wondered if you'd still got . . .?'

A wry smile came to Jude's full lips as she said, 'You mean the chaise longue?'

'Yes.'

Jude moved across to remove a light-blue woollen blanket she'd bought in Morocco and reveal the article under discussion. The chaise longue had come from a little antique shop in Minchinhampton, picked up when she'd been on a trip to the Cotswolds with her second husband. It had been a stage of her life when Jude had been moving away from the husband and towards the idea of becoming a healer. She had thought the chaise longue might possibly do service as a treatment couch, but when she'd got it home she found it to be too low for such a purpose. She had hung on to it, though, and it had moved with her from address to address when other pieces of furniture had been abandoned.

She didn't know how old it was, and the antique dealer who sold the thing to her had been pretty vague on the subject. 'Mid to late Victorian, possibly Edwardian' was as specific as he had got. The base, he said, 'might be mahogany', though Jude thought it was probably a cheaper wood stained to look like mahogany. The upholstery, he felt sure, was not original, but Jude had become quite fond over the years of the purplish flowered print, even though it was usually covered with the Moorish drape. She liked using the chaise longue in the winter months, moving it near the fire, making sure she had an adequate supply of tea, crumpets and books before snuggling under the cover.

Many chaises longues have a supporting arm along one side, but Jude's didn't. And this had proved of great benefit in its life outside Woodside Cottage.

Because her chaise longue was a much borrowed piece of furniture. And it was always borrowed by the same kind of people – amateur dramatic groups. A chaise longue was so versatile. Any play set in any historical period looked better with a chaise longue as part of its setting. And Jude's armless chaise longue was much loved by directors, because they could set it facing the audience on either the right- or the left-hand side of the stage.

Not even counting the times it had been borrowed before, since Jude came to Fethering her chaise longue had featured in most of the church halls of the area in a variety of thespian endeavours. It had been a shoo-in for a part in *Robert and Elizabeth*, the musical about the poet Browning and his wife, and appeared in more than one stage version of *Pride and Prejudice*. Jude's chaise longue had also taken the stage in *The Winslow Boy*, *Arsenic and Old Lace* (twice) and virtually the entire *oeuvre* of Oscar Wilde. It had even, tarted up in gold foil, provided a suitable surface for the Egyptian queen to be poisoned on by an asp in *Antony and Cleopatra*.

And now, Jude intuited, it might be about to make an appearance in George Bernard Shaw's *The Devil's Disciple*.

So it proved. Storm wondered tentatively whether it might be possible for the SADOS to impose on Jude's generosity to borrow . . .? The permission was readily given. Jude's sitting room also contained a sofa which could be moved near the fire for the tea, crumpet and book routine, so the chaise longue would not be missed. The only questions really were when would it be needed, and how should it be got to where it needed to be got to.

The answer to the first was as soon as possible, because when Davina Vere Smith was directing she liked to use all the furniture and props right from the beginning of rehearsals. And the chaise longue needed to be got to St Mary's Church Hall in Smalting. Once in situ it could stay there because there was a storeroom the SADOS were allowed to use for their props and things. In fact, they were lucky enough to be able to hold most of their rehearsals in the Hall, which was of course where the performances would take place in May.

'That's very convenient for you,' said Jude. 'So what, will someone come and pick the chaise longue up from here?'

'Yes, that would be good, wouldn't it?' Storm agreed. 'Trouble is, I've only got my Smart car and it'd never fit in there. And Gordon – that's Gordon Blaine, who's in charge of all the backstage stuff for SADOS – well, normally he'd pick it up, but his Land Rover's got some problem that he's busy repairing at the moment and . . . You can't think of any way of getting it to St Mary's Hall, can you, Jude?'

'Well, I don't have a car myself.'

'Of no, of course you don't. Sorry, I'd forgotten. But you haven't got a friend, have you? A friend you could ask to . . .?'

'Yes.' A smile played round Jude's lips. 'Yes, there is someone I could ask.'

TWO

'I've never had any time for amateur dramatics,' announced Carole Seddon. 'Or indeed for the people who indulge in them.'

'I'm not asking you to indulge in anything,' said Jude patiently. 'I'm just asking you to help me deliver a chaise longue.'

'Hm.'

'It's only in Smalting. Early evening Sunday. The whole operation will take maybe an hour of your time.'

Carole looked dubiously at the uncovered chaise longue. 'I'm not sure that'll fit in the Renault.'

'Of course it will. If you put the back seats down.'

'I don't know. It's quite long.'

'That's possibly why it's called a chaise longue.'

'Oh, very funny, Jude,' said Carole without a hint of a smile.

'I happen to know that it will fit in the back of the Renault. It has had such a peripatetic life since I bought it that it has on occasions fitted into the back of virtually every vehicle that's ever been invented – except a Smart car, which would be a squeeze too far. But if you'd rather not do it, just say and I'll get someone else to—'

'Oh, I didn't say I'd rather not do it.' This was classic Carole Seddon. Jude knew her neighbour very well and was used to the obscure processes that had to be gone through in making arrangements with her. Carole may have disapproved of amateur dramatics, but she still had a very strong sense of curiosity. So long as she was accompanied by Jude, the opportunity of invading the stronghold of the Smalting Amateur Dramatic and Operatic Society was not one that she would readily forego. She'd never actually met any amateur thespians. If she were to meet some, they might well provide justification for her prejudice against them.

'So you will do it?'

Carole let out a long-suffering sigh. 'Oh, very well.' Having made that concession, she now deigned to show a faint interest in the SADOS. 'What play is your chaise longue going to feature in?'

'*The Devil's Disciple.*'

'Doesn't mean anything to me.'

'George Bernard Shaw.' Carole's grimace didn't need the support of words. 'Not your favourite, do I detect?'

'I once spent a very long time sitting through *Heartbreak House.* I've known shorter fortnights.'

'Yes, he can be a bit of an old windbag. But there are still some good plays. *Pygmalion, Major Barbara, Saint Joan . . .* they still just about stand up.'

'I'll take your word for it. And what about *The Devil's Disciple* – does that still stand up?'

Jude shook her head. 'Haven't seen it. Never actually heard the title until Storm mentioned it.'

Carole could not restrain herself from saying, 'Is your friend really called "Storm"?'

'Whether she was actually christened it, I don't know. But "Storm" is the name by which she's known.'

'Oh dear. Well, I suppose it goes with the amateur dramatics.'

'Yes,' agreed Jude, suppressing a giggle at the Caroleness of Carole.

'And will the good burghers of Smalting really come out in their thousands to see a minor work of George Bernard Shaw?'

'That,' said Jude, 'remains to be seen. But it doesn't matter a lot to us, because our only involvement in the production will be delivering a chaise longue.'

Little did she realize how wrong that assertion would prove to be.

Following Storm's instructions, relayed by Jude, Carole nosed the Renault into the car park by the church, within walking distance of a fairly new Sainsbury's Local.

The hall next to St Mary's in Smalting was a clone of thousands of other church halls throughout the country. Built in stout red brick towards the end of Victoria's reign, it had over the years hosted innumerable public lectures, wedding receptions, jumble sales, beetle drives, children's parties, Women's Institute coffee mornings and other local events. More recently its space had also accommodated, according to shifting fitness fashions, classes in Aerobics, Swing Aerobics, Pilates and Zumba. The hall, as Carole and Jude had cause to know from the time when they were investigating the discovery of some bones under a beach hut in Smalting, was also the regular venue for the Quiz Nights of the Smalting Beach Hut Association.

Like others of its kind, St Mary's Hall had been in a constant process of refurbishment, though it was never refurbished quite as well as it should have been. The most recent painting of the doors and windows in oxblood red had not been enough to counter the institutional feeling of its cream walls. And nothing seemed to remove the hall's slightly shabby aura or its enduring primary school smell of dampness, disinfectant and dubious drainage.

Storm's instructions to Jude had been exact. If they arrived at six, the read-through of *The Devil's Disciple* would definitely be over by then. And so it proved. The two women had manhandled the chaise longue out of the Renault, but once they were inside the hall, they were encumbered with help. Storm came swanning across to greet them with a shriek of 'Jude, *darling*!', which made Carole's face look even stonier. For the read-through Storm's hair had undergone another transformation. It was now black, centrally parted and with little curls rather in the manner of Betty Boop. She scattered introductions over Carole and Jude like confetti, far too quickly for the information to be taken in, and organized a couple of men to take the chaise longue into the storeroom.

'Can't thank you enough, Jude darling. We will look after it very well, I promise.'

'I'm sure you will.'

'And now, look, since we've finished the read-through, we were all just about to adjourn to the pub. You will join us, won't you?'

'Well, I don't think—'

Cutting across Carole's words and ignoring the semaphore in her expression, Jude replied, 'Yes, we'd love to.'

They only knew one pub in Smalting, the Crab, and that wasn't really a pub. It was far too poshed-up to be the kind of place that a local could drop in for a pint. It was almost exclusively a restaurant, and the tiny bar area was designed only for people sipping a pre-prandial aperitif.

But fortunately it wasn't the Crab that Storm Lavelle led them to. Almost adjacent to St Mary's Church was a pub called the Cricketers (though why it was called that nobody had ever thought to ask – it was miles from the nearest cricket ground), and it was clear as soon as they walked in that the SADOS members were familiar guests. And welcome guests. The landlord, a perky, bird-like man called Len, seemed to know most of the amateur actors by name. Given the declining numbers of visitors to pubs, the Cricketers was glad of any group who would fall in regularly after rehearsals on a Tuesday, Thursday and Sunday.

Early that particular Sunday evening the amdram crowd seemed to account for most of the pub's clientele. Or maybe, just because they all talked so loudly and flamboyantly, they gave the impression of having taken over the place.

Carole Seddon felt extremely old-fashioned. She hadn't wanted to come to the pub and now she was there all she wanted was to be back in her neat little house, High Tor. Also, although she would never admit to being 'a slave to the television schedules', there was a programme on Sunday nights that she didn't like to miss. About midwives, it combined the unrivalled ingredients of contractions and nuns. Carole sneaked a look at her watch. Only twenty past six. Too early to use the show as an excuse for an early departure. Not of course that she'd ever have revealed the real reason why she wanted to get back.

Jude had moved forward to the bar and just ordered two large glasses of Chilean Chardonnay when she was intercepted by a large man with a ginger beard, whom they'd been vaguely aware of overseeing the transfer of the chaise longue to the storeroom.

'Let me get those,' he said in a voice with a trace of Scottish in it. 'A small thank you to you for sacrificing your furniture to our tender mercies and bringing it over here.'

He thrust a twenty-pound note at the barman and the two women thought they were justified in accepting his generosity. He turned to a young woman also queuing at the bar. 'Let me get you one too, Janie.'

'Oh, you're always buying me drinks.'

'And it's always my pleasure. What're you having?'

'Vodka and coke, please.'

'Your wish is my command. Add a vodka and coke, Len.' The barman nodded. 'And a predictable pint of Guinness for me, please.'

While the bearded man was getting their drinks, the girl introduced herself as 'Janie Trotman'. She was slender, dark, quite pretty, dressed in shiny leggings and a purple hoodie. 'I'm playing Essie,' she volunteered.

'Sorry. I don't know the play,' said Jude.

'It's the only young female part, so I suppose I'm lucky to get it.'

'You don't sound too sure about that.'

'Well, I'm certainly not sure about the play. Having just sat through the read-through, it all seems a bit long-winded to me.'

At that moment a short, dumpy woman with improbably red hair bustled across to them. 'Hello, you two look new,' she said to Carole and Jude. 'I'm Mimi Lassiter, Membership Secretary. Also part of the crowd in Act Three, you know, one of the Westerbridge townsfolk.'

'Nice to meet you. I'm Jude. And this is my friend Carole.'

'Ah, good evening. We've got quite a lot of new members in for *The Devil's Disciple*, because it's such a big cast, though Davina has cut the numbers down a bit. And I'm just going round, checking with the newcomers that they are actually members of SADOS. Now I know you're fully paid up, Janie.' The girl nodded. 'The subscription rate for acting members is—'

'Let me stop you there,' said Jude. 'We're nothing to do with the production.'

'No, we certainly aren't,' Carole endorsed.

'Oh?'

'We've just been bearers of a chaise longue which I'm lending to be part of the set.'

Mimi Lassiter looked seriously disappointed. 'So you're not even in the crowd scenes?'

Jude assured her that they weren't.

'And does that mean,' asked Mimi almost pathetically, 'that you don't want to join SADOS?'

'Certainly not,' replied Carole, as if she'd just been asked to do something very dirty indeed.

'Oh.' Discomfited, the Membership Secretary drifted away.

By now the bearded man had got their drinks which he handed round with old-fashioned gallantry. He introduced himself to Carole and Jude as 'Gordon Blaine – I'm in charge of the heavy backstage stuff for the SADOS – building sets, that kind of thing.'

'Oh yes, Storm mentioned you,' said Jude. 'Your Land Rover's broken down.'

He looked a little affronted by that. 'It's more in a process of refurbishment. I'm putting in a new engine. Haven't quite finished yet. So thanks for the use of your car.'

'It's my car actually,' said Carole tartly.

'Sorry. Then thank *you*,' he said without rancour.

Jude noticed that Janie Trotman was kind of lingering on the edge of their group, as if she wouldn't mind getting away. But maybe she thought, having accepted a drink from Gordon Blaine, she must stay with him for at least a little while.

'Sorry,' he was saying, 'didn't get your names.'

They identified themselves and Jude, to compensate for Carole's frostiness, asked, 'So, Gordon, will you be building the set for *The Devil's Disciple*?'

'Oh yes.'

'And designing it too?'

'No, no. I'm not given the name of "designer",' he replied with careful emphasis. 'Lady over there is "the designer".' He gestured to a thin woman in her thirties, whose short blond hair was dyed almost white. 'I merely interpret the squiggles she puts on the page and turn them into a practical set which won't fall over. And from all accounts, *Disciple* is going to be a real bugger to build.'

'Oh?' said Jude. 'Why? I'm afraid I haven't read the play.'

'Nor have I,' said Gordon with something approaching pride. 'I only arrived at the end of the read-through. I never read the plays we do. Just do as I'm told and get on with whatever I'm instructed to do by the director and the designer.'

'So why is *The Devil's Disciple* going to be such a bugger?' asked Jude, not feeling she was sufficiently part of the SADOS to abbreviate the play's title to '*Disciple*'.

'Well, apparently it's got lots of sets. There's the Dudgeons' house and then the Andersons' house . . . which aren't too bad because you can use one basic structure and differentiate the two locations by a bit of set dressing. But then in Act Three there's also the inside of the Town Hall and the outside of the Town Square where the scaffold is set up. Logistical nightmare.'

'So how are you going to manage it?'

'Don't worry, I'll manage it,' he replied with almost smug confidence. Jude had readily identified Gordon Blaine's type. He was the kind of man who would build up the difficulties of any task he was given and then apply his miraculous practical skills to succeed in delivering the impossible. In her brief contact with the professional theatre, she had met a good few characters like that, mostly involved in some backstage capacity.

'I think the only way it can be done,' Gordon went on, 'whatever fancy ideas the designer may have, is for me to build a basic box-set structure and then—'

He might clearly have gone on for quite a while had they not been interrupted by the appearance of Storm Lavelle, bringing in her wake a tall, good-looking man in his forties. His long hair flopped apologetically over his brow, and there was an expression of mock-innocence in his blue eyes.

Seeing the man approach, Janie Trotman took the opportunity to detach herself from the group round Gordon Blaine and go to join some of the younger members of the company. Whether this was a pointed avoidance of the newcomer neither Carole nor Jude could not judge.

'Jude!' Storm emoted, loud against the background hubbub. 'I really do want you to meet Ritchie.'

'You haven't properly met my friend Carole who—'

But the introduction was lost as Ritchie Good – it must have been him, there couldn't be two Ritchies in SADOS – took Jude's hand in both of his and said, 'Where have you been hiding all my life?'

It was one of the corniest lines in the world, but she admired the way it was delivered. He imbued the words with a sardonic quality, at the same time sending up their cheesiness and leaving the small possibility that they could be heartfelt.

'I've been hiding all over the place,' Jude replied evenly. 'Currently in Fethering.'

'Oh, lovely Fethering, where the Fether rolls down to the sea,' he said, for no very good reason.

'Ritchie's our Dick Dudgeon,' said Storm enthusiastically. 'He's just done a terrific read-through.'

'Well, you were no slouch yourself, Storm. It's only possible to give a good performance when you're up against other good actors.'

Jude was amused by the solipsism of the compliment. While apparently praising his co-star, he was also putting himself firmly in the category of 'good actors'.

'Well, I thought you were wonderful,' Storm insisted. 'You really *were* Dick Dudgeon. I was nearly tearing up in the last act.'

'Oh,' Ritchie said airily, 'I was just demonstrating a few shabby, manipulative tricks. My performance will get a lot more subtle as we go through the rehearsal process.'

'I'm sure it will,' said Storm devoutly.

Oh dear, thought Jude. She had seen the symptoms in her friend before. It looked as though Ritchie Good was in serious danger of receiving the full impact of Storm Lavelle's adoration. And Jude didn't think it was an encounter that would have a happy outcome.

'Oh, look, there's Elizaveta,' said Ritchie, waving across the bar. 'Must go and say hello to her.'

Storm took Jude's arm. 'You must come and meet Elizaveta too. She is just *so* funny.'

And the three of them swept away. Leaving Carole with Gordon Blaine.

Her nose, susceptible to frequent dislocation, was once again put out of joint. She was taken back to the agony of school dances, where her prettier friends had all been very friendly to her until they'd been swept away by the handsome boys. And she'd been left either pretending that the last thing on her mind was dancing, or stuck with one of the nerdy ones. Like Gordon Blaine.

'There's a little trick I used,' he was saying, 'when I was building the *Midsummer Night's Dream* set for the SADOS. Obvious, but it was surprising how few people thought of it. You see, by hingeing the flats at the back so that they could open up to reveal the cyclorama, and using gauzes for the scenes in the woods, I . . .'

Carole Seddon's eyes glazed over.

THREE

'So I said to the director: "Do you want me to do it *your way*, or do you want me to do it *right*?"'

This was a cue for sycophantic laughter from the group around Elizaveta Dalrymple. Jude had heard the line before – it had been attributed to various Hollywood stars – but clearly the *grand dame* of the SADOS was presenting it as her own coining.

Elizaveta Dalrymple must have been a very beautiful young woman and in her seventies she was still striking. She wore a kaftan-style long dress in fig-coloured linen, which disguised her considerable bulk. Her dyed black hair was swept back from her face and fixed by a comb with a large red artificial flower on it, suggesting the image of a flamenco dancer. Her make-up was skilfully done, though it could not cover the lines on her face – bright red lips and lashes far too luxuriant to have grown out of any human eyelid.

The manner in which she had spoken her line suggested that she had spent rather too much time watching Maggie Smith.

Storm took the natural break given by the laugh as an opportunity to introduce Jude.

'Ah, I didn't notice you at the read-through.' Elizaveta Dalrymple gave the impression that there were a lot of people she didn't regard as worth noticing. 'Presumably you're doing something backstage, are you?'

'No, I'm not involved in the production at all. Just lending my chaise longue for the set.'

'Ah, chaises longues,' said Elizaveta in a voice intended to be thrilling. 'How much fun one has had on chaises longues. A long time ago, of course.' She chuckled fondly. 'And a lot of it actually with Freddie.' She allowed a moment for murmurs of appreciation for SADOS's late founder. 'Who was it who said: "Marriage is the longing for the deep, deep peace of the double-bed after the hurly-burly of the chaise longue?"'

Jude said, 'Mrs Patrick Campbell', because it was something she happened to know, but the pique in Elizaveta Dalrymple's face suggested her question had been rhetorical and not one to be answered by mere chaise longue owners.

To reinforce her disapproval, she turned away from Jude to Storm. 'I thought you did a lovely little reading this afternoon as Judith. And the American accent will come with practice.'

Rather than bridling at being so patronized, Storm smiled meekly, saying, 'Thank you very much, Elizaveta. And your Mrs Dudgeon was wonderful.'

'Yes, it's something when an actor like me ends up playing a grumpy old woman who dies offstage during Act Two.' The grande dame smiled. 'I'm thinking of it as a character part.' That got a laugh from her coterie of admirers. 'I really wasn't going to do it. I really do keep intending to give up "the business".' You're just an amateur, Jude wanted to scream, acting is not your profession. 'But Davina twisted my arm *once again.*'

Elizaveta Dalrymple turned an expression of mock ruefulness to a dumpy woman with a long blond pigtail, who was dressed in black leggings and a high-collared gold lamé top. This, Jude remembered from the flurry of introductions when she'd joined the group, was Davina Vere Smith.

'Oh, you were dying to do it, Elizaveta,' protested the director of *The Devil's Disciple*. 'There was nothing going to keep you away from this production, away from anything that SADOS does.'

'Don't you believe it, Davina. I really do think there has to come a time when one has to retire gracefully. And I think I've reached that time.' The coterie protested violently at this suggestion. 'I'd rather go at a time of my own choosing than get to the point where I can no longer remember the lines and the old acting skills start to dwindle.'

'That day'll never come,' insisted the most toadyish of the coterie, a young man who had been introduced as Olly Pinto. He was nearly very good-looking, but the size of his shield-like jaw gave him a cartoonish quality. 'Your reading this afternoon showed that you're still at the height of your powers.'

'Oh . . .' Elizaveta Dalrymple simpered at the compliment.

'And yours was lovely too, Olly. Your Christy's going to be great.'

The young man grimaced. 'It's not much of a part,' he said.

'There are no small parts,' said Elizaveta magisterially, 'only small actors.'

Again she made it sound as if the line was her own, though Jude knew it had been around for years, usually attributed to Stanislavsky. Again Elizaveta Dalrymple received a laugh of approbation from her coterie.

'Well, I think you're going to show that Mrs Dudgeon is far from a small part,' said Olly Pinto, still sucking up.

'I suppose if I can still do something to help out SADOS . . . it's what Freddie would have wanted me to do.' Elizaveta Dalrymple left a silence for a few more respectful grunts. Then she turned to the director. 'Were you pleased with the way the read-through went this afternoon, Davina?'

'Yes, pretty good, really. Obviously a few absentees. Three of my soldiers have got flu and my Major Swindon is still off skiing. I suppose, like most amateur productions, I'll be lucky if I get the full company on the first night.'

Elizaveta Dalrymple clearly thought she had been silent for too long. 'I'm determined to have *fun* playing Mrs Dudgeon. And it'll be nice to give my old American accent a little run for its money.'

'It's very good,' said her toady. 'Did you ever live in the States?'

'Good heavens, no,' said Elizaveta on a self-deprecating laugh. 'But I always have had a very good ear. I'm just one of those lucky people who can pick up accents . . . like that.' Her eye lingered pityingly on Storm Lavelle. 'Of course, there was a time when I'd have been natural casting for Judith Anderson, but those days are gone . . .'

Jude couldn't understand why her friend didn't knock the malevolent old woman's block off, but Storm was still listening intently, as though at the feet of a guru. And when Elizaveta said she would invite Storm to one of her 'drinkies things', Jude's friend looked as if she'd just been made a Dame.

'Of course,' Elizaveta Dalrymple went on, 'my American accent was really given a workout when Freddie and I did *On*

Golden Pond. I remember there was someone from Boston in the audience, and he couldn't believe that I hadn't been brought up in the States. He said he'd never heard—'

But her reminiscences were interrupted by the appearance of Len, the Cricketers' landlord, at the edge of their group. 'Department of Lost Property,' he said, and he held out a star-shaped silver pendant on a silver chain. 'I think it got left here during the pantomime. Someone must've dropped it. So I thought I'd wait till you all came back and see if anyone claims it. Somebody said it might be yours, Elizaveta.'

'Well, yes, I do have one that looks very like that. May I have a look?' The barman handed the necklace across. Elizaveta Dalrymple turned it over to look at the back. 'Yes, this must be mine. It's funny, I hadn't noticed . . .' She reached up to her neck to find a silver chain around it. She pulled at it and out of the top of her kaftan dress came a silver star, similar in size to the other one. 'Oh no, I've got mine.'

She offered Len's pendant round to her group. 'Anyone claim this? It's not yours, is it, Davina?'

'No,' said the director. 'I don't wear jewellery like that.'

Elizaveta Dalrymple made an elaborate shrug and handed the unclaimed pendant back to Len. 'Be worth asking round the other SADOS members.'

'Yes. And could you mention it at rehearsal?'

'Certainly.'

'I'll keep it behind the bar till someone claims it.' And the landlord drifted away, ready to offer the necklace to other groups.

'Let me know if anyone does claim it,' Elizaveta called after him. Then she turned back to her coterie. 'A rather amusing story about jewellery came out of the production of *When We Are Married* that Freddie and I did. You see, there was someone in the cast who—'

But she was cut off in mid-anecdote by the appearance in their little group of a tall, balding man dressed in black jeans, black shirt and a black leather blouson. In his wake came a pretty but nervous-looking red-haired woman in her forties wearing grey leggings under a heavy off-white jumper.

'Elizaveta,' said the man. 'Lovely reading, as ever. You too, Storm, great stuff.'

'I am duly honoured.' Freddie Dalrymple's widow made a little mock-curtsey. 'To have a compliment from the great George Bernard Shaw expert.'

Jude had recognized the man from Storm's description before introductions were made, and he did indeed prove to be Neville Prideaux.

The woman identified herself as 'Hester Winstone'. She had a glass of orange juice, Neville was drinking red wine.

'And what part are you playing in *The Devil's Disciple*?' asked Jude.

'Oh, nothing,' the woman replied dismissively. 'I'm not important. I'm just the prompter.'

'I've seen amateur productions where the prompter has been *extremely* important. In fact, sometimes I've heard more of the prompter than I have of the actors.'

'Well, that's not the kind of production you'll ever see from SADOS,' said Elizaveta cuttingly.

Jude felt suitably reprimanded. She grinned at Hester Winstone and was rewarded by a little flicker of a smile. But the prompter seemed ill at ease, not quite included in the circle of thespians, but still for some reason needing to be there.

At the arrival of the newcomers, Jude noted that Ritchie Good had detached himself from the circle around Elizaveta Dalrymple and drifted off to chat to another group. She wondered if she was witnessing some masculine territorial ritual. Had Neville Prideaux's appearance threatened Ritchie Good's position as alpha male?

'Well,' Neville said, 'I hope this afternoon's reading has convinced everyone I was right to champion *The Devil's Disciple* . . . against considerable opposition.'

The way he looked at Elizaveta Dalrymple as he said this suggested that at least some of that opposition had come from her.

'Oh yes,' she said, 'I think SADOS will probably get away with it.'

'We'll do more than get away with it. It's a very fine play.'

Elizaveta twisted her mouth into a little moue of disagreement.

'I can't help remembering that Freddie always described Shaw as "a left-wing windbag".' Her coterie awarded this a little titter.

'But,' Neville objected, 'we agreed at the Play Selection Committee Meeting that SADOS ought to be doing more challenging work.'

'I'm not arguing with that, Neville love. When Freddie founded the Society, he was determined that we should present material that was "at the forefront of contemporary theatre".'

'And yet it ended up, like every other amdram in the country, doing the usual round of light West End comedies and Agatha Christies.'

'No, I don't think that's fair, Neville.' Clearly nothing that contained the mildest criticism of the hallowed Freddie Dalrymple was fair. Jude also got the impression that Neville and Elizaveta were reanimating an argument which they had visited many times before. 'We have done some very contemporary material,' Elizaveta went on. 'When we did *Shirley Valentine*, that was quite ground-breaking for Smalting – I mean, doing a play based in Liverpool.'

And also one with a socking great part for you in it, thought Jude. The idea of Elizaveta Dalrymple using her 'very good ear' for accents to tackle Scouse was engagingly incongruous.

'I also still think,' the grande dame continued, 'that this time round we should have done *Driving Miss Daisy*.'

And who might have played Miss Daisy? Jude asked herself.

'I mean, that's a play that really tackles serious issues.'

'So does *The Devil's Disciple*,' insisted Neville Prideaux.

'But *Driving Miss Daisy*'s about racial prejudice – anti-Semitism, colour prejudice.'

'Whereas *The Devil's Disciple* is about nothing less than the conflict between Good and Evil. It's also about honour and honesty and bravery and religion and the entire business of being a human being. Anyway, Elizaveta, the other big argument against doing *Driving Miss Daisy* is: where on earth are you going to find a black man in Smalting to play the chauffeur?'

Jude had been aware for a while that Hester Winstone had

been trying to attract Neville's attention, and at this moment she interrupted the argument. Looking at her watch, she said, 'Sorry, Neville, I've got to be going.'

'Fine,' he said, without even looking at her. 'See you at the next rehearsal.'

The prompter detached herself from the group. She still looked nervous and unhappy. The next time Jude looked, Hester Winstone was no longer in the pub.

'Well, anyway,' said Elizaveta Dalrymple, as if putting an end to the topic, '*The Devil's Disciple* is the play we're doing and I'm sure the production will be well up to SADOS's high standards.' She vouchsafed a smile to Davina Vere Smith, as if bestowing her blessing on the enterprise. 'I just wonder, though, how many people in Smalting will want to buy tickets . . .?'

'. . . and, you see,' Gordon Blaine was still going on to Carole, 'I've worked out a rather cunning way of doing the gallows at the end of the play.'

She looked in desperation around the bar, but saw no prospects of imminent rescue. Jude was still in the middle of the group around the melodramatic old woman with dyed black hair. Ritchie Good, the tall man who had chatted up Jude, was by the pub door in whispered conversation with a red-haired woman who looked as if she was about to leave.

There was no escape as Gordon continued, 'It's important that it looks authentic, but it's also important that the structure would pass a Health and Safety inspection. And Dick Dudgeon has to have the noose actually around his neck so it looks like he's really about to be hanged, so what I'm going to do is to have a break in the noose where the two ends are only joined by Velcro and then the—'

'Oh God,' said a languid approaching voice, 'is Gordon boring you with his technical wizardry?'

The words so exactly mirrored Carole Seddon's thoughts that she couldn't help smiling at their speaker. Even though it was Ritchie Good.

'Carole was actually very interested in what I was saying,' said Gordon Blaine defensively.

'Yes, yes, it was fascinating,' she lied.

'Anyway, I've got things to get on with.' And with that huffy farewell, Gordon moved away from them.

'Looked like you needed rescuing,' said Ritchie.

'Thank you very much.'

'And sorry, in all those introductions I didn't get your name . . .?'

'Carole.'

'Ah. Right.' It never occurred to him that she hadn't taken in his name. 'So . . .' He took Carole's hand in both of his and said, 'Where have you been hiding all my life?'

FOUR

Having not wanted to go to the Cricketers in the first place, Carole found that an hour and a quarter had passed before she finally managed to extricate Jude and leave the place. Their departure was now quite urgent. In little more than half an hour Carole's saga of convents and placentas would be starting.

The St Mary's Hall car park was in darkness as they came out of the pub, but when they crossed the beam of a sensor an overhead light came on. In spite of the time pressure of her television programme, Carole characteristically said she must put up the back seats of the Renault before they set off. Anything out of place disturbed her, and the car must be returned to its customary configuration. Carole was the kind of woman who had a tendency to clear away her guests' dinner plates almost before they'd finished eating.

While she repositioned the back seats Jude stood waiting. It was a mild evening for February, the first that offered some prospect of spring eventually arriving. She looked around the car park. The range of Mercedes, BMWs and Audis suggested that the members of SADOS didn't have too much to worry about financially.

Out of the corner of her eye Jude caught sight of a movement behind the windscreen of a BMW quite nearby. Looking closer, she recognized the face of Hester Winstone, the *Devil's Disciple*'s prompter.

And the overhead light caught the shine of tears on the woman's cheeks.

Instinctive compassion took Jude towards the car. The closer she got the more sense she had of something being seriously wrong. Hester was slumped a little sideways in the driver's seat and her eyes were closed. Peacefully closed, as though she were asleep.

Jude had no hesitation in snatching open the car door. As she did so, the prompter's arm flopped to the side of her seat.

And from her wrist bright red blood dripped on to the surface of the car park.

FIVE

'I still think we should call the police,' muttered Carole. 'Or at least send for an ambulance.'

'Hester specifically asked me not to,' Jude whispered back. They were in the sitting room of Woodside Cottage and the subject of their conversation had just gone upstairs to the loo.

'Yes, but she's not rational. People who try to kill themselves are by definition not rational.'

'It wasn't a very serious attempt to kill herself. Those nail scissors couldn't have done much damage. The cuts are only surface scratches.'

'Maybe they are this time, but people who do that kind of thing are very likely to try again. Someone in authority should be informed.'

'Carole, I'd rather just talk to Hester for a while, find out what her state of mind really is.'

'Not great, if she's trying to top herself,' said Carole shortly.

'Please. I'd just like to talk to her.'

Jude's words only added to Carole's sense of pique. 'I'd

just like to talk to her.' Nothing on the lines of 'We should talk to her.' Not for the first time that evening, Carole felt excluded. She'd been stuck at the Cricketers with the world's most boring man, Gordon Blaine, while Jude went off with a bunch of people who had, by definition, to be more interesting. Then in the car park her neighbour had overruled her about getting someone from SADOS to look after Hester Winstone. It had also been against Carole's advice that Jude had driven Hester back to Woodside Cottage in the BMW.

To compound these multiple affronts, the business of doing a temporary bandaging job on the would-be suicide in the car park meant that Carole had missed at least half of her chronicle of wimples and waters breaking.

'Very well,' she said huffily to Jude. 'Well, I must go. I've got things to do.'

'The children are off at boarding school,' said Hester Winstone, 'and my husband's away at the moment.'

'Where?' asked Jude.

'He's on a cricket tour in New Zealand.' Jude didn't take much of an interest in the game, but she knew that there seemed to be Test Matches happening somewhere every day right around the world.

'What, watching cricket?'

'No, playing.'

'Really?' That was a surprise. Assuming that Hester Winstone was in her late forties, then her husband might be expected to be the same age or a little older. And though Jude knew that some men continued to play cricket into their fifties and sixties, she didn't expect many to be involved in international tours.

Hester seemed to sense her need for explanation. 'It's a group of them, a kind of ad hoc team called the Subversives. One of the blokes works in the travel industry and he sets up the tours. They've been doing it for years. Some of the players are pushing seventy.'

'How long do the tours last?'

'Oh, never more than a month. Mike will be back next Friday.'

Hester Winstone seemed remarkably together and business-like for a woman who had within the last two hours slit her wrists. Jude recognized that she was embarrassed and trying to talk about anything except the reason why she had ended up in Woodside Cottage.

'And have you been involved with SADOS for long?'

'Oh no. *Disciple* is the first show I've done with them. No, I just thought, now I've got more time on my hands . . .'

'Have you done amateur dramatics before?'

'Not really. Well, a certain amount at school, and I started to do a bit at college, but since then . . . life's rather taken over . . . you know, marriage, children . . .'

'How many children do you have?'

'Two. Boys, both boarding at Charterhouse. Younger one started in September. Mike was there, so there was never any thought of sending them anywhere else. It's a very good school for sport.'

'Are your boys keen on cricket too?'

'Oh yes,' Hester replied, a note of weariness in her voice. 'And football and tennis and squash.'

'What about you? You do a lot of sport?'

A wrinkling of the lips suggested the answer was no. 'I play a bit of genteel tennis with some friends, that's about the limit of my involvement. Unless, of course, you count the hours I have put in making cricket teas, ferrying Mike and the boys to various matches and tournaments, helping to score in pavilions, shrieking encouragement on chilly touchlines.'

'Sounds like you've served your time.'

'Hm. Maybe.'

Jude was again struck by the incongruity of this normal – even banal – conversation going on with a woman whose right wrist was dressed with a bandage covering the cuts she had inflicted on herself. They weren't very deep, but even so they must reflect some profound malaise within Hester Winstone. But maybe she just came from that class of women who'd been trained from birth to avoid talking about life's unpleasantnesses.

'From what you say,' Jude began cautiously, 'you could be suffering from Empty Nest Syndrome.'

'Oh, I don't believe in Syndromes,' said Hester Winstone dismissively. 'All psychobabble, so far as I'm concerned.'

'Hm,' said Jude gently, 'but, whether it's a Syndrome or not, things aren't right with you, are they?'

'What do you mean?'

'Look, you cut your wrist in the car, didn't you?'

'Oh yes, I just got over-emotional.' She dismissed the incident as if it were some minor social lapse, like sneezing before she'd got her handkerchief to her nose.

'But why did you get over-emotional?'

For a moment Hester Winstone was about to answer, but then she reached for her handbag, saying, 'I must be getting home. Really appreciate your helping me out.'

'I'm sorry,' said Jude firmly, 'but I really don't want you to go home straight away.'

'What do you mean?' She sounded affronted now. 'What business is it of yours?'

'It's my business,' came the calm reply, 'because I found you in your car, having just cut your wrists. And I don't really want you to be on your own until I'm sure you're not about to finish what you started.'

'And what makes you think I'd do that?'

'Because you've done it once.'

'Oh, that was an aberration. As I said, I just got over-emotional.'

'Listen, Hester, I don't have any medical qualifications, but I work as a healer so I do come across a lot of people who've got troubles in their lives. And I'd be failing in my duty to my profession – not to mention in my duty as a human being – if I were just to let you go straight home.'

'But I'm fine.'

'Look, just think how I'd feel if I heard on the local news tomorrow that you'd committed suicide.'

'But I'm not about to commit suicide.'

'That's exactly what someone planning suicide would say.'

Hester Winstone was suddenly on the verge of tears as she said, 'Can't you just leave me alone!'

'No, I really don't think I can.' There was a silence, broken only by Hester's suppressed sobs. 'Look, if you won't agree to talk to me, I'll have no alternative but to call an ambulance.'

'But I don't need an ambulance. You've seen my wrist – it's only a scratch.'

'The fact remains that it's a scratch which you inflicted on yourself. If you were to go home, you'd be on your own, wouldn't you?'

'Yes,' Hester admitted grudgingly.

'Well, is there someone who could come and be with you? A family member? A neighbour?'

'No, there's no one. Anyway, I don't want people knowing about what's happened. If Mike ever got wind it, it would be an absolute disaster.'

'Don't you think you should tell your husband?'

'No, he wouldn't understand.'

'But surely, if you're unhappy enough to slit your wrists – even if you didn't do it very efficiently – then your husband ought to know.'

'No, he mustn't.'

'So when he comes back next Friday, how are you going to explain the big scar on your wrist?'

'Oh, I've worked that out. I'll say I cut it when I was opening a tin of dog food.'

'And will he believe you?'

'It would never occur to Mike not to believe me.'

'I still think you should tell him what happened.'

'No, Mike's no good with that sort of stuff. It'd confuse him – and upset him.'

'If he's the cause of your unhappiness, then perhaps he needs to be upset.'

'I didn't say he was the cause of it.'

'No. But you haven't said what else is the cause, so I'm just having to make conjectures based on the very small amount of information you have given me.'

'You have no right to make conjectures about my life. I'm going to go.'

'Hester, I'll tell you why I have a right to make conjectures about your life. Because I found you in your car having just cut your wrist. That means, whether you like it or not, I have that information. What I do with that information is up to me. A lot of people would have just rung for an ambulance – or even the police – straight away, regardless of whether you wanted them to or not. Carole and I didn't do that. We brought you back here and tidied you up. And I'm quite happy for no one else to know what happened . . . *so long as you persuade me that you're not about to do the same thing again.*'

'What – you're blackmailing me into talking to you?'

'I don't like your choice of word, but if that's what you want to call it, fine. I just want to feel reassured about your mental state.' Hester Winstone was silent. 'Anyway, suppose Carole and I hadn't come into the car park just then . . .? Would you have cut your wrists some more? Did you want to be discovered there by someone in SADOS?'

The slightest of reactions from the woman suggested Jude might have touched a nerve there. 'I don't know what I was thinking. I wasn't very in control,' Hester mumbled, acknowledging for the first time since Carole had left the two women together that there was something wrong.

'Look, I don't know you,' said Jude. 'I know nothing about your life apart from what you've told me in the last few minutes, but for someone to cut their wrist – however ineffectively – suggests a very deep unhappiness.'

'Maybe,' Hester Winstone conceded.

'Whether that's caused by the state of your marriage, or your boys being away at boarding school or some recent bereavement or a long-term depressive condition or the menopause, I don't know. But if you do want to confide in someone, I have the advantages of not knowing your social circle, so nothing you say will go further than these four walls. I also promise not to be judgemental. And enough people have said it to me that I think I can confidently state I'm a good listener. Not to mention an experienced healer. So if you do want to tell me anything . . . well, the ball's in your court.'

Hester twisted her hands together in confusion. 'It's tempting.'

'Then why not give into temptation?'

After a moment the reply came. 'No, I can't. Sorry.'

'Well,' said Jude, 'shall I tell you what I, as an impartial observer of what I saw happen in the Cricketers, think may have caused the sudden deterioration of your mood?'

'You can try. But we were only in the same group of people for a couple of minutes, so you can't have seen much.'

'I had been aware of you in the bar before we were actually introduced. I noticed your body language.'

'God, I didn't know I had any body language.'

'Oh, you did. Hard thing to avoid, body language.'

'And what was mine saying?'

'It was saying you were feeling neglected . . .'

'Oh?'

'Or possibly rejected.'

'Really? By whom?'

'Neville Prideaux.'

'Oh God.' Hester Winstone's hand shot up to her mouth. 'Was it that obvious? Does that mean everyone in SADOS knows?'

'I wouldn't worry too much about that. From the impression I got of those I met this evening, they're all too preoccupied with themselves to notice what's going on with other people. It was easier for me to observe things as an outsider.'

'So what exactly did you observe? From my body language?'

'You seemed to be trying to engage Neville's attention. He seemed to be very deliberately avoiding eye contact with you, and constantly moving to other groups in the pub, so that you wouldn't get a moment alone with him.'

Hester Winstone was silent. Tears were beginning to well up in her hazel eyes.

'But, as I say, I'm sure nobody else noticed,' Jude reassured her. 'It's just, being introduced to a group of people for the first time, you see things in a detached way . . . you know, before you get to know any of them.'

Hester nodded, hoping, but not convinced, that what Jude had said was true.

'So you've got a bit of a history with Neville Prideaux, have you?'

'A very brief history. I hadn't met him a month ago.'

'But you did meet him during the time that your husband's been in New Zealand?'

'Yes,' the woman said wretchedly.

'And he came on to you?'

'It wasn't as obvious as that. Not like Ritchie. He . . . Neville . . . he kind of took me seriously. At least appeared to take me seriously.'

'You mentioned Ritchie. So he came on to you, did he?'

'Well . . .'

'He came on to me the minute I was introduced to him,' said Jude.

'Yes, he does that to everyone.' Hester Winstone coloured. 'He's a very attractive man.'

'He certainly thinks he is.'

'But he really is,' Hester insisted, and Jude was forced to admit it was true. Though Ritchie Good's chat-up line had been crass beyond words, Jude had still felt a tug of attraction towards him.

She banished such thoughts from her mind and said, 'One thing I don't quite get is that today was the first rehearsal for *The Devil's Disciple* . . .?'

'Yes.'

'. . . and it's only in the last few weeks that both Ritchie and Neville have come on to you . . .?'

'Well, as I say, with Neville it wasn't so much "coming on".'

'All right. But how did you come to be involved in SADOS before this production started rehearsing?'

'Ah well, it was the end of the panto . . .'

'Oh?'

'SADOS always do their pantomime at the end of January. And it was round then that Mike went off to New Zealand . . . and I was kind of at a loose end, so I got in touch with SADOS to see if there was anything I could do to help out, and they needed some people for front of house during the panto, so that's how I became involved.'

'And were Ritchie and Neville both in the show?'

'Not acting, no. Ritchie just came to see one performance and then he kind of chatted me up in the Cricketers afterwards.'

'And did you mind him chatting you up?'

'No, I was flattered . . . just having someone taking some notice of me.'

Jude recognized this as another comment on the state of Hester's marriage, but didn't pursue it. Instead she asked, 'And what about Neville?'

'He wasn't acting in the panto, but he'd written the lyrics for the songs, so he was around quite a lot during the run.'

'And you kind of "got together"?'

Hester Winstone blushed furiously. 'One evening after the show we'd had a few in the Cricketers, and my car was being serviced, so Neville offered to give me a lift home, and I invited him in for a drink and . . . I don't think anything would have happened if we hadn't been drinking.'

'And did it happen again?'

'No, just the once. And then suddenly Neville seemed to lose interest. Didn't reply to my texts or calls.'

'And you were hurt because you loved him?'

'I don't know about love. Maybe I convinced myself at the time that was the reason. I don't know. I just felt dreadful. I can't think why I let it happen.'

'You were lonely.'

'Yes, maybe, but that's no excuse, is it? And in my head I've gone through so many scenarios about how I would tell Mike, but that was assuming that Neville still wanted me and . . . I don't know. I'm just so confused.'

'From what you say, it sounds as if you've never been unfaithful before.'

'Good Lord, no.' Hester sounded appalled by the very idea. 'And I wouldn't have done, I mean, not unless I thought I actually was, at least at that moment, in love with Neville. And now I feel just so confused. And Mike's back next week, and I'll have to tell him.'

'Why?'

'Well, I can't not, can I?'

'Of course you can,' Jude asserted. 'In my view far too many people rush to tell their partners about their infidelity. In very few cases does it do any good, and in many it destroys a perfectly salvageable relationship.'

'Do you really believe that?' And there was a spark of hope in Hester Winstone's hazel eyes.

'I most certainly do.'

'But when I see Mike, I'm sure I'll just blurt it out.'

'Well, curb the instinct. Don't give him more ammunition with which to criticize you.'

'But I haven't said he does criticize me.'

'I extrapolated that, Hester.'

'Oh, did you?' She sounded a little crushed. And guilty. But also reassured. Jude's recommendation that she shouldn't tell her husband about her lapse had clearly brought her comfort.

'Oh dear, I don't know what to do.' But now Hester sounded weary rather than desperate.

'Well, I'll tell you exactly what you're going to do. You are going to sit here while I open a bottle of wine and pour you a drink. Then I'll cook us some supper. Then I think you should probably stay here the night.'

Hester grimaced. 'Love to, but I've got to get back for the dogs. If they aren't let out . . . well, you can imagine what will happen . . .'

'I think I can. What about the drink and the supper?'

The woman grinned as she replied, 'That'd be wonderful.'

'And when you go back home, you'll be all right, will you?'

'Yes, I'll be fine,' said Hester Winstone.

And Jude believed her.

SIX

The following morning over coffee at High Tor Jude gave Carole an edited version of her conversation with Hester Winstone. Though the woman wasn't a client, their time together had been almost like a therapy session, so Jude kept the details of the infidelity to herself. She just said that Hester was clearly in a bad state, but talking things through had, she hoped, helped. It would have been different if she and Carole were working on a case together. Then she would have recounted everything that had passed between them. But there was no crime involved here, just a cry for help from a very unhappy woman.

Carole, needless to say, couldn't wait to express her views of the SADOS members. 'Really! Who do they think they are? When I was growing up, we had a word for people like that, and it was "show-offs". Can't they see how ridiculous they appear?'

Jude shrugged. 'They're just doing something they enjoy. I don't see there's much harm in it.'

'Well, I'd hate to be involved with a group like that.'

'No problem. No one was rushing to make you join them, were they?'

'No,' Carole conceded.

'Have you ever done any acting?'

'No.' There was a shudder at the very idea.

'Not even at school?'

'Well, I was in a Nativity Play.'

'What part?'

Carole coloured at the recollection as she said, 'I was the Ox.'

'One of the great parts,' said Jude with a grin.

'I've never been so embarrassed in my life. And I think my parents were at least as embarrassed as I was. The Seddons have never been people for putting their heads above the parapet.'

'No, I can believe that,' said Jude.

It was later that afternoon in Woodside Cottage, while she was reading a book about kinesiology written by a friend of hers, that Jude's phone rang. The male voice at the other end was rich, confident and vaguely familiar.

'Is that Jude?'

'Yes.'

'Oh, good, I'm glad I got the right number.'

'Mm.' She still couldn't place him.

'We met yesterday evening in the Cricketers.'

'Oh yes?'

'My name's Ritchie Good.'

'Ah. And to what do I owe the honour of this call?'

'I just wanted to talk to you.'

'Well, you seem to have achieved your wish.'

'Mm.' He let a silence dangle between them. 'You made quite an impression on me.'

'I'm flattered. Slightly surprised, because we can't have spoken for more than a couple of minutes.'

'It often doesn't take long.'

Jude groaned. 'That's almost as corny as your "Where have you been hiding all my life" line.'

'At least you remember it.'

'Only for its cheesiness.'

'Touché. Anyway, I was wondering if we could meet for a drink or something.'

'A drink might be all right. I'm not so sure about the "something".'

'Let's start with a drink then . . .'

Jude didn't really know why she was playing along with him. If she hadn't already decided that Ritchie Good was nothing but an ego on legs, this phone conversation would have convinced her. And yet here she was, responding in kind to his rather elaborate innuendo. Maybe it was just that it had been a long time since she'd flirted with a man. She was still smarting after the end of a pretty serious relationship with a man called Piers Targett, so wasn't looking for anything beyond casual. But having a drink with an attractive bullshitter . . . well, there might be worse ways of spending an idle hour.

So she found herself agreeing to meet Ritchie Good at six o'clock in the Crown and Anchor.

The fact that she had chosen Fethering's only pub as a rendezvous was a measure of how little Jude was anticipating any kind of relationship. Had the assignation been with anyone who really interested her, she would opted for another venue, a place from where the news of her tryst did not immediately go straight round the village. There was security for her in the Crown and Anchor. It put her on her home base, and there'd be people she knew there – Ted Crisp the landlord, his bar manager Zosia and some of the regulars.

Jude also told herself that she might get more information from Ritchie about Hester Winstone and what had reduced her to a suicidal state. The woman had, after all, said that Ritchie had chatted her up. But Jude knew that was really only an excuse. There was also the fact that he was a very attractive man.

He was late. Jude was already installed in an alcove with a large Chilean Chardonnay, and had already heard Ted's Joke of the Day ('Where are the Seychelles?' 'I don't know – where are the Seychelles?' 'On the Seyshore.').

Ritchie Good apologized for his tardiness. 'Sorry, I got held up at work.'

'What do you do?'

'I work in a bank.'

'Oh, are you one of those pariahs of contemporary society who keeps getting whacking bonuses?'

'I wish. No, I work in the Hove branch of HSBC. On the Life Insurance side.'

'Ah.'

'I see you've got a drink.' No suggestion he should buy her another one. Then again she had only had a couple of swallows from the glass. 'I'll get something for myself.'

He came back from the bar with what Jude knew, because she'd overheard him ordering it, was half a pint of shandy. 'Can't drink much,' he said, 'because I'm rehearsing tonight.'

'I thought *The Devil's Disciple* rehearsed on Tuesdays, Thursdays and Sundays.'

'Yes, they do. Tonight isn't for that. I'm playing Benedict in the Fedborough Thespians' *Much Ado*.'

'At the same time as you're doing *The Devil's Disciple*?'

'Yes. Davina knew the deal when she persuaded me to do Dick Dudgeon. The *Much Ado* is on at the end of March, so I'll have to miss a few *Disciple* rehearsals round then.'

'So how long have you been a member of SADOS?'

'The Saddoes?' he said, enjoying the mispronunciation. 'I'm not actually a member.'

'But you have done shows for them before?'

'Oh yes, I've done shows for most of the local amdrams, but I've never been a member of any of them.' He smiled a complacent smile. 'Sooner or later they all need me to help them out.'

'So you audition for all of them in turn, do you?'

He chuckled. 'I don't do auditions. I get asked to play parts.'

'Is that usual in the world of amateur dramatics?'

'Not usual. But it's how I work. All amdrams have a problem with gender imbalance. There are always more women available. That's why they're always looking for plays with large female casts. Getting enough men's always tough. Getting enough men who can actually act is harder still. So no, I don't audition. I wait till I'm asked to play a part.'

Jude hadn't been aware that there was a star system in amateur dramatics, but clearly there was. And, at least in the Fethering area, Ritchie Good was at the centre of it. The original big fish in a small pond. She almost winced at the conceit of the man.

'Anyway,' he said, 'we don't want to talk about me.' A statement which Jude reckoned might be one hundred per cent inaccurate. He brought the practised focus of his blue eyes on to her brown ones. 'I was really bowled over by meeting you last 'night, Jude.'

'Were you?'

'Yes, it's not often that I see a woman and just . . . pow! You had a big effect on me. I kept waking up in the night thinking of you.'

'Oh yes?'

'Would I lie to you?'

'You really shouldn't set up questions like that for me, Ritchie. They're too tempting.'

'Are you saying you think I would lie to you?'

'I'm damn sure of it.'

'Oh.' He looked a little discomfited. Perhaps his chat-up lines usually got a warmer response. 'Anyway, I thought it would be nice to meet.'

'And here we are – meeting. Is it as nice as you anticipated?'

His face took on the hurt expression of a small boy. 'You're a bit combative, Jude.'

'I wouldn't say that. I just have a finely tuned bullshit detector.'

'Ah. So you reckon I'm a bullshitter?'

'Isn't self-knowledge a wonderful thing?'

'And the possibility doesn't occur to you that I might be sincere?'

'You have it in one.'

'I do find that a bit hurtful,' he said in a voice that was playing for sympathy. 'I'm sorry, it's just that I'm a creature of impulse. I see someone I fancy, I want to get to know that person, find out more about them.'

Jude was silent. She believed his latest statement as little as she had believed his previous ones. Ritchie Good was not, in her estimation, 'a creature of impulse'. She reckoned everything he did was a product of considerable calculation. And she was interested to know the real reason why he had arranged this meeting. His implication that, on first seeing her in the Cricketers, he had experienced a sudden coup de foudre did not convince her.

'So,' she said, taking the conversation on a completely new tack, 'first proper rehearsal for *The Devil's Disciple* tomorrow?'

'Yes.'

'Is it going to be good?'

'Dick Dudgeon's a very good part,' said Ritchie Good. It was the archetypal actor's response. Never mind about the rest of the production, I've got a good part.

'Have you worked with Davina before?'

'Oh yes, a few times. I like her as a director. She's very open to everyone's ideas.'

Jude didn't think she was being over-cynical to translate Ritchie's last sentence as: she listens to my ideas and lets me play the part exactly as I want to.

Time to home in on what she really wanted to ask him. 'I was having a chat with Hester last night . . .'

'Oh?' There was a slight tension in him, a new alertness at the mention of the name. 'What, in the Cricketers?'

'No, actually after she'd left. We met in the car park.' Which was as much as she wanted to say about the circumstances of their encounter.

'Really? Was she all right?' Which struck Jude as a slightly unusual question from someone who'd been in the same pub with the woman the evening before.

'Oh, fine,' she said, finessing the truth. 'Have you known her long, Ritchie?'

'Met her once before last night. I went to see the SADOS panto a few weeks back. They're always pretty dreadful, but I feel I should go out of loyalty. The trouble is, it's basically knockabout slapstick, but Neville Prideaux insists on writing these dreadfully pretentious lyrics for the songs, and the two elements just don't fit together. You know, his lyrics are all about the cigarettes of hope being stubbed out in the ashtrays of dreams. God knows who he thinks he is – Jacques Brel? But that's how they've always done the panto in recent years, and SADOS are not very good at change. Then again, Neville seems to have an unassailable position in the society. They all seem to think the sun shines out of his every available orifice.'

'What's his background? Was he involved in professional theatre?'

'Good Lord, no. Schoolteacher all his life. At some public school, I can't remember the name. Head of English and in charge of all the drama. Directed every school play, ran the Drama Department like his own private fiefdom, as far as I can gather. And now he's retired, so he's vouchsafing SADOS the benefit of his wisdom and experience.'

The sarcasm in his last words reminded Jude of what she had felt in the Cricketers, that there was considerable rivalry between Ritchie Good and Neville Prideaux, both big beasts in the local amdram circles.

'Anyway,' asked Ritchie, 'do you know Hester well?'

'Met her for the first time yesterday evening.'

'In the Cricketers car park?'

'Well, I'd been introduced to her in the pub, but it was in the car park that I got the chance to talk to her.'

'What about?' Ritchie's urgency was making him drop his guard of nonchalance.

'Oh, this and that,' Jude lied casually. 'The production of *The Devil's Disciple* . . . SADOS . . . how long she'd been involved . . . that kind of thing.'

Ritchie Good nodded, and Jude thought she detect relief

in his body language, as he moved on to talk about the play. 'Be interesting to see how *Disciple* goes down in Smalting. Shaw's gone out of fashion, but he does write good parts for actors. Bloody long speeches, mind you. I didn't know the play when Davina asked me to play Dick Dudgeon, but the minute I read it I knew I had to do it. Rather let down the Worthing Rustics, whom I'd vaguely promised that I'd play Higgins in their *Pygmalion*, but I've done the part before, and Dick Dudgeon was much more interesting . . . you know, to me as an actor.'

'I'm sure,' said Jude. 'I don't know the play, I'm afraid, but I assume that Dick Dudgeon is the lead part.'

'Yes. Well, Judith's a decent part too.'

'The one Storm Lavelle's playing?'

'Mm. I hadn't met her before the read-through, but she's not a bad little actress. Needs a bit of work on the American accent, but I dare say I can help her out there.'

'And Judith is . . . not Dick Dudgeon's wife?'

'No, she's married to the Pastor, Anderson. She starts off hating Dick Dudgeon, but by the end is rather smitten. Davina gave me the choice of playing Anderson or Dudgeon, but there was no contest. Anderson's a goody-goody, whereas Dick's . . . well, "The Devil's Disciple". No question Dick Dudgeon is the sexier role.'

'Which I suppose you would regard as typecasting,' suggested Jude slyly.

Although she had intended the remark as satirical, Ritchie took it at face value. 'Yes, very definitely.'

'And who's playing Anderson?'

'Oh, I've forgotten the guy's name, but he's perfectly adequate.' Perhaps, thought Jude, the perfect example of damning with faint praise.

'And is Neville Prideaux in the production?'

'Yes, he's playing General Burgoyne. Only appears in Act Three. Rather a showy part, suits Neville down to the ground.' Clearly no opportunity was going to be missed to have a dig at his rival.

There was a silence. Then Jude, never one to beat about the bush, said, 'I'm still not clear why you wanted to meet me.'

'I told you. You made an instant impression on me. I couldn't not see you again.'

The delivery was as polished as the lines, but once again Jude found them unconvincing. 'And after this meeting, what then . . .?'

'I hope it's the first of many.' Jude rather doubted whether it would be. 'Why is it,' he protested, 'that people round here are so hidebound? You meet someone you really click with . . . and what do you do about it? For most people – nothing. Well, I don't subscribe to that approach. If I meet someone who makes a big impression on me, I want to see more of them, want to get to know them, want to find out whether they're feeling a little bit of what I'm feeling . . .?'

To someone less full of himself, Jude would have been gentler, but she had no problem saying to Ritchie Good, 'Well, I'm afraid I don't feel anything for you.'

'Oh.' He was clearly taken aback; her reaction was perhaps not one he frequently encountered.

'I mean, I can see you're attractive . . .'

'Thank you.'

'. . . and your conversation's quite entertaining . . .'

He nodded his gratitude.

'. . . but I can't imagine being in a relationship with you.'

'Why not?'

'I quite like one-to-one relationships.'

'So?'

'Well, I can't see you being very good at concentrating solely on one woman.'

'Try me.'

'No, thanks.' Jude turned the full beam of her brown eyes on him. 'Are you married?'

'Well, yes, but the marriage has—'

'Oh, don't tell me. Which expression were you going to use, Ritchie? "The marriage has been dead for years"? "It's only a marriage in name these days"? "We're more like brother and sister than husband and wife"?'

He looked very disgruntled. 'You've got a nasty cynical streak, Jude.'

'Not normally. Only when I encounter someone who prompts cynicism.'

There was a silence. Then Ritchie asked, 'Is it only now you know I'm married that you've become cynical about me?'

'No, I was cynical about you before that. Mind you, I assumed you were married all along.'

'Why?'

'Your type always are.'

'Hm,' said Ritchie Good, and it was the 'Hm' of a man about to cut his losses. He looked at his watch, swallowed down the remains of his shandy and announced, 'I'd better be off to rehearsal.'

'Right. Oh, one thing . . .' said Jude as he rose from the table.

'Yes?'

'Where did you get my phone number from?' It was in the directory, but very few people knew under which of her former husbands' surnames it appeared.

'Storm Lavelle gave it to me,' replied Ritchie. And Jude reckoned it was one of the few things he'd said during their encounter that was true.

He hovered for a moment, wanting perhaps to place a farewell kiss on her cheek but unwilling to bend down into the alcove where she still resolutely sat. 'Well, I'll call you,' he said finally.

But Jude very much doubted if he would. And she certainly didn't mind if he didn't.

SEVEN

'But what I still don't know,' she said to Carole, 'is why he really wanted to meet up with me.'

'I thought it was your feminine charms,' came the frosty response. 'I thought you'd "made a great impression" on him.'

'No, that was just flannel. That's how he talks to all women. He's one of those men who never stops trying it on.'

'I believe you. He actually had the nerve to ask me in the Cricketers "where I'd been hiding all his life".'

Jude had to suppress a giggle at the way Carole put the words in quotes. After Ritchie had left, she had phoned her neighbour to come down and join her at the Crown and Anchor for a drink. And that drink, she knew, might well lead to having supper in the pub. She hadn't put the idea forward yet, but she knew it would be greeted by a considerable barrage of disapproval before Carole finally agreed to eat out.

'It still seems odd, though, that he actually wanted to meet me.'

'Not so very odd. You said he's one of those men who never stops trying it on. And if he comes on like that to every woman he meets, maybe he does get the odd one who actually responds.'

'Possibly. He's an attractive man.'

'Huh,' said Carole Seddon as only Carole Seddon could. 'Well, was there anything else he talked about, apart from just chatting you up?'

'He talked a bit about how he is the star of all the local amdrams and they're all falling over themselves to get him to play the leads in their productions. And he talked about *The Devil's Disciple.*'

'Anything else?'

'Well, he did ask about Hester . . .'

'What about her?'

'He asked if she had been "all right" last night. Which I found rather odd.'

'Why? Obviously he was worried that he'd upset her.'

'But when had he upset her?'

'Just before she went out to the car park.'

'Really?'

'Oh, you probably couldn't see from where you were at the bar.'

'No, I just saw her being cold-shouldered by Neville Prideaux.'

'Well, I saw Ritchie Good stop Hester on the way to the door. He didn't say much, but whatever it was it seemed to upset her. She broke away from him and rushed out of the pub.'

'Oh, really?' said Jude.

And suddenly there were two men whose behaviour towards her might have made Hester Winstone feel suicidal.

Nothing more was heard from anyone to do with SADOS for the next week. Jude was unsurprised to have no call from Storm Lavelle. She knew of old that, once her friend became involved in rehearsals for a play, she hardly noticed what might be happening in the rest of the world. It was only after the performances had finished that Storm would be back on the Woodside Cottage treatment table, bemoaning all the short-comings of her life.

Jude was also unsurprised to hear nothing more from Ritchie Good. She had had no expectation of hearing back from him again, but his silence once again made her question why he had contacted her so urgently in the first place. If his motive was purely sexual, then perhaps her combative banter had scared him. What he'd thought might be another easy conquest had turned out to be a trickier proposition, so maybe he'd just backed off. But Jude still couldn't help thinking that the important part of their conversation had been his anxiety about Hester Winstone.

Her investigative antennae were alerted by the situation, but she knew there was no case to explore. Hester Winstone, a woman possibly unhappy in her marriage, had made a very unconvincing suicide attempt. It had really been the classic cry for help. Jude doubted whether, after the shock of the first incision, Hester would have had the nerve to make another cut. So there was really nothing to investigate.

For the rest of the week Jude got on with her business of healing, while Carole continued her business of disapproving of most things. And presumably in Saint Mary's Hall in Smalting, on the Tuesday, the Thursday and the Sunday, rehearsals for *The Devil's Disciple* continued in the usual way.

On the following Monday morning Carole came to Woodside Cottage for coffee. By arrangement, of course. Carole was not the kind of person who ever 'dropped in' for coffee – or indeed for anything else. 'Dropping in' on people was the kind of habit that Carole Seddon associated, disparagingly, with 'the

North'. Except at times of great urgency, even though she only lived next door, she would never have appeared on Jude's doorstep without having made a preparatory phone call. So the arrangement to meet for coffee that Monday had been made some days before. Carole had an appointment at Fethering Surgery for a blood pressure test – 'just a routine thing, not serious – just something that came up at one of those Well Woman appointments they insist on dragging you along to.'

Carole's health had in fact been remarkably good throughout her life, and retirement from the Home Office had not changed that. She ate sensibly and fairly frugally (except when coerced by Jude into the Crown and Anchor). She drank little (except when coerced by Jude into the Crown and Anchor). And long walks on Fethering Beach with her Labrador Gulliver ensured that she got plenty of exercise and sea air.

But if Carole Seddon were ever to have anything wrong with her, she would certainly not tell anyone. She had a strong animus against people 'who're always going on about their health' or 'imagine that you're interested in their latest operation'. Carole had been brought up not to 'maunder on' about that kind of stuff. Her ideal relationship with the medical profession would be never to have anything to do with any of them. (In fact, at times her ideal relationship with all of mankind would be never to have anything to do with any of them.)

She was not a stupid woman, however, recognizing that growing older one should keep an eye on one's health. So if at a Well Woman appointment she was told she needed to go back to the surgery for a blood pressure test, back to the surgery she would go.

But that didn't stop her from moaning about the experience afterwards. 'You'd think they'd get some system of dealing with appointments in that place,' she said as Jude presented her with a cup of coffee in the jumbled sitting room of Woodside Cottage. 'I'd have been here half an hour ago if those doctors just got vaguely organized. I mean they have all this technology, checking in on a screen when you arrive at the surgery, appointments being flashed up in red lights on another screen, but none of that changes their basic inefficiency. I can't remember a time when I've actually got into an appointment there at the time scheduled.'

'Well, what did the doctor say?'

'Oh, I wasn't even seeing a doctor. Just one of the nurses for the blood pressure test. Nothing important.'

'Are you sure?' asked Jude.

'Yes,' Carole replied, ever more determined not to be one of those people 'who're always going on about their health', and firmly moving the conversation in another direction. 'I noticed as I was walking past Allinstore –' she referred to Fethering's only – and uniquely inefficient – supermarket – 'that they're advertising a new delicatessen counter. If that's as successful as all their other modernization efforts—'

Having dealt with the NHS, Carole's move into a rant about Allinstore was only prevented by the ringing of Woodside Cottage's doorbell. Jude went through to the hall. Carole heard the door being opened and the sound of a masculine voice, but her finely tuned gossip antennae were not up to hearing what was being said. Jude returned to the sitting room with a chubby, balding man, probably round the sixty mark, wearing a blazer with burgundy corduroy trousers and carrying a bottle of champagne. The colour of his face was not a bad match with the trousers.

'Carole, I'd like you to meet Mike Winstone.' In response to her neighbour's puzzled expression, she added the gloss, 'Hester's husband.'

'Oh, hello, how nice to meet you.'

'The pleasure's mutual,' he said in a hearty public school accent. 'And it seems I should be offering you thanks too.'

'What for?'

'I gather you also helped Jude out when Hester threw her little wobbly.'

'Oh. Yes.'

'Sorry about that.' He guffawed. 'Can't be keeping an eye on the better half all the time, can I?'

'Particularly not from New Zealand,' said Jude with some edge.

'What? No, right. She told you I was off, playing cricket, did she?'

'Yes.'

'Ridiculous at my age, isn't it? Just this bunch of old over-grown schoolboys. Call ourselves the Subversives. Old fogeys now, but we have dreams – still waiting for that call from the England selectors, eh?' This again was apparently worthy of a guffaw.

'As you see,' Jude intervened, 'we're having coffee. Would you like a cup or . . .?'

'Bought you some champers by way of thank-you.' He waved the bottle. 'Still cold, fresh out the fridge. Why don't we crack that open?'

'Well, it's a bit early . . .' Carole began, but she was overruled by Jude saying:

'What a good idea. I'll get some glasses.'

Left alone together, Mike Winstone favoured Carole with a bonhomous beam. 'You interested in cricket, are you?'

Her recollections of the game came from the very few occasions when she'd watched her son Stephen play while he was at school. Those games only lasted a couple of hours, but they'd still seemed interminable. What watching a full five-day Test Match must be like was too appalling for Carole to contemplate. Thank goodness Stephen had never shown any real aptitude for the game – or indeed for any others – and devoted himself increasingly to his studies.

'No, I'm afraid not,' she replied.

'You're missing a lot, you know, Carole. Very fine game, subtle mix of the very simple and the really quite complex. Lot of women getting interested in it now too, you know, and I must say some of them don't half play a good game.'

Jude returned with the glasses before Carole was required to amplify her views on cricket. Which was probably just as well.

Mike Winstone expertly removed the foil, wire and cork from the champagne, then filled the three glasses. Passing two to what he referred to as 'the ladies', he raised his own. 'As I say, thanks very much for helping out "her indoors" in her moment of need.'

'Our pleasure,' said Carole.

'So she told you all about it?' asked Jude, a little puzzled because Hester Winstone had so firmly assured her that she wouldn't let her husband know about the suicide attempt. He was, she'd said, 'no good with that sort of stuff'.

'Oh yes,' Mike replied confidently. 'No secrets between Hest and me. Got to tell the truth when you're incarcerated in a marriage – worse luck.' He guffawed again.

'So did she tell you as soon as you got back?'

'Well, we were having a chinwag about everything we'd both been up to while I'd been in the Antipodes and then I notice this dressing on Hest's wrist and I said, "What've you been up to, darling – trying to top yourself?"' This was deemed to merit another huge guffaw.

'And she told you?' asked an incredulous Jude.

'Yes. And I said, "Good heavens, Hest – what a muppet you are!" Because, you know, she's always been scatty, but cutting her wrist when she was opening a tin of dog food . . . well, doesn't that just take the biscuit – or should I say "dog biscuit"?' Another rather fine joke, so far as Mike Winstone was concerned.

Jude nodded agreement, at the same time desperately trying to think how to find out the details of the story Hester had told her husband.

Fortunately Mike provided the information himself. 'Anyway, when she told me about cutting herself, of course, I realized it tied in with what happened last Sunday – not yesterday, Sunday before.'

'Ye-es,' said Jude tentatively.

'You see, I'd rung Hest on the landline that evening. Good time from the Antipodes – I'm just getting up about the time she's thinking of bed, but I didn't get any reply. Which I thought at the time was a bit odd . . . until Hest explained that she was here with you.'

'Hm.' Jude still wanted a bit more than that . . . which Mike again supplied.

'She told me all about what happened in the car park . . .'

'Really?'

'Yes . . . how she'd nipped out early on the Sunday evening to do a bit of shopping . . .'

'Right.'

'At Sainsbury's.'

'Of course,' said Jude, waiting to see where Hester's fabrication would take them next.

'And how she came over all funny in the car park and fainted or something, and you wondered what had happened.'

You never said a truer word, thought Jude.

'Anyway, I'm so glad you were there. Well, you too, Carole.' He raised his glass again to both of them. 'Very kind of you to take her in, Jude.'

'No problem.' She still hadn't got the complete picture, but Hester Winstone's version of events was becoming clearer.

'Better you than some officious member of the Sainsbury's staff who'd probably have called an ambulance and started God knows what kind of palaver. Poor old thing. Hest must've lost a lot more blood than she thought.'

'Oh?'

'From the cut. For her to have keeled over like that.'

'Ah yes.'

'I've never known her to faint in the . . . what? Twenty-five years odd we've been married. Still, it's probably partly her age.'

'Are you talking about the menopause?' asked Carole who, in her view, hadn't said anything for far too long.

'Well, erm . . .' Mike Winstone coloured. He was clearly not at ease in discussing what he would no doubt have referred to as 'ladies' things'. 'Well, Hest is getting rather scattier than usual.' He raised his glass to them for an unnecessary third time. 'Anyway, this is just to say: thanks enormously.'

'As I say, no problem. Anyone would have done the same.' Jude reckoned she now had the complete text of what Hester Winstone had told her husband. 'You see someone keel over on a cold evening in Sainsbury's car park, you go and help them. It's human nature.'

'Well, I'm glad it was you who did it, anyway. You clearly made quite an impression on Hest.'

'How is she, by the way?'

'Hest? She's right as rain. Scatty as ever, like I said, but fine. Our boys have got an exeat from school this weekend, so she's looking forward to seeing them. Oh, there's never anything wrong with Hest for long. She doesn't let things get to her.'

Jude caught Carole's eye and could see that the same thought was going through both their minds. Namely, that Mike Winstone didn't know his wife at all. So long as he was secure in his cocoon of cricket and general bonhomie, he could keep himself immune from other people's problems.

'She mentioned,' said Carole casually, 'that she's involved in some amateur dramatic group . . .'

'Oh yes, the "Saddoes".' He used the same pronunciation that Ritchie Good had. And clearly, from the darkening of his expression, he wasn't a great enthusiast of the society. 'Mm, Hest said she'd got time on her hands now the boys are both at Charterhouse and I said, fine, give you a chance to play more tennis, have a serious go at whittling down the old golf handicap. But what does she go and do? Join this bunch of local poseurs in the amdram.'

'You don't sound very keen on the idea.'

'Well, to be quite honest, Carole, I'm not. I mean, I remember at school there was a bunch of boys who spent all their time putting on plays and, quite honestly, they weren't the most interesting specimens. I certainly made many more friends among the sporting types than I did with that lot. I mean, you go on enough minibus trips to cricket matches and football matches with chaps and you really get to know them well. I made some damned good chums through sport, certainly never made any from amongst the drama lot.'

'But presumably they made friends with other people doing drama?' suggested Jude.

'Oh yes, of course they did.' He flipped a limp wrist and said in the voice all schoolboys use to suggest homosexuality, *'Very good friends.'*

Jude made no reaction to this, but said, 'I gather Hester's going to be prompting for the new production of *The Devil's Disciple.'*

'Something like that, yes. I don't remember the name of the play. But no, good for her,' he said without total conviction. 'If that's what Hest wants to do, then I'd be the last one to stand in her way. They say it's important in a marriage for the partners to have different interests. And there's nothing that could be more different from cricket than amateur dramatics!' This was judged to be another guffaw-worthy line.

'You will give Hester our best wishes, won't you?' said Jude.

'Oh, absolutely. Course I will.' He coloured again. 'And, erm, one thing . . .'

'Yes?'

'I'd appreciate it frightfully if you didn't mention anything to anyone about Hester's, erm . . . little lapse.'

Which both Carole and Jude thought was an odd thing for him to say. And which could have suggested Mike Winstone knew more about what had really happened to Hester than he was letting on. And also maybe explained why he had been so keen to talk to Jude and Carole.

EIGHT

'Something really dramatic's happened!'

'Oh yes,' said Jude, not holding her breath. She knew of old that Storm Lavelle was capable of considerable hyperbole. In her priorities 'something really dramatic' could be something that anyone else would have regarded as of very minor significance.

It was the Thursday morning, three days after Mike Winstone's visit to Woodside Cottage. Jude had been quite surprised to have a call from Storm. Knowing the obsessive concentration her friend brought to amateur dramatics, she hadn't expected to hear anything till after *The Devil's Disciple* had had its last performance.

'It's Elizaveta Dalrymple,' Storm announced.

'What? Is she ill?'

'No, it's worse than that.'

'Why? What's happened?'

'Oh God, it was at rehearsal on Tuesday night.' Storm left a pause, clearly intending to enjoy the narrative she was about to unleash. 'I mean, so far things have been going pretty all right with the production. We've spent the first week just blocking, really, and there hasn't been too much tension. Well, a bit between Davina and Ritchie, because, well, she is the director, but he's pretty firm in his opinions about the way he wants to do things, regardless of what she thinks.'

That chimed in with Jude's recollection of her conversation with Ritchie Good in the Crown and Anchor. Clearly he was one of those actors who regarded directors as minor obstacles in the preordained path of his instinctive genius.

'But, anyway,' Storm went on, 'it's all been fairly amicable, though there's a bit of resentment of Ritchie . . . you know, because he's been kind of parachuted into the production, and there are some people who've been members of SADOS for a long time and feel that parts should only go to bona fide members of the society. I mean, Mimi Lassiter obviously, because she's Membership Secretary. But also people like Olly Pinto, who really reckons he should have been playing Dick Dudgeon, because he's kind of served his time in the SADOS, playing supporting parts, and he's thinking it's about time he should get a lead. And he's stuck with being Christy, Dick's brother, who doesn't really have a lot to do, so Olly's still cheesed off about that. But basically everything's been pretty friendly . . . until last night.'

Jude didn't say a word, allowing Storm to control the drama of her story in her own way.

'Well, needless to say, it involved Elizaveta.' Jude was not surprised. Clearly the widow of the SADOS' founder thought it her right to be the centre of everything that went on in the society. 'And, you know, she's playing Mrs Dudgeon, Dick Dudgeon's mother. And she's playing it very well. I mean, Mrs Dudgeon is basically a malevolent old bitch . . .'

'Typecasting,' Jude suggested quietly.

'Well, maybe, yes. But she's only in the first act and she has a bit of a scene with Dick Dudgeon, but not a lot, and anyway a discussion came up on Tuesday night about costume . . . and I don't know if you know, but George Bernard Shaw is very specific about what he wants his plays to look like.'

'Oh yes, all those interminably long stage directions.' During her brief acting career, Jude had been in a production of *Caesar and Cleopatra.*

'And anyway, Elizaveta was saying, like, she didn't agree with how Shaw described Mrs Dudgeon, and she thought the character would naturally look rather smarter than the way he wanted her to be. The stage directions don't say much about her actual clothes, just that she's shabby and cantankerous and she wears a shawl over her head. Anyway, Elizaveta was very much against the idea of the shawl.'

'Vanity?'

'I suppose so, Jude. Elizaveta's very proud of her hair.'

'It's certainly a good advertisement for whoever did the dyeing.'

'Yes. And she said everyone in the SADOS' audience recognized her by her hair and if it was covered with a shawl nobody would know it was her playing the part.'

'Don't they have programmes? Couldn't they have looked up the cast list there?'

'Well, yes, you'd have thought so, but no one mentioned that. Anyway, Davina said it wasn't important at that point, we'd got months to sort out the costumes and we should be getting on with rehearsal. But Elizaveta said it was a point of principle and it should be decided right then.'

'Sounds like it was a bit of a power struggle between actor and director.'

'That's exactly what it was. And Davina's fairly biddable as a director – you know, she doesn't really stand up to people, tends to go with the flow. She was certainly doing that with Ritchie. She'd go along with whatever he suggested.'

'Which no doubt made Elizaveta jealous, and she wanted to be treated the same way?'

'Spot on, Jude. Particularly as she's always been great mates with Davina and she doesn't take kindly to being sort of shut out of things. So, anyway, then Ritchie gets involved. He starts saying that we're wasting valuable rehearsal time . . . which is a bit rich coming from him, because most of the interruptions we've had up till that point have been due to him arguing with Davina about how he wants to do things.

'And of course Elizaveta doesn't like this, and then Ritchie

makes things worse – quite deliberately, I think – by saying that
we shouldn't be spending so much rehearsal time worrying
about the play's *minor* characters. Well, that's like a red
rag to a bull to Elizaveta. She goes into this great routine
about never having been so insulted in her life, and about
the fact that she's generously giving of her time to help
SADOS out by playing the *minor* role of Mrs Dudgeon. And
pretty soon she's listing all of the major roles she's played for
the society, even quoting some of the rave reviews she's had
from the *Fethering Observer* and the *West Sussex Gazette*. Then
she gets started about Freddie, her ex-husband, and how he
started SADOS and how there wouldn't have been any SADOS
without him, and how it wasn't the place of "jumped-up
actors" who *"weren't even members of the society"* to start
criticizing the work done by Freddie Dalrymple.'

'And how did Ritchie take all this?'

'Well, by now he's getting pretty annoyed too, and we all
kind of realize that what we're witnessing is a scene that's
been brewing up since the moment we started rehearsal – that
it's a kind of power struggle, Ritchie and Elizaveta fighting
over which one of them has more control of Davina. And then
it turns out that there's a bit of history between Ritchie and
Elizaveta.'

'Really?' Jude thought instantly of the man's habit of coming
on to every woman he met. 'Surely not an affair or—?'

'Oh God, no! The history was more between Ritchie's
mother and Elizaveta. Apparently his mum was big in local
amdram circles, playing lots of major roles, round the time
that Freddie Dalrymple was setting up SADOS. And there was
some kind of rumpus about Ritchie's mum wanting to join the
new society and Elizaveta using her influence with Freddie to
keep her out.'

'Elizaveta not wanting a rival for all the leading parts?'

'Exactly. So, anyway, last night at rehearsal the argument
between Ritchie and Elizaveta is batting to and fro, kind of
over Davina's head, and finally Ritchie loses his temper and
says, "Oh, come on, forget all your bloody airs and graces.
My mother knew you before you managed to trick Freddie
Dalrymple into marrying you – when you were plain Elizabeth

Jones, serving behind the counter of the fish and chip shop right here in Smalting!"

'Well, that did it! That really caught the nerve. So there's a lot more from Elizaveta about having never been so insulted in her life. And then she says that, under the circumstances, she can no longer continue in this production of *The Devil's Disciple* – and she walks out!'

'Flouncing, I dare say.'

'Very much so, Jude. Flouncing, slamming doors, completely throwing her toys out of the pram. So suddenly we're without a Mrs Dudgeon.'

'But surely there are lots of people in SADOS who can play it? Amateur dramatic societies may have problems recruiting young men, but there's always a glut of mature women.'

'I know, but the trouble is they're all on Elizaveta Dalrymple's side.'

'What do you mean?'

'The older members of the society are mostly founder members or people who joined in the first few years. They're fiercely loyal to the memory of Freddie Dalrymple. Some of them, I gather, are more ambivalent about Elizaveta. She aced them out of too many good parts for them to support her too much. But once it became known that Ritchie Good had insulted the sainted Freddie . . .'

'And how did they know this?'

'From Elizaveta, of course. She must have spent the whole day yesterday on the phone to the mature women in the society. And she's persuaded all of them to boycott this production of *The Devil's Disciple.*'

'Ah, has she?'

'Yes. Davina also spent most of yesterday ringing round every woman in the society who was vaguely the right age – and that became more elastic as she got desperate – but Elizaveta had got to every one of them first. The boycott was unbroken.

'And it's not just Mrs Dudgeon she's worried about. Elizaveta's got supporters throughout the society. I mean, Olly Pinto for one. He's playing Christy and he's great mates with

Elizaveta. I haven't heard whether he's walked out too, but it wouldn't surprise me.'

'But you're not about to go, are you, Storm?'

'Oh, good heavens, no. Judith's the best part I've ever been offered. No way I'm going to give that up. Anyway, I've always found Elizaveta Dalrymple a bit of a pain. No, I'll see it through.'

'And Ritchie will, presumably?'

'You bet. I wouldn't be surprised if he doesn't think what's happened is a personal triumph.'

'One rival ego removed?'

'Oh, I wouldn't say that. Ritchie hasn't really got a very big ego. When you get to know him, he's actually quite shy. He just has an accurate assessment of his own talents.'

Oh dear, thought Jude. Storm's defensive words might well indicate that Ritchie Good was the next man she was about to throw herself at. And if she did, there was no question that it would end in tears.

'Well,' said Jude, 'exciting times we live in.'

'Yes.' There was a silence. 'So, obviously, there's only one question I have to ask you.'

'What?' came the puzzled reply.

'Davina asked me if I would.'

'Er?'

'Jude, will you step into the breach and play the part of Mrs Dudgeon?'

NINE

'You're absolutely mad,' said Carole. 'What on earth do you want to get involved with that lot for?'

'They're harmless.'

That was greeted by a customized Carole Seddon 'Huh.'

'And they're stuck for someone to play Mrs Dudgeon. It's not going to take much time out of my life.'

'Not "much time"? Rehearsals three days a week? That

sounds like quite a big commitment to me. You wouldn't catch me doing it. I couldn't afford the time.'

For a moment Jude was tempted to ask what her neighbour couldn't afford the time *from*. Although Carole always carried an air of extreme busyness, it was sometimes hard to know what she actually *did* all day . . . apart from keeping High Tor antiseptically clean, completing the *Times* crossword and taking Gulliver for long walks on Fethering Beach.

But Jude didn't give voice to her thoughts. The look of distaste on Carole's face suggested that her neighbour's involvement in *The Devil's Disciple* had brought back atavistic fears of 'showing off' and traumatic memories of being The Ox in the School Nativity Play.

'I just thought I could help them out,' said Jude.

Another 'Huh. Well, I still think you're out of your senses. It's one thing lending them your chaise longue. Lending yourself is something else entirely.'

Suspicion appeared in the pale-blue eyes behind the rimless glasses. 'And you're not joining them because of that man?'

'Which man?' asked Jude, though she knew who Carole meant.

'That smooth talker who you met for a drink last week.'

Jude grinned. 'I can assure you my taking the part has nothing to do with Ritchie Good. If I'm doing it for anyone other than myself, then I'd say it was Storm Lavelle – she's the one who asked me. In fact, thinking about it, I wouldn't be surprised if Ritchie Good is rather annoyed by my arrival in the company.'

'Oh?'

'Because when we met I did prove rather resistant to his charms. He's not used to women reacting like that to him, and I don't think he likes it very much.'

'Huh.'

'Though actually, Carole, there is another reason why I want to be involved in this production.'

'Oh really? What's that?'

'Hester Winstone. I'm still rather worried about her . . . particularly since meeting her husband. I'd quite like to keep an eye on Hester.'

'Well, rather you than me, Jude.' Carole positively snorted.

'The day I get involved in amateur dramatics you have my full permission to have me sectioned.'

So it was that Jude took over the part of Mrs Dudgeon in the SADOS' production of *The Devil's Disciple*. She had an early evening healing session booked on the Thursday, so didn't attend her first rehearsal till the Sunday. Sensitive to atmosphere, she could feel the definite air of triumph emanating from Ritchie Good. He was pleased to have seen off Elizaveta Dalrymple.

Nor was he the only one who seemed relieved by the old woman's absence. Davina Vere Smith, despite her reputation as a 'close chum' of Elizaveta, was relaxed and apparently had given up any pretence that she was in charge of the production. She meekly took on board Ritchie's notes and suggestions, even when they applied to performances other than his own. The actor was yet again doing a play on exactly the terms he desired.

Davina accepted all that, but what did annoy her was the regular list of absentees from every rehearsal. Two were involved in a Charity Marathon and one had shingles.

Olly Pinto, self-appointed toady to Elizaveta Dalrymple, did not leave the production, as Storm had suggested he might. But all the time there was something chippy about him, especially in relation to Ritchie Good. He grimaced a lot behind Ritchie's back, and muttered words of dissent at a level that was not quite audible.

Olly also talked a lot about Elizaveta and Freddie Dalrymple. He had been fortunate enough to meet the blessed Freddie just before he died, and reminiscences of the two of them were constantly on his lips. Elizaveta Dalrymple may have walked out of the production, but Olly Pinto ensured that no one in the *Devil's Disciple* company was allowed to forget her.

Able to observe everything at close hand, Jude was again struck by Storm Lavelle's talent. She really was making something of Judith Anderson. Since Jude didn't have her own transport, Storm ferried her to and from rehearsals in her Smart car – Fethering was virtually on the route from Hove. And in the course of those journeys the two women talked a lot – well, to be more accurate, Storm talked and Jude listened a lot. All her friend talked about was the play and how she was approaching the part of Judith Anderson. So far, she seemed too preoccupied with her acting to waste any energy throwing herself at Ritchie Good. Which was a considerable relief.

But Jude did tend to arrive at rehearsals in a state of mental exhaustion from all the listening she'd had to do.

Jude's observations of Hester Winstone at rehearsals were less encouraging. The prompter still seemed very nervous and unhappy. Both Ritchie and Neville Prideaux virtually ignored her and, having met Mike, Jude didn't reckon Hester was getting much support at home either. She tried to be friendly, but her suggestions of going for a drink together at the Cricketers after rehearsals were met with polite refusals. Hester Winstone was continuing to do her job as prompter, but apparently no longer wished to be involved in the social side of SADOS.

And then of course Jude herself had to get back to the idea of acting. The stuff she had done in the past had arisen directly out of her work as a model. There's an enduring idea amongst agents and producers that someone beautiful enough to be photographed professionally must also be able to act. Though it can work in the cinema where short takes and clever editing can disguise complete lack of talent, the inadequacy of models is more likely to be exposed by a full evening on the stage of a theatre.

But Jude had actually been quite good, she had discovered a genuine aptitude for acting, and she was surprised at how much she enjoyed coming back to it and playing Mrs Dudgeon. Also, in her early twenties she had been cast only for her beauty – in other words in straight roles. She had suspected back then that the actors in character parts were having more fun and, as Mrs Dudgeon, she found that to be true. There was a great freedom to be derived from playing a crotchety old curmudgeon, so different from her own personality.

Jude was unsurprised that Ritchie Good made no further attempt to come on to her, and indeed behaved as if their meeting in the Crown and Anchor had never happened. Any attraction she might have felt towards him quickly dissipated in the course of rehearsals. Seeing what a control freak he was in his discussions with Davina Vere Smith – they had long since ceased to be arguments – Jude was turned off by his egotism.

But she remained intrigued by him. There was something about his personality that didn't ring true, something that had struck her in the Crown and Anchor and had only been re-inforced by further acquaintance. His habit of coming on to women was clearly a knee-jerk reaction, but Jude wondered how far he wanted any kind of relationship to develop. Had she proved more amenable when they met in the pub, seemed keener on spending time with him, would they have ended up under her duvet in Woodside Cottage that evening? She somehow doubted it.

Neville Prideaux, Jude could see as she watched him at rehearsals, was a more subtle operator. Jude kept remembering that it was Ritchie who'd chatted up Hester Winstone, but it was Neville who had actually gone to bed with her. He didn't have Ritchie's obvious attractiveness, but maybe he was the more ruthless seducer.

Since his character of General Burgoyne only appeared in Act Three of *The Devil's Disciple*, Neville was not at as many rehearsals as most of the company. As an actor, Jude found him impressive technically, though she wasn't moved by him. But perhaps that was the right way to play General Burgoyne. The right way to play Shaw, anyway. His characters were all, in the view of many playgoers, more like mouthpieces for opinions than people one could engage with on an emotional level.

The impression Neville Prideaux gave out of orderliness and detachment was strengthened by the time Jude spent with him during the inevitable post-rehearsal sessions in the Cricketers. She kept being reminded of Ritchie Good's rather bitchy comments about how, during his days as a schoolmaster, he'd run the drama department like his own 'private fiefdom'. Neville was probably as much of a control freak as Ritchie, but the characteristic manifested itself in different ways. He never took issue with Davina at rehearsals, meekly taking her notes and doing what she told him, but he still contrived to play General Burgoyne exactly the way in which he wanted to play the character.

One evening in the Cricketers Jude was with Neville Prideaux when the subject of Elizaveta Dalrymple's defection came up. 'Have you known her long?' asked Jude. 'Were you with SADOS in the early days?'

'Oh, good heavens, no. I only joined up after I retired . . . what, six years ago.'

'And I gather you have some kind of role as the society's dramaturge?'

'It's nothing as formal as that. Nothing official. It's just that there aren't perhaps that many people round SADOS who know a great deal about drama, and having spent my entire career researching and exploring the subject, I do feel I have something to contribute.'

'Well, it's nice to have a hobby in retirement.'

Jude's words had been no more than a bland conversation-filler, but Neville Prideaux reacted to them with some vehemence. 'I hardly have time for hobbies,' he retorted. 'I'm busier since I've been retired than I ever was as a teacher.'

'Oh?'

'I run workshops and drama classes. And then of course there's *my own writing.*'

He spoke of this with some awe, which made Jude feel perhaps she ought to know about something he'd written. Better to confess ignorance, though. 'Sorry, I don't know about your writing . . . except Ritchie said you'd written some lyrics for the SADOS' panto. Is that the kind of stuff you do?'

'Oh, good heavens, no. That's just recreational stuff. No, basically I'm a playwright.'

'Ah. Have you written lots of plays?'

'Not as many as I would have wished. There was no time when I was teaching, so I've only really been able to concentrate on it in the last six years.'

'With any success?'

'Oh, I've had some very positive responses,' Neville Prideaux replied. Jude didn't think she was being too cynical to read this answer to her question as a 'No'.

'And,' he went on, 'the SADOS' Play Selection Committee are very keen to do one of my plays next season, but I'm not convinced that that's a very good idea.'

'Oh? Why not?'

'Well, I just feel a production down here might be too low-key. I think the play would probably benefit from exposure in a larger arena.'

Like the West End? thought Jude. But she didn't ask the question. She was already getting a pretty clear view of the dimensions of Neville Prideaux's ego.

'And what's the play about?' she asked.

'Oh, there are a lot of themes,' he said rather grandly. 'It's set in a school – or apparently set in a school.' Well, that's the only setting you know, thought Jude. 'But obviously the school has considerable symbolic resonance.'

'Obviously,' she echoed, prompting Neville to look at her rather sharply, assessing whether she might be sending him up. Jude's face maintained an expression of total innocence which had proved very useful to her over the years.

'Anyway,' said Neville, 'it's very difficult to talk about one's work – particularly in the drama. A play can only be fully realized and judged when it is acted out in front of an audience.'

Jude nodded agreement. 'And how do you think the current one's going?'

'Play? *The Devil's Disciple*?'

'Yes.'

'Well, I think it gets better in Act Three.' When the character of General Burgoyne comes in, was Jude's thought – i.e. when you're on stage. 'And I think Ritchie's losing a lot of the nuance in Dick Dudgeon's character – particularly in Act One.'

'I thought he was coming across quite strongly.'

'Oh, yes, it's a competent performance, one can't deny that. Ritchie has a few acting tricks and tics to wheel out. But every part he plays is exactly the same. He never gets below the surface of a character.'

'But I thought that was the right way to play Shaw. His characters don't have great emotional depth.'

Neville Prideaux shook his head in sage disagreement. 'That's a very arguable statement, Jude. I mean, yes, GBS is more in the Ben Jonson tradition than the Shakespearean, and he looks forward to Brecht in some ways. His characters are "types" if you like, rather than psychologically complex individuals, but he doesn't go for the full Brechtian *verfrem-dungseffekt*. I would agree with you, there is emotional distance in Shaw's plays, but there's a high level of psychological engagement too.'

Jude felt she knew what it must have been like to be a sixth former in one of Neville Prideaux's classes.

'And the trouble is,' he continued, 'that Ritchie doesn't get near that psychological engagement. His Dick Dudgeon is nothing more than an assemblage of character tics. But he's not going to change. He doesn't listen to criticism. The only thing someone like Ritchie Good listens to is his own enormous ego.'

Well, it takes one to know one, thought Jude.

A little later on in the pub she was approached by Mimi Lassiter, her hair an even less likely shade of red. 'Now, Jude,' she said, 'now that you're playing Mrs Dudgeon, you can't deny that you're an Acting Member of SADOS.'

'I wouldn't attempt to.'

'So I'm afraid you have to join the society and pay a subscription.'

'I'm very happy to.'

'Everyone who acts in a SADOS production has to be a member.'

'Except Ritchie Good.'

'Hm.' An expression of displeasure crossed the little woman's face. 'Yes, I'm still arguing with Davina about that. Now, as an Acting Member, your subscription will be . . .'

Jude paid up.

TEN

'Though I say it myself,' announced Gordon Blaine, 'I'm not unpleased with the result. Obviously it did present various engineering challenges, but none I am glad to say that proved beyond my capabilities.'

A month had passed. It was a Sunday at the end of March. They'd reached the stage where Davina would have liked all of the cast to be 'off the book' – in other words, knowing their lines. Some of them had achieved that milestone, others were still fumbling. Hester Winstone was kept busy in her role as prompter.

Jude was a member of the virtuous group; she was 'off the book'. She had been surprised how easy she had found committing Mrs Dudgeon's lines to memory. And of course, given the old lady's early departure from the action, there weren't too many to learn.

Though they usually worked on the stage of St Mary's Hall, on this particular Sunday the rehearsal was taking place in the auditorium. The curtains were firmly closed, but from behind them various thumps, hammerings and muttered curses had been heard in the course of the afternoon. Gordon Blaine was building his gallows.

He'd been hard at work since the Saturday morning. Though all the components of the device had been made in his work-shop at home, he was actually assembling them in situ. And, assuming he got it finished in time, the structure was due to be dramatically revealed to the *Devil's Disciple* company at the end of the afternoon's rehearsal.

With this coup de théâtre in prospect, there was around St Mary's Hall an air of excitement mingled with a bit of giggling. Gordon Blaine, the SADOS Mr Fixit, was clearly something of a joke amongst the members, and Jude could understand why. Though it was Carole rather than she who had received the full blast of Gordon's monologue the first evening they had gone to the Cricketers, that did not represent a permanent escape from him. Gordon Blaine was around quite a few rehearsals and he was very even-handed in the distribution of his conversation; he made sure that no one evaded their ration of it. And Jude, being new to the society, had certainly got her share.

The SADOS Sunday rehearsals started at three (so that those who needed to could enjoy their family lunch) and finished on the dot of six. Then everyone rushed to the Cricketers. Maybe this schedule had been established in the time of fixed licensing hours, but it had continued into the era of all-day opening.

That Sunday afternoon, as six o'clock drew nearer, the level of giggliness increased. Davina Vere Smith was facing an uphill battle, trying to get some concentration out of the actors involved in the opening scene. Jude was rock solid on her lines, but Janie Trotman as Essie, along with the actors playing Anderson and Christie, kept breaking down and cracking up with laughter. At about five to six, Davina gave up the unequal struggle and declared the rehearsal over.

As if on cue, Gordon Blaine had then appeared through the curtains to make his announcement. Having duly patted himself on the back for completing his task in the face of insuperable difficulties, he continued for a while talking up his prowess as an engineer.

Jude looked around the assembled company. There was still a level of excitement there, but as Gordon began to speak, the giggles were threatening to take over. Nearly everyone seemed to have stayed for the forthcoming revelation. Glancing round the room, the only significant absentees Jude was aware of were Ritchie Good and Hester Winstone.

The former's disappearance was explained as soon as Gordon Blaine, with an inept attempt at flamboyance, went into the wings to draw back the curtains. Onstage stood a very convincing-looking gallows, beneath which was a small wooden cart. On the cart, with the noose around his neck, stood Ritchie Good. The *Devil's Disciple* company let out a communal half-mocking gasp of appreciation and started a small round of applause.

Stepping back onstage, Gordon Blaine beamed at this appreciation of his talents. 'Thank you,' he said. 'Yes, not a bad bit of work, though I say it myself.'

From behind his back he produced a noose identical to the one hanging from the arm of his gallows. One end was neatly tied in a loop; at the other was a metal ring, clearly designed to hook on to something. Gordon stretched the noose with his hands, demonstrating its strength and solidity. 'Simple piece of equipment, really, isn't it? But very effective for ridding the world of undesirables.' He chuckled a little, indicating that what he'd just said was a Gordon Blaine joke.

'Still, we don't want to have any accidents in our *Devil's Disciple*, do we? Particularly to a fine actor like Ritchie Good. So just in case we have any Health and Safety inspectors in the building, let me give you a demonstration of the means by which, in the use of this apparatus, unpleasant accidents may be avoided.'

He moved ponderously across the stage and took up the T-shaped pulling handle of the wooden cart. 'A few words, did we agree, Ritchie?'

'Yup. Ready when you are.' And the man with the noose around his neck went into Dick Dudgeon mode, though preferring his own words to the ones George Bernard Shaw had written for this dramatic moment. '"It is a far, far better thing that I do now . . ." Oops, sorry, wrong play. That's *A Tale of Two Cities*. No, what I want to say to you all is that I've been through everything in my mind over and over again and I've decided –' he gestured to the noose around his neck – 'that this is the best way out.'

There was a ripple of laughter at his melodramatics. Ritchie Good, ever the showman, was enjoying his moment in the spotlight.

'Also I'd like to say that public hangings used to be one of this country's most popular spectator sports, until some wet blanket of a do-gooder decided that they weren't an appropriate divertissement for the Great Unwashed to gawp at. So you're very honoured, ladies and gentlemen, fellow members of SADOS, to have this much-loved entertainment re-created for you, here in St Mary's Hall, Smalting. And with that – let my hanging commence!'

At what was clearly a prearranged cue, Gordon pulled the cart away from beneath his feet. Ritchie Good's hands shot up to grasp the strangling rope around his neck, and for a moment he swung there, choking and kicking out into the nothingness.

The gasp which followed this had no element of irony in it. People rushed forward to the stage.

But before he could be rescued, Ritchie released his grip on the noose and dropped down to the floor, as neat as an athlete finishing a gymnastic routine. His mocking laughter revealed that the whole thing had been a set-up, and he looked boyishly pleased with the trick he had played on everyone. 'Not bad, is it? Full marks to Gordon!'

Mr Fixit glowed and did a half-bow to acknowledge the rattle of applause. Then he moved across to demonstrate the cunning secret of his handiwork. The noose was no longer a loop, but two parallel pieces of rope. 'Oh, the magic of Velcro,' said Gordon, as he pressed the two ends together and reformed the circle.

'Very clever,' said the sardonic voice of Neville Prideaux, 'but in fact unnecessary. In the text of Shaw's play the cart never gets moved. Dick Dudgeon may have the noose around his neck, but he's in no danger of ever getting hanged. Then he's saved by the arrival of Pastor Anderson.'

Gordon Blaine looked almost pathetically nonplussed at having his moment of triumph diminished. But Ritchie Good came quickly to his rescue. 'Well, speaking as the person who actually has the rope around my neck, may I say I'm very pleased about the sensible precautions Gordon has taken. Accidents do happen. I could black out while I'm up there, or the cart could break or somebody could push it away by mistake. No, thank you very much, but I'm happy to stay with my Velcro rope. And I'm equally happy that General Burgoyne is unable to see through his plan of getting me hanged.'

Though he was talking entirely in terms of *The Devil's Disciple*, Ritchie Good still managed to make his last sentence sound like a criticism of Neville Prideaux, and a point scored in the ongoing rivalry between the two men.

As she watched the action, Jude had been standing next to Mimi Lassiter, who looked seriously shocked by the scene they had just witnessed. 'Are you all right?' asked Jude.

Mimi didn't answer the question, just announced in an appalled voice, 'He said "fellow members of SADOS" – and he hasn't even paid his subscription.'

Clearly she took her duties as Membership Secretary very seriously.

Over by the stage, where the curtains had once again been closed, there was much clapping on the back for Gordon Blaine, along with congratulations on another feat of stagecraft and offers to buy him a drink. He said he and Ritchie would join the others after he'd made a couple of adjustments to his precious gallows.

And the rest of the company, predictably enough, adjourned to the Cricketers.

As Jude crossed the car park towards the pub, she saw Hester Winstone standing by the side of a flash BMW, in heated conversation with someone through the driver's side window.

'I just want to stay and have a drink,' Hester was saying.

'And I just want you to come home.' The voice was recognizably her husband's. 'Look I've already had to rush my Sunday lunch to get you here for the beginning of the bloody rehearsal. Then I come into the rehearsal room and see some idiot showing off pretending to be hanged – and I see no sign of you. And now you're here and I'd have thought the least you can do is come home now the bally rehearsal's finished.'

'You go home. I'll get a cab.'

'Well, that's a waste of money when I'm here to give you a lift. I'm already stuck with paying the insurance excess on the repairs caused by you pranging your bloody car. On top of that . . .'

Jude couldn't hear any more of the conversation without becoming too overt an eavesdropper, so she continued her way into the Cricketers.

ELEVEN

The macabre demonstration they had seen had lifted the spirits of the *Devil's Disciple* company. This was partly due to the jokey double act which Gordon and Ritchie had just presented for them, but also to the feeling that they were finally making progress on the production. They were around halfway into their rehearsal schedule, some of the cast were actually 'off the book', and now they were being shown how bits of the set would work. *The Devil's Disciple* was beginning to gather momentum.

Jude had found that sessions in the Cricketers had become considerably more relaxed since the departure of Elizaveta Dalrymple and her cronies. Elizaveta was one of those women who not only needed always to be the centre of attention but who also carried around with her a permanent air of disapproval. And, given her place in SADOS history, though she didn't voice it in so many words, there was an implication of disdain for everything the society had done since the demise of its founding father Freddie Dalrymple. And yet, despite this inevitable decline in standards, Elizaveta Dalrymple had appeared magnanimous enough to offer her services and do what she could for SADOS.

So, without her condescension and prickliness, without everyone kowtowing and worrying about her reaction to things, the atmosphere in the Cricketers after rehearsals had improved considerably. The inevitable glass of Chilean Chardonnay in her hand, Jude found herself looking round quite benignly at her fellow actors. She had come to recognize that most of their flamboyance and ego derived from social awkwardness and, as ever attracted to people by their frailty, she realized that she was getting fond of most of them. To her considerable surprise, she discovered that she was enjoying her involvement in amateur dramatics. She giggled inwardly at the thought of breaking that news to Carole.

Feeling it was her turn to buy a round for the small circle she stood with, Jude looked for the African straw basket which contained her wallet, and realized to her mild irritation that she must have left it in St Mary's Hall.

To joshing cries about 'the Alzheimer's kicking in', Jude left the Cricketers and made her way back to the rehearsal room. The March evening was comfortingly light, finally promising the end of the miserable weather that seemed to have been trickling on forever.

Security at St Mary's Hall was not very sophisticated. The keys were kept behind the bar of the Cricketers and one of Davina Vere Smith's duties as director was to open the place and lock up at the end of rehearsals. Frequently, because cast members were slow to leave the hall, Davina didn't do the locking up until when she was leaving the pub to go home.

So it proved that Sunday evening. Jude slipped in without difficulty and went through the foyer area to the main hall. She switched on one row of lights and noticed, without thinking much of it, that the stage curtains were almost closed, with just a thin strip of light showing.

The straw bag was exactly where she thought she'd left it, propped against the wall by the trestle table on which the kettle, coffee mugs and biscuit tins were kept.

Jude was about to leave the hall when she thought she should perhaps turn off the stage working lights. Though not obsessive about green issues, she tried whenever possible to save electricity.

There were pass doors on either side, but the simplest route up on to the stage was by the steps in the middle (much used for audience participation when the SADOS did their pantomimes). Jude stepped up, pushing the curtains aside, in search of the light switches.

But what she saw on stage stopped her in her tracks. The wooden cart had been pushed to one side. From the noose on the gallows dangled the still body of Ritchie Good. His face was congested, his popping blue eyes red-rimmed.

This time he wasn't play-acting.

TWELVE

Jude's mobile was in her basket. She knew she should ring the police straight away. But Ritchie Good was unarguably dead, and a few minutes' delay was not, so far as she could see, going to make a lot of difference to the official investigation. She moved closer to the hanging corpse and looked up at the rope tight around his neck.

It was as she suspected. The noose which had strangled Ritchie Good was not the fake one with the Velcro linkage. It was the unbroken one whose strength Gordon Blaine had demonstrated in the run-up to his coup de théâtre.

Jude moved far enough away to see the top of the gallows. Fixed there was a large backward-facing hook, on to which the ring at the end of the noose had been fixed. From it the rope ran through a channel at the beam's end, so that it could dangle in its appropriate position over the cart.

For anyone who knew the structure of the gallows, switching the two nooses would have been a matter of moments. But who on earth could have done it? And how had they persuaded Ritchie Good so helpfully to have stood once again on the cart and placed the noose around his neck?

Though still in a state of shock, Jude found her mind was buzzing with possibilities. She tried to think back over the last half-hour, to remember who had appeared in the Cricketers and in what order. Also who had left the pub, and who hadn't even gone in in the first place.

While these thoughts were scrambling through her mind, Jude became aware of a noise in the empty hall. She heard a low whimpering, sounding like an animal, and yet she knew it to be human. It was coming from the small annex to the side of the stage, which during their productions SADOS used as a Green Room.

She moved softly through and found Hester Winstone collapsed on a chair, incapable of stopping the flow of her tears.

The woman looked up as she heard Jude approaching and said brokenly, 'It's my fault. I'm the reason why he's dead.'

THIRTEEN

J ude would have liked to talk to Hester, to offer comfort, to find out what exactly her words had meant, but they were interrupted by a scream from inside the main hall. Jude rushed through to find an aghast Davina Vere Smith.

The director must have come into St Mary's Hall to lock up, then, just like Jude, have gone to turn the lights off on stage. Where she too had been confronted by the grisly sight of Ritchie Good's dangling body.

Once she had recovered from her initial shock, Davina had no hesitation about ringing the police straight away. Somehow drawn by bad news, a few other SADOS members had drifted over from the Cricketers. The sight of Ritchie's corpse prompted all kinds of emotional displays, making it difficult for Jude to talk privately to the still-weeping Hester Winstone.

And once the police and an ambulance had arrived, such a conversation became impossible. Two uniformed officers came first, but they were quickly calling up plain clothes reinforcements. The paramedics from the ambulance were allowed to confirm that Ritchie Good was dead, but then the police asked them to keep off the stage. Soon after they left St Mary's Hall. Moving the body would happen later, after photographs and other essential procedures.

Jude was struck by how little information the police have when they first arrive at the scene of a crime (or indeed an accident). They'd probably never heard of SADOS; they'd need an explanation of the rehearsal process which had brought everyone to St Mary's Hall. And that was before they started even getting the names of the individuals involved.

But the two officers, later backed up by detectives, showed great patience in their questioning as they began to build up a background to the events of that afternoon. Their job was not made any easier by the histrionic tendencies of the SADOS members. All of them seemed to have something to contribute, and in many cases it was something that placed them centre stage in the day's drama.

Eventually St Mary's Hall was cleared. The police had by then established the identity of the victim. They had also taken names, addresses and contact numbers from everyone present and said that further follow-up questions might be necessary at a later date. The SADOS members were then left in no doubt that it was time for them to leave. Which – with some reluctance, they were enjoying the theatricality of the situation – they did.

They were also forbidden to tell anyone about what they had witnessed in the hall that afternoon. But if the police thought that instruction was likely to be followed, then they had never met anyone involved in amateur dramatics.

Jude was kept till last. As one of the first into the hall after Ritchie Good's death, she was told that a full statement would be required from her. Not straight away – the police needed time to examine the scene of the incident – but the following day, either at her home or the local police station, according to her preference.

'But I'm free to go now, am I?' she asked.

'Yes. You'll get a call in the morning.'

'And . . .' Jude looked across to where the weeping Hester Winstone was being comforted by a female officer. 'What about . . .?'

'No, Mrs Winstone won't be leaving straight away,' said the detective.

During the drive back to Fethering in her Smart car Storm Lavelle went into full drama queen mode. 'I mean, it's just such a *shattering* thing to happen. Ritchie's such a good actor, it's such a *waste*! And God knows what's going to happen to *The Devil's Disciple* now.'

Jude was relieved to hear that her friend seemed more worried about the production than heartbroken about Ritchie Good's death. Storm must've been too busy with rehearsals to have any time to start throwing herself at Ritchie.

'What, you mean they're likely to call the whole thing off out of respect for Ritchie?'

'Oh, good Lord, no. The show must go on.' She spoke the words devoutly; they were, after all, the basic principle of amateur dramatics. No matter what disaster might occur during the rehearsal period, *The Devil's Disciple* would still be presented to the paying public in St Mary's Hall on the promised dates.

'No, Jude, Davina'll just juggle the cast around. Presumably Olly Pinto will be boosted up to Dick Dudgeon . . . which will please him no end, because he always thought he should have been playing the part in the first place. And, I don't know, one of the boys playing the soldiers will get boosted up to take on Olly's old part of Christy.'

'Will it make a lot of difference to you, playing Judith Anderson to a new Dick Dudgeon?'

'I don't think it will that much, actually. I mean, Ritchie's a very good actor, but you never feel he's really engaging with you onstage. You know, he's thought through how he's going to play his part and that's what he does, regardless of what he's getting back from the rest of the cast. Ritchie's a great technician, but he isn't the kind of actor with whom you can get any kind of emotional roll going. He's very self-contained. It's a bit like having a very cleverly programmed robot on stage with you.'

Jude was interested to hear how closely Storm's assessment of Ritchie Good's acting skills matched that of Neville Prideaux. And Storm's was more objective; she wasn't motivated by jealousy.

'What do you think killed him?' asked Jude, in a manner that was meant, but failed, to sound casual.

'Well, obviously, strangulation by the noose round his neck.'

'Yes, but why did it happen?'

'An accident. He and Gordon must've been doing some adjustment to the gallows and unfortunately—'

'Gordon wasn't there. He was in the group that came straight over to the Cricketers at the same time as I did.'

'Oh well, Ritchie may have just been fiddling about with it.'

Storm seemed so remarkably incurious about the circumstances of the death that Jude didn't feel inclined to raise suspicions by asking further questions. Instead she said, 'The police want me to make a statement for them tomorrow. Have you got to do the same?'

'No, they just took my address and mobile number. Said they might be in touch, but didn't make it sound very likely.' There was a silence, then Storm said, 'Hester looked in a pretty bad way, didn't she?'

'Yes. So far as I could work out, she'd found Ritchie's body just before I had. She was in a terrible state of shock.'

'Hm. And she started off pretty neurotic, didn't she?'

'Is that the impression she gave?' asked Jude, surprised at her friend's powers of observation. Then she reminded herself that Storm was also a healer, used to analysing the sufferings of her clients.

'No, on the surface she was fine, but I did get the impression that she was very tense, holding a lot in.'

'Yes, I felt that too.'

'So,' said Storm, 'if Hester doesn't recover, we'll be short of a prompter. And, judging from this afternoon's display, just when her services will be most in demand.'

'Oh, surely there are lots of SADOS members around who could do that?'

'You'd think so, wouldn't you? But a lot of the potential prompters, mature ladies who're unlikely to be cast in plays any more . . . well, they're part of the contingent that walked out with Elizaveta Dalrymple.'

'And might they not be lured back?'

'Oh, Good Lord, no. Not until *The Devil's Disciple* boycott is complete. Anyone who breaks through the picket line on that will receive the full blast of Elizaveta's anger.'

'I'm surprised that would worry anyone. I got the impression that she was rather a spent force in the SADOS.'

'A spent force she may be, but there are still a lot of members terrified of getting the wrong side of her. They might be excluded from the guest list for her famous "drinkies things".'

'Oh dear. Well, maybe Hester will make a full recovery and no replacement prompter will be needed.' But as she said the words, Jude wasn't feeling as positive as she sounded. After all, what Hester Winstone had said to her in the Green Room could have been interpreted as a confession to murder. Whose consequences could make her unavailable for *Devil's Disciple* rehearsals, as well as many other areas of her life.

'Anyway, if Hester is ruled out,' said Storm, 'you wouldn't by any chance have a friend who might step into the breach as prompter, would you?'

Jude could hardly prevent herself from giggling at the thought, as she replied, 'Yes, you know, I think I might.'

FOURTEEN

On the Monday, by arrangement, the police had come to Jude's home to take her statement. She had described to the best of her recollection exactly what she had witnessed the previous day at St Mary's Hall. She had told the truth, but not quite the whole truth, omitting to report Hester Winstone's words about the death being her fault. Jude had glossed over that, saying that Hester was too hysterical to say anything coherent.

Her motives for telling the lie were instinctive and benign. She recognized Hester's mental fragility and didn't want to get her into any more trouble than she already was.

But she decided not to tell her neighbour what she'd done. Perhaps because of her Home Office background, Carole strongly disapproved of lying to the police.

Now that there was a corpse involved, Carole Seddon suddenly found the doings of SADOS a lot more interesting. Her voice was full of suppressed excitement as she asked, 'You say Ritchie Good was hanged, Jude? Was his neck broken?'

'I don't think so.'

'Then it would have been a very painful death.'

'Oh?'

'Humane hangmen usually arrange it so that the force of the drop breaks the victim's neck. Then death – or at least unconsciousness – is more or less instantaneous. If the neck isn't broken, the victim dies slowly of strangulation. It can take ten – or in some cases up to twenty – minutes. Pretty nasty way to go.'

Jude looked at her friend in surprise. 'Is that something you learned at the Home Office? I know there was a lot of back-stabbing there; I didn't know they went in for strangulation too.'

'Ha, ha, very funny. No, it's just information I picked up,' Carole replied airily. She had an increasing interest in the mechanics of crime, and had started filling directories on her laptop with the fruits of her research on the subject. But it was not a hobby she ever talked about, even to Jude.

It was the Tuesday, two days after Ritchie Good's death. They were having coffee at Woodside Cottage. The two women hadn't seen each other for a few days. Carole's daughter-in-law Gaby had been struck down at the weekend by a particularly nasty bout of a sickness bug and Granny had been summoned to the rescue in their house in Fulham. Since Carole absolutely worshipped her granddaughter Lily, this was no hardship for her. And with Gaby confined to bed, she even got over her customary unease at staying anywhere other than High Tor. She had taken Gulliver with her, and she was much entertained by the bonding between dog and granddaughter.

Because of her absence from Fethering till the Tuesday afternoon, this was the first Carole had heard about the death in St Mary's Hall. Jude recognized the sparkle of interest in her pale-blue eyes as she asked, 'So do you reckon that this Ritchie Good person was murdered?'

'I really don't know. It's an odd one. I've been going through the facts, revisualizing everything I saw on Sunday night. And it strikes me there are two major questions that need asking. First, who switched the safe noose with the Velcro joint in it for the real, unbroken one? And, second, why on earth did Ritchie allow the noose to be put around his neck?'

'Are you sure he didn't put it there himself?'

'Why would he do that?'

'To commit suicide. Come on, you saw more of him than I did, Jude. I just exchanged a few words with him in the

Cricketers. Did anything he said to you make you think he might have depressive tendencies?'

'Absolutely not. I don't think I've ever met a man so armoured in self-esteem as Ritchie Good. He wouldn't want to deny the world the pleasure of his company. He would have regarded that as a terrible deprivation for everyone else on the planet. No, what happened to him is a complete mystery.'

'Intriguing, though,' said Carole, and behind their rimless glasses there was even more sparkle in her pale-blue eyes.

'Hello, Mike Winstone.' The voice answering Jude's call had its bonhomie firmly fixed in place.

'Hello, it's Jude. Remember, you came round with the champagne to say thank you . . .?'

'Yes, yes, of course. How the devil are you?'

'Fine, thanks. And you?'

'Never better.'

'I was actually ringing about Hester . . .'

'Oh yes?' For the first time there was a less welcoming tone in his voice.

'When I last saw her on Sunday she was in a terrible state.'

'Well, she's fine now,' said Mike Winstone curtly.

'But it looked as if she was about to be taken away by the police.'

'She did go with them to the station, where she made a statement and then was allowed to come home.'

'So is she there now? Would it be possible for me to speak to her?'

'No, I'm afraid that wouldn't be possible.'

'But she is there, is she?'

'No. No, she's not.' He spoke as if he had just thought of the answer. 'Hester's gone to stay with a friend.'

And that was all Jude got out of him. Except for the impression that he was lying.

FIFTEEN

A text had gone round to all the *Devil's Disciple* company to say that the Tuesday rehearsal was cancelled. The police were yet to finish their investigations at St Mary's Hall, but there was a hope the SADOS could resume their schedule on the Thursday. They'd receive a confirmatory text from Davina Vere Smith if that proved to be the case.

Jude was not surprised by the cancellation, but it did raise the question of *what* the police were investigating. An accident? Or something more serious? She couldn't get out of her mind what Hester had said in St Mary's Hall after Jude discovered Ritchie Good's body.

If only she could contact Hester . . . Partly to find out what had happened to her at the police station, what she'd been asked, what she had told them. But more than that, the healer in Jude was worried by the state in which she had last seen the woman. Though the incident in the car park had been almost too trivial to count as a suicide attempt, it still raised the possibility that, when faced with increased stress, the woman might try again.

Jude hoped the 'friend' that Mike had said Hester was staying with was of the sensitive and nurturing kind. And yet at the same time the suspicion recurred as to whether the 'friend' even existed. Was it just a covering lie from her husband for the fact that Hester was in police custody? Or had she actually been at home with him when he had taken Jude's call?

If so, she didn't think Mike Winstone would necessarily come out very well in the sensitive and nurturing stakes. Jude was seriously worried about Hester.

Later in the day, after she'd had coffee with Carole, she had a call from Davina Vere Smith. 'You got the text, did you?'

'Yes, thanks. Any news yet from the police on whether Thursday's rehearsal's likely to be on?'

'When they were last in touch, things were looking quite hopeful.'

'Good. And how're you going to replace Ritchie?'

'Olly Pinto will be playing Dick Dudgeon.'

'He'll be pleased.'

'What do you mean by that?' asked Davina rather sharply.

'Just that Olly seems to think he should have had the part in the first place.'

'Mm. Maybe you're right. Yes, Olly has served his time in supporting roles. And at least he is a member of SADOS, which is more than Ritchie ever was.' There was an undercurrent of resentment in these words. Jude was reminded once again of Ritchie's outsider status in the society. His behaviour had only been tolerated because of his talent. In the world of amateur dramatics loyalty to an individual group counted for quite a lot. And there was a nit-picking punctiliousness about details like whether someone involved in a production had actually paid his subscription or not.

With this came another thought, that Davina might actually relish working with Olly Pinto more than she did with Ritchie Good. The younger man would probably be more malleable, more inclined to listen to the director's ideas about the play and less likely just to follow his own agenda. Jude wondered how many more members of the *Devil's Disciple* company might regard Ritchie's death as something of a bonus.

'Anyway, Jude, the reason for my call –' oh yes, of course, there must be a reason – 'is that it seems Hester Winstone won't be able to take any further part in the production.'

'Ah. Do you know anything about where she is? Or indeed how she is?'

'No. I spoke to her husband. He said she was staying with a friend.' At least Mike's story was consistent.

'He didn't say any more?'

'No, Jude.'

'Didn't say what was wrong with her?'

'He didn't say that there was anything wrong with her. All he said was that Hester wouldn't be able to continue being our prompter for *The Devil's Disciple.*'

'Ah.'

'And he seemed quite gleeful as he passed on the news.'
Jude could picture that. Mike Winstone had always resented
his wife's involvement in SADOS. 'Which does put me in a
bit of a bind.'

'In what way?'

'Well, it means we haven't got a prompter. And just at this
stage of the production, when I'm trying to get everyone off
the book . . . we need one more than ever.'

'I can see that.'

'And the trouble is that there are plenty of SADOS members
who might be happy to take on the role, but they're all friends
of Elizaveta's.'

'Ah, yes.'

'And since Elizaveta's boycotting the production – and
incidentally being very shirty with me – none of them will
help me out. They're all part of her inner circle, you know,
the lot who were always going to little "drinkies things" at
Elizaveta and Freddie's . . . which I used to be, but I've
somehow blotted my copybook with Elizaveta. Anyway, if
she makes it a three-line whip on the potential prompters, none
of them would dare go against her.'

'Mm.'

'But I was talking to Storm Lavelle, who surprisingly now
seems to be a fixture at Elizaveta's "drinkies things" –' Jude
found herself starting to grin as she realized which way the
conversation was heading – 'and she said you had a friend
who might be prepared to step into the breach . . .?'

'Well, I could ask her,' said Jude, suppressing a giggle.

'What – me? Are you asking me to get involved in *amateur
dramatics*?' The way the last two words were spoken, they
could have been some unhealthy sexual practice.

Jude had gone round to High Tor as soon as she'd ended
the call from Davina Vere Smith. She was mischievously
intrigued as to how the proposal would be greeted. And her
neighbour's reaction did not disappoint.

'I thought,' Carole went on, 'I had made clear my views
on *amateur dramatics*.'

'Oh yes, you certainly have. But I thought, you know, helping people out when they're in a bit of a spot . . .'

'There are people I might help out when they're in a spot, but not people who indulge in *amateur dramatics*.'

'So your answer to taking over as prompter is no?'

'Definitely.'

'That's rather a pity.'

'Why?'

'Well, I thought you might be able to help me on the investigation.'

'The investigation?'

'Into Ritchie Good's death.'

Carole's expression changed instantly from disapproval to alert interest. 'Oh yes, I hadn't thought of that.'

'And, if you were, kind of . . . embedded in the production of *The Devil's Disciple* . . . well, we'd both be on the spot . . . and able to investigate, wouldn't we?'

'That is a thought, yes.' Carole was clearly intrigued. 'You said earlier this afternoon that you didn't know whether it was murder.'

'No, but it's certainly suspicious.'

'Yes.' Carole nodded slowly, but with mounting enthusiasm. 'Suspicious, hm . . .'

'Well, come on, there is something odd about it. The doctored noose was definitely changed for the real one. I suppose it's possible Ritchie himself might have done that, but it doesn't seem likely.'

'So you reckon someone in the *Devil's Disciple* company did it?'

'Seems the most likely possibility, yes.'

'Hm.' Carole tapped her steepled hands together in front of her mouth as she tried to control her racing thoughts. A spark of excitement had been ignited in her pale-blue eyes. 'Ooh, it's frustrating not to know all the people involved.'

'Well, there's a very good way of getting to know them,' said Jude teasingly.

'What, you mean if I took over from Hester Winstone as prompter?

'Exactly.'

'Oh, I don't think that's for me,' said Carole Seddon, in characteristically wet blanket mode.

It was only half an hour later that the phone rang in High Tor.

'Is that Carole Seddon?'

It was a female voice she didn't recognize. 'Yes,' she replied cautiously.

'Good afternoon. My name's Davina Vere Smith.'

'Oh yes?'

'I gather Jude's asked you about taking over as prompter for the SADOS *Devil's Disciple.*'

'Yes. And I told her I'm afraid I can't do it.'

'I wonder if you could be persuaded.'

'I doubt it,' said Carole.

It was pure curiosity that had made her agree to meet Davina Vere Smith in the Crown and Anchor that evening. Ted Crisp greeted her in his customary lugubrious style. 'On your own, are you? No Jude?'

Carole had been intending to have a soft drink, but Ted had already started pouring a large Chilean Chardonnay, so it seemed churlish to tell him to stop. 'I'm meeting someone.'

'New boyfriend?'

'No,' came the chilling reply. Carole knew that Ted's words had reminded both of them of their brief and unlikely affair. The thought that it had happened still gave her a frisson of disbelief . . . and excitement.

'Do you know the best way to serve turkey?' asked Ted.

Carole, not expecting a culinary question at that moment, replied that she didn't.

'Join the Turkish army!' said Ted heartily.

It took Carole a moment to register that it was one of his jokes. 'Oh, really,' she said, with annoyance that was only partially feigned.

'Excuse me, are you Carole?'

She turned to face a short woman with blond (almost definitely blonded) hair bunched into a pigtail. She wore grey leggings and a purple cardigan, unbuttoned enough to reveal an extremely well-preserved cleavage. A star-shaped silver pendant hung around her neck.

'Yes. You must be Davina.'

'Mm. I saw you in the Cricketers when you brought over Jude's chaise longue.'

'But we weren't introduced then, were we?'

'No.' Davina pointed to the wine glass Ted Crisp had just placed on the counter. 'Is that yours?'

'Yes.'

'I'll pay for it.'

'Oh, there's no need for you to—'

'Of course I will.' Davina grinned at the landlord. 'And I'll have a large G and T, please.'

When they were settled into one of the alcoves, the director said, 'Feels odd to me, being here on a Tuesday.'

'Oh? Why?'

'Tuesdays are always SADOS rehearsal days. But today . . . well, did Jude tell you what happened on Sunday?'

'Yes. I was very sorry to hear about it.' A conventional expression of condolence, though even as she said it, Carole wondered why she felt obliged to say the words. She had only met Ritchie Good once and she hadn't taken to him then.

'It was a terrible shock for everyone.' But Davina's response also sounded purely conventional. She didn't appear to feel any grief for her lead actor's demise. 'And it's going to cause a lot of readjustment in my production of *The Devil's Disciple*.'

'I'm sure it will.'

'Which is why I wanted to meet you, Carole.'

'Yes, you said.' The words came out more brusquely than intended.

'Jude thought you'd make a really good prompter.'

'I've no idea whether I would or not. I've never had anything to do with amateur dramatics.' Still a bit frosty.

But Davina Vere Smith persevered. 'I'm sure you'd enjoy it if you did agree to join us. The SADOS are a very friendly bunch.'

Bunch of self-dramatizing poseurs, was Carole's unspoken thought. What she said was, 'As I told Jude, it's really not my sort of thing.'

'Then why did you agree to meet me? If you've already made up your mind to say no?'

It was a good question. Carole was forced to admit to herself that she was more than a little intrigued by the whole SADOS set-up. Particularly now there was an unexplained death in the company. She decided to change the direction of the conversation to a little probing. 'Going back to what happened to your actor on Sunday . . . What was his name?' she asked, knowing full well.

'Ritchie Good.'

'Yes. Presumably it was some kind of ghastly accident . . .?'

'Oh, it must have been, yes. Not that you'd think that from the theories some of the *Devil's Disciple* company are coming up with.'

'You mean some of them think it wasn't an accident?'

'From the texts and phone calls I've had in the last twenty-four hours you'd think they're all auditioning for the part of the detective in an Agatha Christie thriller.'

'Some of them think it was murder?'

'And how!' said Davina Vere Smith.

Which was what persuaded Carole Seddon to take over the role of prompter in the SADOS production of *The Devil's Disciple*.

When Jude was informed of the decision, she didn't think it was the moment to bring up her neighbour's previous assertion that 'The day I get involved in amateur dramatics you have my full permission to have me sectioned.'

SIXTEEN

I t was striking to Jude how little Ritchie Good was mentioned after the Thursday rehearsal following his death. Carole hadn't been there that evening, but she noticed the same once she started attending rehearsals. The Thursday, only four days after the tragedy, had witnessed a lot of emotional

outpourings (some of them possibly even genuine), as members
of the *Devil's Disciple* company expressed their shock at what
had happened.

Very little actual rehearsal got done that evening, which was
annoying for the director because prurient interest had ensured
that, for the first time, every member of her cast had turned
up. But whenever Davina Vere Smith tried to focus their attention on the play, someone else would have hysterics, or go
into a routine about how they 'couldn't do the scene without
imagining doing it with Ritchie'.

Even Olly Pinto did a big number about how dreadful he
felt. This wasn't the way that he had wanted to get the part
of Dick Dudgeon. He was going to suffer every time he said
one of the lines that rightfully belonged to Ritchie Good. But,
nonetheless, he would pull out all the stops to match up to
Ritchie's performance. He would do his best 'for Ritchie'. In
fact, he asked Davina at one point during that emotional
Thursday evening rehearsal whether they could put in the
programme the fact that he would be 'dedicating' his performance to 'the memory of Ritchie Good'.

But that was it, really. One evening of unfettered emotion
and then everyone wanted to get on with doing the play.
The members of the *Devil's Disciple* company returned to
their default preoccupation: themselves. The surface of
SADOS had closed over, as if Ritchie Good had never
existed.

Not much was said about him during the following
Sunday's rehearsal, though they did get the news from Davina
that Gordon Blaine had been questioned by the police. At
what level this questioning had taken place she did not know,
but they'd been to his house rather than taking him to the
station. This information caused a surprising lack of discussion amongst the *Devil's Disciple* company. But there was a
general view that Gordon's being questioned was logical.
After all, he had built the structure which had killed Ritchie
Good.

As she was leaving St Mary's Hall at the end of her first
rehearsal, that Sunday, Carole was approached by Mimi

Lassiter. 'Oh, now you're in the production you must be a member of SADOS.'

'Must I?'

'Yes, nobody can be in a SADOS production if their subscription's not up to date.'

'Unless they're Ritchie Good,' said Carole, who had heard from Jude about his non-membership. Mimi Lassiter's face darkened. 'He wasn't a member, was he?'

The Membership Secretary agreed that he wasn't. 'And look what happened to him,' she said with something like satisfaction.

They were now out in the car park. Carole looked at Mimi Lassiter, dumpy with her dyed red hair. No wedding ring, post-menopausal, archetypal small town spinster. Then she noticed that Mimi was carrying a Burberry raincoat exactly like her own.

Carole took out her car key and unlocked her clean white Renault. As she did so, she realized that parked next to it was the identical model, also white. 'Well, there's a coincidence,' she said.

'Just what I was thinking,' Mimi Lassiter agreed.

'What, you mean . . . that one's yours?'

'Yes.'

Carole Seddon felt very uncomfortable. The same Burberry raincoat, the same white Renault. Both post-menopausal. And she'd just mentally condemned Mimi Lassiter as an archetypal spinster. Was that how the denizens of Fethering saw her too?

But Mimi was not to be distracted from her cause. 'Now the subscription of Acting Members is—'

'But I'm not an Acting Member,' Carole objected. Unpleasant memories of the School Nativity Play welled up in her. Ooh, that itchy Ox costume. 'You'll never catch me acting,' she said with some vehemence. 'I am the prompter.'

'Yes, well, that's still covered by Acting Membership. Everyone who's actually involved in the production—'

'Backstage as well?'

'Yes, backstage as well. They're all in the category of Acting Members.'

'Well, it's a misnomer, isn't it?'

'What?'

'Acting Member. Acting Member implies that people in that category actually act. It should be Active Member.'

'I think it's fairly clear that anyone who's involved in—'

'Anyway, what other categories of membership are there?'

'Well, there's Supporters' Membership. That's usually for people who have got too old to continue as Acting Members but are still involved with the society. And then there's Honorary Membership, but that was really only set up for Freddie and Elizaveta . . . you know, because they actually started SADOS and there needed to be some recognition of their enormous contribution to the—'

'So how much do I have to pay for an Active Membership?'

'Acting Membership.'

'It really shouldn't be called that,' said Carole.

'Well, it always has been called that!' Mimi Lassiter was very worked up. Clearly she didn't like anyone questioning the way she operated as Membership Secretary. 'And the subscription for Acting Membership is . . .'

Carole paid up.

Olly Pinto, in the role of Dick Dudgeon, had just asked if Essie knew by what name he was known.

'*Dick,*' replied Janie Trotman, in the role of Essie.

He then told her that he was called something else as well. But before he could say, '*The Devil's Disciple,*' he was interrupted.

'That's wrong,' said Carole. It was the Sunday rehearsal a fortnight after Ritchie Good's death, and she was beginning to feel at ease in her new role of prompter.

'I'm sure it's right,' said Olly Pinto, on the edge of petulance.

'No. You said you were *called* something else as well, whereas what George Bernard Shaw actually wrote did not include the words: "*I am called*".'

'Well, it means the same thing.'

'It may mean the same thing, but what you said is not the line that Shaw wrote.'

'All right,' said Olly Pinto, well into petulance now. 'I'll take it back to where I ask Essie what they call me.' And he delivered the line that Shaw wrote.

'What?' asked Janie Trotman.

'That was your cue. I was giving you your bloody cue!'

'Keep your hair on. I'm not the one who's cocking up the lines.'

'I am not cocking up the lines! Look, I've taken on the part of Dick Dudgeon at very short notice and I'm doing my best to—'

'All right, all right,' said Janie, who'd heard quite enough of Olly Pinto's moaning. '*Dick.*'

'What?' he asked.

'You gave me my cue. I'm giving you the line that comes next. *Dick.*'

'Well, I didn't know you'd started, did I?'

'All right. Well, I have started. *Dick.*'

Again Olly Pinto tried to get out the line where he mentioned he was called '*The Devil's Disciple*'.

Again Carole interrupted him. 'You said "*as well*". Shaw actually wrote "*too*".'

'Oh for God's sake!' snapped Olly Pinto. '"*As well*" – "*too*" – what's the bloody difference? They both mean the same.'

'They may mean the same, but George Bernard Shaw chose to write one rather than the other. And the play SADOS is doing is the one written by George Bernard Shaw, not by members of the cast.'

Olly Pinto looked as if he was about to take issue, but decided against it. Hester Winstone had been very timid as a prompter. She wouldn't give the line until one of the actors virtually asked her for it. And she had seemed happy to accept any kind of paraphrase of George Bernard Shaw's words. Whereas with this new one . . . blimey, it was like being back at school.

Carole Seddon was surprised to find she was really enjoying her job as prompter. With the text of *The Devil's Disciple* in her hand, she had the advantage over the actors. And even the most flamboyant of them looked pretty silly when they couldn't remember their lines.

Also, although she would never have admitted it to a living

soul, she was glad to have the prospect of fewer evenings alone with Gulliver in High Tor, reading or watching television (even about convents and confinements).

Carole and Jude's conviction that they were engaged on an investigation grew weaker and weaker. Whenever they tried raising the subject with members of the cast, asking for their ideas as to who might have switched the two nooses, nobody seemed to be that interested. Getting *The Devil's Disciple* on was much more important than Ritchie Good. He was already old gossip.

Despite his problems with the lines, Olly Pinto was really relishing his elevation to the role of Dick Dudgeon. Previously at coffee breaks during rehearsal it had been Ritchie Good round whom the junior members had gathered. Now it was Olly. He wasn't a natural to take on the casual insouciance of an amdram star, but he was getting better at filling the role.

And he mentioned Elizaveta and Freddie Dalrymple and their 'drinkies things' significantly less often. Now he'd got the part that he reckoned had always been his due, he didn't need the imprimatur of their distinguished names. Olly Pinto was now unquestionably the star of *The Devil's Disciple*.

At one point, in the course of that Sunday rehearsal, Jude, returning from the Ladies during a coffee break and passing the Green Room, overheard a snatch of conversation.

'Oh, for heaven's sake, don't start that,' said a peevish voice she identified as Janie Trotman's.

'Come on, I'm not doing any harm. It's just that I do find you stunningly attractive.' It was Olly Pinto's voice, steeped in sincerity.

'Even if that were true, it doesn't give you an excuse to come on to me.'

'Janie, I'm just—'

'Oh, I get it. Now you've got Ritchie's part, you reckon you can take on his personality too, do you?'

'It's not like that.'

'Chat up everything in sight, eh? Get them interested and then drop them like hot cakes? Well, you're not going to succeed with that, Olly. Certainly not with me. For one simple reason. Ritchie *could* get women interested because he was attractive. You can't because you aren't.'

'There's no need to be offensive.' The note of petulance that she'd heard at rehearsal was back in Olly Pinto's voice.

Also he was using that as an exit line. Jude hurried back to the main hall to avoid being caught eavesdropping.

What she had heard was very interesting, though.

Carole had now attended four rehearsals of *The Devil's Disciple*, but she hadn't joined the mass exodus to the Cricketers after any of them. When her neighbour raised the subject, Carole insisted that she was 'not a pub person'. But Jude remembered the very same words being used about the Crown and Anchor in Fethering when they first met. Carole had fairly quickly become something of a 'pub person' there, and Jude reckoned it was only a matter of time before she also became a post-rehearsal regular at the Cricketers. Her natural nosiness would ensure that.

The first Sunday she attended rehearsal Carole had given Jude a lift in her Renault. Now they were both involved, that seemed to make more sense than having Storm Lavelle go out of her way to pick Jude up. Anyway, there wouldn't be room for three of them in the Smart car. That Sunday Jude had dutifully gone back to Fethering in the Renault immediately after the end of rehearsal, foregoing a drink at the Cricketers. She had wanted to go there, though, not only for the convivial atmosphere, but also in hopes of reactivating the investigation into Ritchie Good's death.

So on the following Tuesday and Thursday Jude travelled from Fethering in the Renault, went to the pub when Carole left and got a lift back home with Storm. Storm was such a chatterbox, particularly when she'd got a few drinks inside her, that she was more than ready to join in conjectures about Ritchie's hanging.

After overhearing the conversation between Janie Trotman and Olly Pinto, there was no way Jude wasn't going to the Cricketers after that Sunday's rehearsal. She hadn't had the chance, with all the *Devil's Disciple* company around, to tell Carole what she had heard, but she was more insistent that her neighbour should come to the pub that evening. Carole once again demurred, though with less conviction than before. Jude reckoned her friend would be a 'pub person' at the Cricketers by the end of the week. But Carole was not to be swayed that evening, so Jude said she'd get a lift back with Storm.

Though the post-rehearsal SADOS company noisily took over the pub and formed into large groups, it was still possible to have a relatively private conversation with someone at one of the side tables. By good fortune Jude found herself at the bar at the same time as Janie Trotman, and an offer to buy the girl a drink assured her attention. The nearest group of actors centred on Olly Pinto, and Janie seemed unwilling to join them, so Jude had no problem in steering her to a table beside the open fire.

They clinked their glasses, Janie's a vodka and coke, Jude's predictably enough a Chilean Chardonnay. 'Olly seems to be stepping fairly effortlessly into Ritchie's shoes, doesn't he?'

Janie agreed. 'Mind you, he'll never be as good as Ritchie. He hasn't got the same amount of talent. Not nearly.'

'No, but I think he'll be all right.'

'He may be, if he learns his bloody lines.' Janie giggled. 'Mind you, Carole the Dominatrix is keeping him up to his work, isn't she?'

Jude giggled in turn, wondering how Carole would react to the nickname.

'She's quite a hard taskmaster, isn't she?' Janie went on.

'Something of a perfectionist, yes.'

'Where on earth did she come from? I've never seen her round any other SADOS shows.'

'I brought her in.'

'Really?'

'Yes, she's a friend of mine. My next-door neighbour, actually. Why're you looking so surprised?'

'I'm sorry, it's just . . . I wouldn't have put you two down as friends. You seem so different. You're so laid back and, well, Carole . . .'

'Opposites attract,' suggested Jude.

'Maybe.' But Janie didn't sound convinced.

'Hm. Anyway, the surface of the water seems to have closed over Ritchie Good, doesn't it? Like he never existed.'

'I think in some ways that's quite appropriate.'

'How do you mean?' asked Jude.

'Well, there always was something slightly unreal about him.'

Jude found that a very interesting observation; it chimed in with the feeling she had got about Ritchie when they'd met in the Crown and Anchor, that he was going through the motions of life rather than actually living it. She asked Janie to expand on what she had meant.

'The way he used to come on to every woman he met, it never felt spontaneous. It was more like . . . I don't know what you'd call it. Learned behaviour, perhaps? Certainly not innate.'

Jude grinned. 'You know the jargon.'

'I've got a degree in psychology,' said Janie.

'And do you use that in your work?'

'Sadly not at the moment. I haven't had a proper job since I left uni. And that was nearly three years ago.'

'I'm sorry.'

'There's nothing I could get round here that'd actually use my qualifications. Unless you reckon that stacking shelves in Lidl gives a unique opportunity to study the patterns of human behaviour.'

'Couldn't you look for something further afield?'

Janie Trotman shook her head ruefully. 'Can't really at the moment. My mother's got Alzheimer's. And my father's desperate that she shouldn't have to go into a home or a hospital. But looking after her is too much for him on his own. So . . .' She spread her hands wide in a gesture that seemed to encompass the limited possibilities of her life.

'Obviously it won't always be like this. My mother will presumably die at some point. I just hope to God she goes before my father. Otherwise I'll be lumbered full time.' There was no bitterness in her words, just a resignation. What she had described was her current lot in life, and that was all there was to it.

'It's why I keep doing the amateur dramatics,' she explained.

'I enjoy it and it gets me out of the house at least three times a week.'

Jude said again that she was sorry.

'It's all right,' said Janie. 'I'm not after sympathy. My parents looked after me when I couldn't help myself . . .' She shrugged. 'Some kind of payback seems logical.'

'Are you an only child?'

The girl nodded. 'And I love both my parents . . . or perhaps in my mother's case I should say I love what she used to be.' Determined not to succumb to a moment of emotion, she went on briskly, 'Anyway, I've told you about my life. What about you, Jude? What do you do?'

She explained that she was a healer.

'Ah. And it'd be too much to hope for, I suppose, that you might have found a way to heal Alzheimer's?'

'I wish. I can sometimes alleviate distress or panic in a sufferer, but cure . . . no.'

Janie grinned wryly. 'I was afraid you'd say that. But at the same time I'm rather relieved you did.'

'Why?'

'Because you don't come across to me like a charlatan.'

'Thank you.'

'I mean, I've looked online endlessly for anything that offers the hope of a cure. And there are plenty of people out there who do just that. If you only buy their patent medication, their dietary supplement . . . then hooray, goodbye to Alzheimer's.'

'Did you buy any of them?'

'I'm afraid I did. When my mother started to decline, I was desperate, I'd try anything. Well, I did try one or two things, and they all had one thing in common. They were entirely useless. So, as I say, there are a lot of charlatans out there.'

'I don't doubt it.' Then Jude redirected the conversation. 'Incidentally, did Ritchie Good come on to you?'

'Of course.'

'When he first met you?'

'Yes. Didn't he come on to everyone when he first met them?'

'Certainly did with me. And Carole too, actually.'

'Really?'

'Don't sound so surprised. Carole is a very attractive woman.'

'Yes, I'm sure she is. But there's something a bit . . . I don't know, a bit forbidding about her. Like, say a word out of line and she'd cut you down pretty quick. If I were a man, I'd think twice before coming on to Carole.'

'But, as we've established, Ritchie Good came on to *every* woman.'

'Hm.'

'How did you react, Janie?'

'When Ritchie first came on to me? Well, I was flattered, I guess. At that stage I hadn't witnessed him coming on to anyone else, so I thought maybe he was genuinely attracted to me. And then of course he was the star of the show, and he was so much older than me, and . . . yes, I was flattered. Also, at the time I was in a rather low state about men.'

'Oh?' Jude smiled sympathetically. 'Relationship just finished?'

Janie nodded. 'Actually, it finished quite a while ago, but I was still feeling raw. I had quite a lot of boyfriends while I was at uni, but there was this one boy I got together with in my third year, and we kind of stayed together after we'd done our degrees. We had a flat together in Crouch End, but then . . . Mummy got ill, and I was having to spend more and more time down here. And, you know, I'd rush up to London for the odd night, but that made me feel guilty and . . . Oh, I don't blame him. I don't think I was much fun to be with at the time. Well, we tottered on like that for . . . over a year, it was . . . and then the inevitable happened.'

'He met someone else?'

'Yup,' replied Janie, trying to make it sound casual, as if the separation was something she had come to terms with. But Jude could tell that she hadn't. 'So, anyway, having an older man, an attractive man coming on to me, telling me I was beautiful, even if he was married, even if he was Ritchie Good . . . well, it gave me quite a boost. And yes, I did fall for him a bit.'

'Did anything come of it?'

'Like what? Are you asking whether we went to bed together?'

'Well, yes, I suppose I am.'

'Then the answer's no. But it was odd . . .'

'Odd in what way?'

'Well, he kind of implied that we would go to bed together. He kept telling me how much he fancied me and trying to persuade me to say yes. And he said he'd book a hotel room for us and . . . well, he persuaded me, I guess. I don't know how much I really wanted to, but, you know, it was the prospect of something different happening in my life, something apart from looking after my mother and attending rehearsals for *The Devil's Disciple*.

'So I said yes. And we fixed the date, and Ritchie said he'd booked the hotel room and . . . Then the afternoon of that day I had a text from him saying he'd decided he couldn't go through with it.'

'Did he give any reason?'

'He said he'd realized that he was just being selfish and, however much he fancied me, it wouldn't be fair to his wife.'

'And how did he treat you after that, Janie? When you met him at rehearsals? Was he embarrassed?'

'Not a bit of it. He behaved as if nothing had happened between us. I mean, he stopped coming on to me, but he didn't try to avoid me or anything like that. And certainly his confidence wasn't affected. In fact, I would have said he was cockier than ever after that.'

'Pleased that he had avoided the pitfalls of sin?' suggested Jude with some irony.

'I don't think that was it. It was almost as if for him the process was complete. He'd got what he wanted out of his relationship with me. He'd persuaded me to agree to go to bed with him and, having achieved that, he had lost interest.'

What Janie Trotman had said confirmed the impression Jude had got when she and Ritchie met in the Crown and Anchor. She didn't know if there was a word to describe a man who behaved like that, but had it been a woman she would have been called a 'cock-teaser'.

SEVENTEEN

'Is that Jude Nichol?'

She was surprised. So few people ever referred to her by anything other than her first name. It was only on official documentation that she used the surname she had gained from her second marriage.

'Yes,' she replied cautiously.

'It's Detective Inspector Tull,' said the voice from the other end of the phone. 'You remember you gave a statement to me and one of my colleagues after the death of Mr Ritchie Good.'

'Yes, of course I remember.'

'And I said then that I might be in touch with you again in connection with our enquiries.'

'Yes.'

'So here I am, being in touch,' he said with some levity in his voice.

'Right, Inspector. What can I do for you?'

'I just wanted to check a couple of details that you put in your statement.'

'Fine. Fire away.' But Jude felt a small pang of panic. She had withheld from the police what Hester Winstone had said to her in the Green Room that Sunday night. Maybe, when interviewed, Hester herself had mentioned it and Inspector Tull was about to expose Jude's lie.

'We've now spoken to all of the people who attended the rehearsal that afternoon,' the Inspector began smoothly, 'and they all seem to tell more or less the same story.'

'That's not surprising, is it?'

'Not necessarily, no. And the sequence of events that everyone agrees on is that before the demonstration of his gallows, Gordon Blaine was holding a real noose as opposed to the fake one. Would you go along with that, Mrs Nichol?'

'Please just call me Jude.'

'Very well, Jude.'

'Yes, I would go along with that.'

'Thank you. And then when the stage curtains were drawn back to reveal Mr Good, he had the fake noose around his neck . . .?'

'Yes.'

'And he was standing on the wooden cart, which Gordon Blaine moved away so that it no longer supported him . . .?'

'Exactly. And Ritchie then grabbed the noose so that the Velcro didn't give way immediately, and he did a bit of play-acting, as if he was actually being hanged.'

'"Play-acting"?'

'Yes, playing to the gallery, showing off.'

'And to do that would have been in character for Mr Good?'

'Completely.'

'So, after the demonstration, everyone went off to the Cricketers pub opposite St Mary's Hall . . .?'

'Yes, I'm honestly not certain whether *everyone* went, but most people certainly.'

'And within half an hour you went back to the hall and found Mr Good dead, hanging from the gallows with the real noose round his neck . . .?'

'As I said in my statement, yes.'

'Yes. So within that half-hour – or however long it was exactly – someone substituted the real noose for the fake one . . .?'

'They must have done.'

'Mm.' The Inspector was silent for a moment. 'When you went to the Cricketers pub that evening, did you notice any members of the group missing? Or did you see anyone leaving the pub to go back to the hall?'

'I wasn't aware of anyone missing or anyone leaving, but that doesn't mean it didn't happen. You know, I was just having a drink with a bunch of people. I wasn't expecting ever to be cross-examined on the precise events of the evening.'

'No, of course you weren't.' Another silence. 'Well, Jude, you'll be pleased to know that your account tallies more or less exactly with what all the other witnesses have said.'

'Good.'

'Did you know Mr Good well?'

'No, I'd only met him since I became involved in the production.' No need to muddy the waters by mentioning drinks à deux in the Crown and Anchor.

'So you probably didn't know him well enough to have a view on whether or not he might have suicidal tendencies?'

'No. But from what I had seen of him, I would have thought it very unlikely.'

'A lot of suicides are very unlikely.'

Jude agreed. She'd seen plenty of evidence of that in her work as a healer. 'I know. It's often impossible to know what's going on inside another person's mind.'

'Hm.'

'Does that mean, Inspector, that you are thinking Ritchie changed the nooses round himself?'

'It's something we're considering . . . along with a lot of other possibilities.' She might have known she would just get the standard evasive answer to a question like that. 'One of the people in your group seemed to think it was the most likely explanation.'

'Oh, who was that?'

'Come on, Jude. You know I won't tell you that.'

'Was it Hester Winstone?'

'Or that.'

'And I suppose you won't tell me if you're about to make an arrest either?'

'How very perceptive of you. Anyway, an arrest implies that a crime has been committed. There seems to be a consensus among the people in your group that Mr Good's death was just an unfortunate accident.'

'Really? No one's mentioned the word "murder"?'

'You're the first.' Once again there was a note of humour in his voice.

'I'm amazed. I would have thought that self-dramatizing lot would have all—'

'You're the first.'

'Well . . .' She was flabbergasted.

'Anyway, Jude, thank you very much for your time. I think it very unlikely that we will have to trouble you again.'

'Does that mean you've closed the investigation?'

'It means I think it's very unlikely that we will have to trouble you again.'

That was it. Inspector Tull's call did not serve to make Jude feel any more settled. She still felt convinced that Ritchie Good had been murdered, and it was frustrating to have just been talking to someone who undoubtedly knew a great deal about the case. Who had, quite properly, resisted sharing any of that knowledge. Her own investigation seemed to have hit a brick wall.

And she did wish she could contact Hester Winstone. She'd love to know what the former prompter had said when she was questioned by the police.

Jude had another unexpected call that Monday. It was round five o'clock and she was just tidying up after a healing session with a woman suffering from sciatica. Her efforts had proved efficacious and she felt the usual mix of satisfaction and sheer exhaustion.

'Hello?' she said.

'Is that Jude?' A woman's voice, cultured, precise.

'Yes.'

'My name is Gwenda Good. I'm the widow of Ritchie Good.'

'Oh.' Jude hastened to come out with appropriate expressions of regret and condolence, but the woman cut through them.

'I believe you were the first person to find my late husband's body.'

'One of the first, certainly.' Jude didn't want Hester Winstone's name to come into their conversation unless Gwenda Good introduced it.

'I would very much like to talk to you about what happened to Ritchie.'

'I'd be happy to talk about it. Do you think there was something suspicious about his death?'

'I don't like the word "suspicious". I would prefer to say "unexplained".'

'Very well.'

Jude felt a spark of excitement. She was a great believer in synchronicity. Earlier that day, after her phone call from Inspector Tull, her investigation seemed to have hit a brick wall. Now, out of the blue, she was being offered the chance to speak to the dead man's widow.

'I'm afraid I don't go out much,' said Gwenda Good. 'I wonder if it would be possible for you to visit me at my home?'

'Certainly . . . that is, assuming you don't live in the Outer Hebrides.'

If the woman at the other end of the line was amused by this suggestion, she didn't show it. 'I live in Fedborough,' she said.

'Oh, that's fine. I'm only down in Fethering.'

'I knew you couldn't be too far away. We have the same dialling code.'

'Yes. Well, when would be convenient for me to come and see you?'

'Would Wednesday morning be possible? Eleven o'clock.'

So that was agreed. When she put the phone down, Jude was struck by how businesslike and unemotional Gwenda Good had been. She didn't sound like a woman who had just lost a much-loved husband.

EIGHTEEN

B ecause the character of Mrs Dudgeon only appeared in Act One of *The Devil's Disciple*, Jude was not required for all the play's rehearsals. But Carole, now indispensable as prompter, had to be there every time. And the following day, the Tuesday, was one of those for which her neighbour wasn't called, so Carole drove to Smalting on her own.

Jude had told her about the phone calls from Inspector Tull and Gwenda Good. Though not much information had come out of the first one, Carole was intrigued by what Jude might find out when she visited Ritchie Good's widow. She was also, not to put too fine a point on it, rather jealous. Now she was embedded in the *Devil's Disciple* company as prompter, she wanted to be fully part of any investigating they managed to achieve there.

So she was determined to use her evening at St Mary's Hall without Jude to good effect. To Davina's annoyance, there was a poor turnout that evening, because of a gastric flu bug which was working its way through the *Devil's Disciple* company. Still, Carole found the evening rather enjoyable. She managed to rap most of the surviving cast over the knuckles for paraphrasing George Bernard Shaw's text, and when the cry of 'Anyone for the Cricketers?' went up, Carole conceded that she would join the throng.

She got a strange satisfaction from making that breakthrough on an evening when Jude wasn't there. Next time they were both present, Carole could go to the pub after rehearsal as if she'd been doing it all her life.

Because of the driving, she had been intending to drink something soft. But when Davina Vere Smith said, 'Let me buy you a drink. No prompter should have to work as hard as you had to this evening', her resolve melted away. She asked for a small Chilean Chardonnay, and Davina bought her a large one.

Carole lingered on the periphery of a group in the centre of which Olly Pinto was doing his Ritchie Good 'Life and Soul of the Party' impression, until Neville Prideaux came and joined her. 'Sorry, Carole, we haven't really had a chance to have a proper chat, have we?' he said.

She was glad to have the chance to talk to Neville, though she put herself on her guard. Jude had brought her up to date with everything she knew about the retired teacher, so Carole was wary of appearing to know too much.

'You were certainly kept busy today,' Neville went on.

'I suppose that's the prompter's role.'

'To be busy? Yes. But not *that* busy.'

'Well, I didn't have to prompt you once.'

'No,' he responded rather smugly. 'I felt, since I'm the one who suggested the play, I have to set an example as General Burgoyne.' A complacent smile, then: 'Olly was absolutely hopeless this afternoon, wasn't he?'

'Hopeless on the lines, do you mean, or as an actor?'

'Let's just stick to the lines for the moment, shall we? He was all over the place. You were having to prompt him on virtually every speech.'

'Yes, but of course he has taken the part over at very short notice.' Carole was not just being defensive for the young man; she had spotted an opportunity to steer the conversation back to Ritchie Good's death.

'He's had a couple of weeks. He ought to be more advanced than he is. Olly's always been a bit iffy on lines. I directed him as Algy in *The Importance*, when Elizaveta gave her Lady Bracknell. Oscar Wilde's lines are so beautifully written, you wouldn't think anyone could cock them up. Well, Olly Pinto managed it. He was paraphrasing everything. He's actually not a very good actor either.'

Neville spoke as if sounding the death knell on Olly Pinto's theatrical career.

'Then why does he get big parts in the SADOS?'

'Oh, a couple of reasons. One, the eternal problem of all amateur dramatic societies: not enough men. The gender imbalance is so skewed that a young man with a very small talent can go a long way. And someone with a bit more talent – even a glib, meretricious talent like that possessed by Ritchie Good – can cherry-pick any part he wants.' Even though his rival was no longer on the scene, Neville Prideaux still spoke of Ritchie with considerable venom.

'You said there were two reasons why Olly got good parts . . .'

'Oh, yes. Well, the other one, of course, is because he's a *creature*. And I use the word in the Shakespearean sense of someone *created* by a more powerful person to whom they are totally subservient.'

'So who fits that role for Olly Pinto?'

'Elizaveta, of course. Elizaveta Dalrymple, undisputed queen of SADOS.'

'I gathered that her right to that title had been disputed.'

'What do you mean, Carole? Oh, that business of her walking out of this production. That won't be forever, I can guarantee you that. SADOS is far too precious to Elizaveta for her really to cut her ties with it.'

'But with regard to Olly, you're saying he owes his success in the society to Elizaveta backing him?'

'Exactly. As I said, he's her *creature*.'

'Or poodle?'

'"Creature"'s better,' said Neville definitively. Carole got the feeling that anything he thought of would always be better than anything anyone else thought of. That was why he'd so enjoyed being a schoolteacher, pontificating to small boys who never dared to question his opinions.

'Oh yes,' he went on, 'Olly is very much Elizaveta's creature. Part of the inner circle who spend all their time going for "drinkies" round at her place. She's got a nice house on the seafront at Smalting, and I gather she's been having these little parties for years. She used to co-host them with Freddie and didn't let his death stop her.'

'When did he die, actually?'

'Oh, I suppose about three years ago.'

'What of?'

'Heart attack, I think it was. He had a flat in Worthing where he used to "prepare his productions". He was found there, I believe. Still, he left Elizaveta very well provided for.'

'Oh?'

'Freddie made a lot of money. That's why he could afford an expensive hobby like SADOS.'

'Doing what?'

'You mean how did he make his money? He was a *pensions consultant*.' Neville loaded the words with contempt. 'Nothing even mildly to do with the arts.' Strange, Carole reflected, how Neville seemed to recognize a hierarchy amongst day jobs. To her mind being a schoolteacher wasn't that much more interesting than being a pensions consultant, but to Neville there was evidently a big difference.

'Anyway,' he went on, 'Freddie had sorted out his own pension provisions very carefully indeed. Elizaveta is extremely well-heeled.' He spoke with a degree of resentment. 'It's why she can always afford to be giving her "drinkies things".'

'I've heard about those, but I don't know much detail.'

'Oh, they're part of her power base, those "drinkies" parties. Elizaveta has a level of deviousness in her that makes Machiavelli look like a rank amateur. She's always been one of those manipulators who likes to "colonize" people. If you're not *for* me, you're *against* me, that's her approach to life.'

'Have you ever been to one of her "drinkies things"?'

'Good Lord, no. I can't be bought by a free glass of champagne.' The statement, intended to sound rather magnificent, succeeded in sounding petty.

'But if Olly Pinto is part of this charmed inner circle, then why didn't he join in Elizaveta's boycott of the production?'

'Interesting point, Carole. I wondered that a bit myself. Then I decided it was for one of two reasons.' He clearly liked dividing things into numbered sections, another schoolmasterly trait perhaps. 'Either it was just sheer greed. He saw a socking great part being offered to him, and he thought, "Yes, I'm going to grab that."

'The other possibility – and I think the one I favour – is that Elizaveta encouraged him to take the part.'

'Why would she do that?'

'Because she knows he's not a very good actor. I think what she hoped for first didn't happen – that her walkout would stop the production stone dead in its tracks. Elizaveta's not used to playing small parts, you see. Most productions she's been in for SADOS, if she'd walked out, it really would have been the end. She didn't realize how easy it would be to find another Mrs Dudgeon.'

'I'm sure Jude would be very flattered to hear you say that,' Carole observed drily.

'Sorry, that didn't come out right.' He was quick to come back with a smooth response. 'I mean how easy it would be to find another *and vastly superior* Mrs Dudgeon.'

'Ha-ha. But, Neville, are you saying Elizaveta encouraged Olly to take the part of Dick Dudgeon because she thought he would ruin the production?'

'I wouldn't put it past her. Another reason she might have done it is so that she has a spy in the enemy camp.'

'So that he reports back to her everything that happens during rehearsals for *The Devil's Disciple*?'

'Once again, I wouldn't put it past her. Elizaveta Dalrymple is a woman of remarkable deviousness. She deeply loathed

Ritchie Good for what he said to her about her past – particularly because he did it so publicly. She'd want to get her own back.'

'Enough to arrange his hanging?' asked Carole, making the question sound more frivolous than it was.

'Ah. Do I detect I'm with that contingent of the *Devil's Disciple* company who believes we have a murder on our hands?'

'I'd never rule out any possibility.'

'Hm.'

'Do I gather, Neville, that you do rule out that possibility?'

'I think an accident is the more likely scenario. As to murder . . .' He acted as though he were contemplating the possibility for the first time. 'Well, if it was, we wouldn't lack for suspects, would we? Was there anyone in SADOS whose back Ritchie Good hadn't put up?'

'I don't really know,' Carole lied. Jude had kept her up to date with everything. 'I haven't been with the group for long.'

'No, of course not. Well, someone with an ego the size of Ritchie's doesn't really notice whose sensibilities he's trampling over. I mean, did you hear what he said to cause the big bust-up with Elizaveta?'

'Yes, I got reports of that from Jude.'

'Ah, your pretty friend, yes.' He said this as though he were a great connoisseur of the feminine gender, and Carole felt an atavistic pang from her childhood, the inescapable fact that she would never be known as 'the pretty one'.

Putting such thoughts firmly to one side, she asked, 'And did Ritchie insult you in the same kind of way?'

'No, he laid off me pretty much.' The smug smile reappeared. 'He recognized that I was a lot more intelligent than he was. And at least as good an actor. So he tended to avoid direct confrontation with me.'

'There was no rivalry between you?'

'Good Lord, no. Well, certainly not on my side. I had no reason to be jealous of Ritchie. I suppose he might well have been jealous of me, though.' Again it seemed that this monstrously egotistical thought was a new one to him. 'Yes, he probably was jealous of me.'

'I wondered if there was ever any rivalry between you over women . . .?'

'Women?'

'Women in the company.'

'How do you mean?' He spoke innocently, but there was a kind of roguishness in his manner too.

'I just wondered whether there might have been any conflict between the two of you over some woman you both fancied . . .?'

'Unlikely.'

'I mean, Ritchie Good apparently had a habit of coming on to every woman he met. He even came on to me,' confided Carole, blushing slightly.

'I don't think that meant much with him. Just a knee-jerk reaction,' said Neville, unaware of how offensive his remark might be. 'Ritchie was all mouth and no trousers. Glib with the chat, but he didn't follow through.'

'Unlike you . . .?' Carole suggested rather boldly.

Neville Prideaux smiled a wolfish smile. 'I generally get what I want. And besides, Ritchie was in a different position from me. He was married.'

'And you are not?'

A thin smile answered the question. 'I got divorced when I retired. A wife who is excellent as a house mistress at a boy's public school did not fulfil the requirements I had for the rest of my life. Now I am more of an emotional freelance.'

'What does that mean?'

'I am not looking for anything long term in a relationship. As long as it's still fun, I will keep on with it. Once it ceases to be fun, I end it.'

Carole found that Neville Prideaux's charm was diminishing by the minute. Otherwise she might not have pushed ahead with her next line of questioning. 'I heard someone chatting at rehearsals and saying that you'd had a fling with my predecessor . . .'

'Sorry?'

'Hester Winstone.'

'Huh.' He looked displeased. 'You can't have any secrets with this lot.' Then he looked defiantly at Carole. 'So what if I did? We're both grown-ups.'

'But I'd heard that Ritchie Good came on to her too.'

'I thought we'd already established that Ritchie came on to anything in a skirt. Why, are you suggesting that Ritchie and I were rivals for Hester's affections, and I murdered him so I could have uncontested access to her?'

This was so close to what Carole had actually been thinking that she had some difficulty making her denial sound convincing.

'Well, I can assure you that wasn't the case. Hester and I shared one night of what could hardly be described as bliss and decided mutually that ours was not going to be *la grande affaire*.'

'Mutually?'

'I decided and told her. She didn't complain. Hester's a very unstable woman.'

Carole didn't disagree. Nor did she think it was the moment to ask Neville whether he thought his behaviour might have contributed to her instability.

'So,' he went on, 'if you're looking for someone who might have murdered Ritchie, I'm afraid you're very much barking up the wrong tree with me.'

'And who do you think might be the right tree?' No harm in asking.

'Well, I actually think you're stuck in a whole forest full of wrong trees. Because I firmly believe that Ritchie's death was an accident. That probably Gordon Blaine was playing about with his precious mechanism and left the wrong noose in place. But, if I were going to waste my time playing amateur detectives . . . I think the question I would ask is: Who has benefited from his death? Who is more relaxed, as if with his decease a huge weight has been lifted off their shoulders?'

'And what would your answer be?'

'Davina Vere Smith.'

NINETEEN

On the Wednesday morning Jude travelled by train for the two stops from Fethering to Fedborough. She felt no guilt in not including Carole in the day's mission. Jude, after all, was the one who had found Ritchie Good's body. Maybe that gave her some obscure right to meet his widow.

On the train she remembered Gwenda saying that she wasn't very mobile, and wondered about her level of disability. But the woman who opened the door of the terraced house in a road off Fedborough High Street showed no overt signs of illness and seemed to move with ease as she hastened to close the front door once her guest was inside. 'Sorry, need to keep out the cold,' she said.

Jude wouldn't have thought it was that cold, even a bit above average temperature for April. She herself was only wearing a cotton jacket over a T-shirt and skirt. The two chiffon scarves wound around her neck were statements of Jude's style rather than for warmth.

And the minute she stepped inside the house, she was glad not to be wearing more. The place was incredibly over-heated, but Gwenda Good was wearing a cardigan over a jumper and fleece jogging bottoms. Over this she had on a plastic apron with a Minnie Mouse image on it. Her hands were in yellow Marigold gloves. She wore her greying hair in a thick plait and had unglamorous black-rimmed glasses.

Jude found it very difficult to assess the woman's age, but certainly reckoned she was a lot older than her late husband.

'Very good of you to come,' said Gwenda Good, and led the way into a small sitting room that faced out on to the street. Wooden Venetian blinds were half-closed and two standard lamps were on to compensate for the gloom. One stood over a small table, on which was a bowl of water, dusters

and sponges and some small china figurines. Gwenda gestured
to them and said, 'Wednesday, that's the day I clean the collection. Oh, do sit down.'

As Jude sat in a leather armchair, she became aware of the
'collection' referred to. And the scale of it. It was clearly no
coincidence that Gwenda had a Minnie Mouse on her apron.
Because the image was reduplicated literally hundreds of times
throughout the sitting room. Shelves covered the two side
walls, and on one of these stood rows of figurines of Minnie
Mouse in a variety of costumes and poses, dressed as a balle-
rina, as Santa Claus, as a tennis player, as a doctor, as a
schoolteacher and many more.

A glass-fronted set of shelves was full to bursting of stuffed
Minnie Mouse toys, again in a wide range of liveries. Another
section featured Minnie Mouse accessories – pencil cases,
backpacks, lunch boxes, packs of cards, board games, jigsaws
and so on. Above these hung an opened Minnie Mouse
umbrella. Jude observed that even the cushion on her chair
wore the distinctive image with its spotted red bow. And the
two standard lamps had Minnie Mouse shades.

For once she was at a loss for words. She couldn't think of
anything nice to say about the aggregation of Minnie Mouses
and yet to behave as if she hadn't noticed it would be perverse.
She ended up saying, rather limply, 'Well, you've got quite a
collection here.'

'Yes, it's not bad,' Gwenda agreed, 'but there's always so
much more out there. It's hard work just trying to keep up.
EBay's made it easier sourcing the goodies, but you have to
keep your eye on the deadlines there, or you could miss
something great. And actually,' she said as if admitting some
shortcoming, 'most of the stuff I've got here is post-1968.'

'Sorry? Why is that significant?'

'Post-1968 is modern. Pre-1968 is vintage.'

'Ah.'

'And the prices are vintage too. You can spend literally
millions if you get into that market.'

Again Jude couldn't think of anything to say. The question
she was burning to ask – '*why* do you collect it?' – didn't
seem appropriate at that moment. So she fell back on a more

fitting expression of condolence. 'I'm very sorry about your husband's death.'

'Thank you.' The words were spoken automatically, without much emotion involved. Gwenda had gone back to sit at her table under the standard lamp, and continued with the cleaning process which Jude's arrival had interrupted. She put each figurine in the water, swirled it round and then wiped it down meticulously with a cloth. Those whose hollow interiors were accessible were carefully dried inside with a sponge.

Gwenda appeared almost to have forgotten that there was anyone else in the room. Jude found it a little odd that she hadn't been offered a cup of tea or coffee. After all, Gwenda was the one who had set up the encounter.

The silence was extended while the punctilious figurine-cleaning continued.

Eventually Jude said, 'You wanted to talk to me about your husband . . .?'

'Oh yes,' said Gwenda, as if being reminded of something she had completely forgotten. She looked a little disgruntled at having her attention taken away from the task in hand. 'You were the one who found him dead – that's right, isn't it?'

'I was the one who raised the alarm, yes,' Jude agreed, again keeping Hester Winstone's name out of it.

'And he was dead when you found him, not dying?'

'He was definitely dead.'

'And I gather just before that he'd been taking part in a demonstration of how the gallows worked.'

'That's right. He was part of a set-up with Gordon.'

'Gordon?'

'Yes. Gordon Blaine. He'd designed and built the gallows.'

'Ah. I don't know the names of any of the people Ritchie did his acting with.' She said this as if it would have been rather bizarre for her to have known them.

'Did you go and see any of the shows?'

'No.' Gwenda sounded surprised that the question needed asking. 'I couldn't, could I?'

This was such a peculiar statement that Jude immediately asked, 'Why couldn't you?'

'Well, for obvious reasons.' Which didn't do much to clarify the situation.

'What do you mean by—?'

But Gwenda was not about to offer explanations. 'Ritchie didn't talk about any of that,' she said. 'Except the women, of course.'

'The women?'

Once again Gwenda just moved on. 'From what you saw of Ritchie's body, would you say his death looked accidental?'

'It seems most likely that it was an accident, yes,' Jude replied cautiously. 'That is, if it wasn't suicide. Do you know whether your husband ever had any suicidal thoughts?'

'Good heavens, no. Ritchie had a very happy life. He liked his work at the bank. He enjoyed his play-acting. And then of course we had a very happy marriage.'

Jude knew it was impossible ever to look inside a marriage and see what's going on, but she would have loved to know how Gwenda Good defined 'happy'. She said, 'You must have been very upset when you got the news of his death.'

'Why?' Again the strangest of responses.

'Well, because your happy marriage was over.'

'It had run its course,' said the widow without sentiment. 'That was when it was destined to end. There's no point in getting upset over things that are preordained.'

This sounded like part of some spiritual package, so Jude said, 'It must be a comfort for you to have your faith.'

'I don't have any faith,' said Gwenda. 'Just a knowledge that everything that happens is preordained.'

'By whom?'

'Oh, I don't know that.'

This was becoming one of the most bizarre conversations Jude had ever participated in, and yet Ritchie Good's widow did not sound at all unhinged. Everything she said seemed to be entirely logical, at least to her.

Jude had heard that Ritchie Good's funeral had taken place the week before and assumed that, since the body had been released, the police investigation into the death had ended. So she asked, 'Was there a good turnout for your husband's funeral?'

'I believe so, yes.'

'You *believe so*?'

'Well, obviously I couldn't be there.'

'Why obviously?'

'I can't leave the house,' replied Gwenda, as if this were something that everyone in the world knew.

'Do you mean you are agoraphobic?'

The woman dismissed the word with a shrug. 'I'm not too bothered what people call it. I have no interest in psychobabble. I just don't leave the house.' This was spoken without any anxiety or self-pity, as a simple statement of fact. Not leaving the house seemed very normal to her.

'Not even to go to the shops?'

'I have everything delivered. I order online. What with that and eBay, I spend quite a lot of time on the laptop.' Again this was made to sound like the most natural thing in the world.

'A few minutes ago,' said Jude, 'you said that Ritchie didn't talk about his amateur dramatics, but he did talk about "the women" . . .'

'Yes.'

'Do you mind if I ask what you meant by that?'

'Not at all.' Gwenda seemed pleased that the matter had been raised. 'The thing is, Ritchie was a very attractive man . . .'

Jude was tempted to say, *Well, he certainly thought so*, but restrained herself.

'. . . and so, obviously, he had lots of women throwing themselves at him.' Gwenda looked straight at Jude for the first time in their conversation. 'Did you throw yourself at him?'

'Hardly.' Throwing herself at men was not Jude's style, though she couldn't deny the initial attraction she had felt for Ritchie Good.

'No, he didn't mention you.'

'Are you implying by that that he mentioned others?'

'Oh yes. Ritchie told me everything. There are a lot of unattached women in amateur dramatic societies, and quite a lot of them came on to him.'

'Don't you think he did some of the "coming on"?' Jude

couldn't forget his automatic 'Where have you been hiding all my life?'

'Oh no. He told me all about it. A lot of the women were very brazen. They would seek him out and try to get him on his own. Ritchie didn't give them any encouragement. And then most of them would quite shamelessly try to get him to go to bed with them.'

Jude, remembering how Janie Trotman had described her involvement with Ritchie Good, thought she could see a pattern emerging. She waited for more from Gwenda.

'And then of course at that point he had to disappoint them. He had to point out that he was happily married. To me.' There was huge complacency in the way she said these words.

And to Jude it all made perfect sense, explaining the gut feeling that she had had when alone in the Crown and Anchor with Ritchie. He was, as she'd thought after her chat with Janie, the male equivalent of a cock-teaser. He would come on to women, chat them up, get them to the point where they would agree to go to bed with him, before suddenly announcing that he couldn't go through with it because of his undying loyalty to his wife.

That was how he got his kicks. And then he would add the refinement of telling Gwenda exactly what had happened – or at least his version of what had happened. And their marriage would be strengthened. In fact, Jude suspected, Ritchie's descriptions of his skirmishes with other women were the dynamo of his relationship with Gwenda. As she had frequently thought before, human imagination can hardly cope with the variety of what goes on inside marriages.

Gwenda Good was still smiling smugly as she dried off a figurine of Minnie Mouse as cheerleader. She didn't seem to feel the need to initiate further conversation.

So, after a lengthy silence, Jude said, 'I'm still not quite clear why you asked me here. Have we talked about what you wanted to talk about?'

'Oh yes,' said Gwenda blandly.

'Well, could you tell me what it was?'

'Of course. I just wanted to know that you agreed Ritchie's death was an accident.'

A part of Jude wondered why that question couldn't have been asked on the telephone. But a more substantial part of her wouldn't have missed the morning she'd just experienced for the world.

'Why was that important to you, Gwenda?'

'Because of the Life Insurance. I didn't want there to be any delay on the Life Insurance, and that could have happened if there was any doubt about the circumstances of his death.'

'Yes, I suppose there could have been.'

'And if there were a question of suicide the cover could be invalid.'

'Well, I just asked you about that, and you said there was no chance that Ritchie would ever have committed suicide.'

'Oh yes, I know that. But I wondered if anyone had been spreading contrary rumours around.'

'From everything that I've heard discussed at rehearsals, nobody seems to think there was any question of suicide.'

'Oh, good.' The smug smile grew broader. 'Ritchie worked in Life Insurance, you see. And so he himself was very well insured. He used to say to me quite often – it was one of our little jokes – "I'd be a lot more valuable to you dead than I am while I'm alive."'

And Gwenda Good laughed. 'So I think when it all comes through,' she said, 'I'll be allowing myself a real splurge on eBay for more of my precious Minnies.'

TWENTY

A s she travelled back on the train to Fethering, Jude went over in her mind the conversation she had just shared. And the more she thought about it, the more bizarre it seemed. Through her work as a healer, Jude had come across mental illness in many forms, but she had never met anyone who behaved like Gwenda. And indeed she wondered whether 'mental illness' was the right diagnosis. Though undoubtedly agoraphobic, the woman did not seem distressed at any level. But there was something definitely odd about her.

The glee with which she'd talked about the Life Insurance windfall about to come her way made Jude wonder for a moment whether Gwenda could have had a hand in her husband's death. Killing someone for their insurance is one of the oldest plotlines in the history of crime (and in its fictional version).

On the other hand, if the woman really never left the house, she couldn't have arranged the murder without the help of an accomplice. The more Jude thought about it, the less likely it seemed that Gwenda had been involved.

Still, she had plenty of news to share with Carole so, on her way back from Fethering Station, she called at High Tor to invite her neighbour round for coffee. And, once inside Woodside Cottage, because it was so near lunchtime, opening a bottle of Chilean Chardonnay seemed simpler than the palaver of making coffee.

After the exchange of their news, Carole asked, 'What do you think of Neville's idea that Davina had a motive to kill Ritchie?'

'Well, he's certainly right that she's more relaxed without him around. He totally destroyed her confidence as a director. She just kowtowed to him, whereas with Olly as Dick Dudgeon, she orders him about all over the place.'

'And, of course, after you, she was the first one into St Mary's Hall to discover Ritchie's body. Maybe she was checking up that her little ploy had worked.'

'Possible.' Sceptically, Jude screwed up her face. 'Doesn't seem likely, though. And your mentioning that reminds me that Hester Winstone was also present. She was in the hall before I got there.'

'Alone with Ritchie – alive or dead. And tell me again, Jude, what was it exactly that Hester said?'

'"It's my fault. I'm the reason why he's dead."'

'Which could be an admission that she had killed him.'

'It could . . . except for the fact that the police released her after interviewing her. I can't imagine Hester was in a robust enough emotional state to lie convincingly, so she must have provided an explanation for her presence in St Mary's Hall that let her off the hook.'

Carole sighed. 'It's a pity we can't contact Hester. I think she could provide answers to many of the questions that are troubling us.'

'I agree. I tried ringing her home again yesterday. Once again the phone was answered by Mike, not very pleased to hear from me. Once again he said Hester was "staying with a friend".'

'Do you think that's true?'

Jude shrugged. 'Could be. No way of finding out.'

'I think we should keep an eye on Davina at rehearsal tomorrow night. See if she gives anything away.'

'What, like confessing that she murdered Ritchie? I don't think it's very likely she'd provide chapter and verse on—'

'Don't be trivial, Jude. You know what I mean.'

'Well, yes, I do, but—'

Jude was again interrupted, this time by the phone ringing. She answered it, and heard an elocuted female voice ask, 'Is that Jude?'

'Yes.'

'How nice to hear you. This is Elizaveta Dalrymple.'

'Oh.' That was a surprise.

'I gather I have to congratulate you, Jude.'

'On what?'

'On taking over from me as Mrs Dudgeon and, from all accounts, being rather splendid in the part.'

'Well, I'm doing my best.'

'I'm sure you are. And also I gather you've got a friend of yours involved too, in the role of prompter. Carole Seddon, isn't that right?'

'Yes, it is.' For someone who was boycotting the production of *The Devil's Disciple*, Elizaveta Dalrymple seemed very well informed about it. Jude wondered who was reporting back to her. Olly Pinto seemed the most likely candidate.

'Anyway,' said Elizaveta, 'I was wondering whether you – and your friend Carole – might be free on Saturday evening . . .?'

'Well . . .'

'It's just for a little "drinkies thing" at my place. Totally informal. Say about six o'clock . . .? Would you be free?'

'Well, I know I am. I'm not sure about Carole.' At the mention of her name Carole looked puzzled. 'But actually she's here. I'll ask her.'

'Oh, she's there?' said Elizaveta. 'I didn't realize you two cohabited.'

'No, we don't. We—'

'Don't worry. Your secret's safe with me.'

Jude suppressed a giggle. It wasn't the moment to put Elizaveta right, to say no, in fact she and Carole were not a lesbian couple. She wondered whether the misapprehension would lead to interesting misunderstandings on the Saturday night. That is, assuming Carole was free.

Jude looked across at her neighbour and said that they were being invited for 'drinkies' at Elizaveta Dalrymple's. And was able to relay the glad news to their hostess that Carole Seddon would be able to come too.

'Interesting,' said Carole when Jude had put the phone down. 'I agree.'

'Neville Prideaux told me that these "drinkies" sessions of Elizaveta's have been going on for years. Something she started when the much-adored Freddie was around. He described them as part of her "power base".'

'So why have we been invited?'

'Well, Jude, I'm sure it's not just for the charm of our personalities. According to Neville, Elizaveta Dalrymple always has an ulterior motive.'

'So we just have to find out what it is.'

'Yes,' agreed Carole. 'We do.'

They were both at rehearsal on the Thursday evening and, as agreed, they kept a watching brief on Davina Vere Smith. It was undeniable that since the death of Ritchie Good she had relaxed considerably in her directorial role. And she enjoyed having Olly Pinto as a punchbag.

He still wasn't on top of Dick Dudgeon's lines, so Carole was once again kept busy as prompter. And the further he got into rehearsal for his leading role, the more clearly his inadequacies as an actor were exposed. He just didn't convince on stage. While he should have been projecting the sardonic insouciance of Shaw's anti-hero, he looked insecure, uncertain not only about his lines but also in his whole demeanour.

Increasingly Carole wondered if what Neville Prideaux had suggested might be right. That, in spite of her boycott, Elizaveta Dalrymple had encouraged Olly to take part because she knew he would ruin the production.

There was one confrontation during that evening's rehearsal which caused Carole and Jude to exchange covert looks. Davina Vere Smith was working on a scene in Act Two, the first time Dick Dudgeon and Judith Anderson are left alone together. Storm Lavelle, who by then had her words indelibly fixed on the interior of her cranium, was being very patient as Olly Pinto stumbled and paraphrased, as ever. And even when he got the lines right, he managed to get the intonations wrong.

Each time they had to go back on the scene, the tension in Davina increased. Eventfully, she could stand it no more and burst out, 'Oh, for God's sake, Olly! Don't you have any idea of the basics of acting?'

'Yes, of course I do. I'm just used to working with more sympathetic directors.'

'Oh, are you? Well, let me tell you, I can be a very sympathetic director when the talent of the people involved justifies my sympathy. Come back, Ritchie Good – all is forgiven!'

'You weren't sympathetic to Ritchie,' objected Olly. 'You were just afraid of him.'

'I was certainly not afraid of him.'

'Yes, you were. You never argued with him. Whatever he suggested, whatever he wanted to do, you just went along with it.'

'That was because I trusted him. Because I'd worked with him many times before on other productions and I respected his instincts. I knew he was a good actor, and it was worth putting up with a few disadvantages – like his ego, for instance – because a really good performance would emerge at the end of the process. Why else do you think I put such effort into persuading him to be in the production?'

It was at this moment that Carole and Jude exchanged looks. Somehow they'd both thought that Ritchie Good had been foisted on to Davina Vere Smith by the power brokers of SADOS. But if it was she who had brought him into the *Devil's Disciple* company, that rather changed their views on the situation.

The last thing Davina would have wanted would be to lose her original Dick Dudgeon.

Jude had a call the following morning from a friend she hadn't heard anything of for a long time. They had first met when Isabel, known universally as 'Belle', worked as a nurse in one of the big London hospitals. It had been on a course about healing. Belle, increasingly disillusioned by the shortcomings and iniquities of the NHS, had a growing interest in alternative therapies, but she found there was still a scepticism about them amongst the more traditional medical practitioners. Her ambition was to see the alternative integrated with the professional.

The two women had seen a lot of each other when, both between marriages, they had lived in London, but since Jude had moved to Fethering their contact had reduced to the occasional phone call. So when Belle rang on that Friday morning in April they had a lot of catching up to do.

They checked up first on each other's love lives. Both were currently unattached, Belle's second marriage having come to 'as sticky an end as the first one – God, men are bastards'. She asked whether her friend had had any recent 'skirmishes' but, normally very open to her intimates about such matters, Jude didn't mention her recent involvement with a real tennis enthusiast called Piers Targett. Even though months had passed since she had last seen him, it still hurt.

'Anyway, what about work?' she asked.

'Big changes,' said Belle. 'I've left the NHS.'

'Really?'

'Yes, it was just getting so dispiriting. They kept bringing in new schedules. I wasn't being allowed to spend the kind of time with patients that I wanted to. I was leaving every shift feeling totally frustrated by the fact that I hadn't achieved as much as I wanted to.

'Anyway, the one good thing that came out of my second divorce was that I got a bit of money from the bastard. Not much, but enough for me to take some time out from being employed, so I gave in my notice at the hospital.'

'Not early retirement?'

'God, no.' Belle was about the same age as Jude. 'I like to think I've got a few more useful years in me. But I took the opportunity to do a couple of courses. Like the healing one when we first met, though I've decided I haven't really got what it takes to be a healer.'

'I thought you were very good.'

'I was OK, but I hadn't got the magic. Not like you have.'

Jude did not demur at the compliment. She knew, when it came to healing, she was blessed with a gift, and she was no believer in false modesty.

'So,' Belle went on, 'I thought I should concentrate on a more practical kind of therapy. I did a course in reflexology, which I found very interesting, but I still didn't think it was quite for me. And then I did a course in kinesiology.'

Whereas when Storm Lavelle talked about going on courses, Jude suspected a level of faddishness in her, she never doubted the complete seriousness of Belle.

'Funny you should mention that. I'm getting very interested in kinesiology,' she said. 'Been reading up about it. I think it really works.'

'Me too.' The enthusiasm grew in Belle's voice. 'No, the further I got into the subject, the more I realized it fitted me like a glove.'

'So have you put a shingle on your door and set up on your own as a kinesiologist?'

'No, I'm not quite ready for that yet. And when my money from the bastard ran out, I needed a regular income, so I got another nursing job.'

'Not back in the NHS?'

'By no means. Private sector. In a convalescent home. I've been there for five months. And I've been intending to ring you all that time, but I've got waylaid by, you know, starting the job, and getting my new house – well, old house but new to me – vaguely habitable. But the reason I wanted to ring you is that we're practically neighbours.'

'What?'

'The home where I'm working is in Clincham . . .'

'Wow!'

'. . . and I'm living in a little village called Weldisham.'

'Oh, goodness me. Just up on the edge of the Downs. It's lovely up there.' Jude remembered when she and Carole had investigated some human bones discovered in a barn near Weldisham. 'Well, since you're so close, we absolutely must meet up.'

'I agree. That's why I was ringing.'

'But tell me first about this convalescent home where you're working. Are you enjoying it?'

'Best job I've ever had. I've been so caught up in it that's another reason why I haven't phoned you. It's a big house just on the outskirts of Clincham, lovely setting, great views looking up towards Goodwood and the Downs. Called Casements. And the patients are, well, what you'd expect – people recovering from operations, a bit of respite care, some who're just run down or have had breakdowns, a few terminal cases. But the doctor who runs it is the kind I've been looking for all my life.'

'You don't mean in the sense of a potential Husband Number Three?'

'Certainly not. Rob is very happily married, I'm glad to say. He's a qualified doctor, but he's really found his métier as director of Casements. What's more, he's the perfect boss for me because he does genuinely believe in mixing traditional and alternative therapies.'

'So you get to do a bit of kinesiology?'

'Yes. Which is great. Rob also has people who come in to do reiki and acupuncture. I mean, none of it's forced on the patients. And of course I do the normal everyday nursing stuff as well. But if any of the patients want to have a go with me on the kinesiology, well, they can. And I must say I've had some really encouraging results. Really think I've helped some of them. I no longer leave work feeling dissatisfied.'

'That sounds brilliant. Well, look, come on, diaries at the ready. Let's sort out a time when we can meet up. Presumably if you're in Weldisham three miles up a country lane, you must have a car. There's a very nice pub here in Fethering called the Crown and Anchor.'

'There's also a nice one in Weldisham called the Hare and Hounds.'

'Yes, I know it.' Jude and Carole had spent quite a bit of time there when they'd been investigating the death on the Downs.

'Oh, before I forget, Jude . . . there was another reason why I phoned you today.'

'Really?'

'Yes. Your name came up yesterday when I was talking to one of the patients here.'

'Oh? Who was it?'

'Her name's Hester Winstone.'

TWENTY-ONE

'Staying with a friend.' Yes, thought Jude, that's exactly how a man like Mike Winstone would explain away his wife's absence. In his shallow world of cricketing heartiness there was no room for uncomfortable realities like mental illness. Belle told her that Hester had been in Casements almost from the moment she had been released by the police after questioning about Ritchie Good's death. She was under the care of a psychiatrist, but she had also accepted Belle's offer of some kinesiology treatment. It was during one of their sessions that Jude's name had come up. 'She was very kind to me,' Hester Winstone had said.

According to Belle, Hester wasn't isolated at Casements. Though she had breakfast in her room, she ate other meals communally with the other patients. She was on a heavy dose of antidepressants, and she was given sleeping pills at night. Belle said she was not a difficult patient. She seemed very withdrawn and, yes, in a state of shock.

Jude had then given a brief outline of the events in Smalting that had led to Ritchie Good's death, and Belle said, hearing that, she wasn't surprised at the state Hester was in. 'So do you think she actually witnessed him dying?'

'I think so. But I can't be sure. I'd really love to talk to Hester about that.'

'Well, why don't you?'

'What do you mean?'

'Come and visit her at Casements.'

'Could I do that?'

'Why not?'

'I thought perhaps she wasn't allowed visitors.'

'Not so far as I know. Her husband comes to visit her twice a week. Regular as clockwork. Two o'clock on Wednesdays and Saturdays.'

'Have you met him, Belle?'

'No, I haven't.'

'So you don't think there'd be any problem if I were to visit her?'

'I wouldn't think so. I'll check with Rob if you like. I think he'd welcome your coming. I think he'd also welcome it if you tried a bit of healing on her.'

'That's a thought. Would you mind asking him, though?'

'No problem. I'll be going in after lunch. My shift starts at two. I'll ask Rob and phone you back.'

'Well, if it's OK, maybe I could come and see Hester this afternoon?'

'I can see no reason why not,' said Belle.

As it turned out she must have phoned her boss straight after their call ended, because she rang back within five minutes, offering to pick Jude up in Fethering at one-thirty and drive her to Casements.

It was good to see Belle again. Jude always found that, whatever time had elapsed since their last meeting, they could pick up together as if they'd only met the day before. But they didn't talk a lot on the journey to Clincham. Jude was preoccupied with her forthcoming encounter with Hester Winstone and, as she did before a healing session, was focusing her energies. Belle knew her well enough to respect the silence between them.

Casements was a large house set back from the road some miles outside Clincham in the Midhurst direction. Its name clearly derived from its large number of windows, all criss-crossed with lead latticework. It looked more like a country house than a hospital.

As she brought her Toyota Yaris to a halt in the staff car park, Belle said, 'I'd like you to meet Rob. I told him you were a healer.'

'Fine.'

The door off the main hall to the Director's Office was open, which seemed to typify the air of relaxed warmth around Casements. Rob himself reinforced that impression. A tall man in his forties, he dressed more casually than the average GP, but there was a shrewdness in his blue eyes which suggested he was aware of everything that was going on around him.

'My friend Jude,' said Belle as they stood in the doorway.

'Great to meet you.' Rob's handshake was firm and welcoming. 'I hear you're a healer.'

'Yes.'

'I can't claim to understand how it works, but I have a great respect for your profession.' Jude wondered how Carole would have reacted to hearing what she did described as a 'profession', as Rob went on, 'And I've seen some remarkable results from the work of healers.'

Jude grinned. 'I can't claim that I know how it works either. But I know *when* it works.'

'Sounds good enough to me. As Belle's probably said, we use a lot of alternative therapies here – though actually I prefer to call them *complementary* therapies. Medical knowledge is improving all the time, but there are still too many things we are clueless about when it comes to curing them. So I'm in favour of trying anything – short of downright charlatanism – that might work.'

'Sounds a good approach to me,' said Jude.

'Were you thinking of trying any healing with Hester this afternoon?'

'Only with your permission. She's your patient, not mine.

I don't want to do anything that might clash with the treatment she's already receiving.'

'I don't see how healing could do that,' said Rob. 'Mixing therapies is not like mixing medications. No, if you think you can help her – and Hester herself doesn't object – you have my permission to use your healing powers on her.'

'I'll see how she feels about it . . . if the moment comes up. But thank you.'

'And I wish you good luck.'

'Oh?'

'The psychiatrist who's working with Hester is finding it hard work. Not that she doesn't cooperate. She's very polite, very accommodating, but there's a whole lot of stuff she's holding in, things she won't talk about.'

'But she's not pretending there's nothing wrong with her?'

'No, she recognizes there's something wrong. She seems almost relieved to be here. But in terms of getting her better . . . Well, until she opens up a bit about what's really trauma-tized her, it's uphill work.'

'I'll see if I can get her talking, though I'm really just here as a friend, not in any professional capacity.'

'I understand that. Anyway, let me know how you get on with her. Drop in here when you're leaving.'

'Of course.'

'There have been quite a few cases in the past where I've thought healing might have some effect.' Rob focused his blue eyes on her. 'I wonder, Jude, would you mind my contacting you if something similar were to come up in the future?'

'I'd certainly be up for having a go. Can't guarantee results, I'm afraid. You never can with healing.'

'You never can with a lot of traditional medicine,' said Rob, smiling.

Hester Winstone's room was at the back of Casements, with latticework windows looking up towards the gentle undulations of the South Downs. It was comfortably furnished, more like an upmarket hotel room than anything to do with a hospital.

And the manner of Hester's greeting to Jude was more suited to a hotel guest than a patient. She was smartly dressed in a tartan skirt and pink cashmere jumper. Her red hair was neatly gathered at the back in a black slide and she was wearing more make-up than she had when attending SADOS rehearsals.

Belle had gone ahead to check that Hester felt up to the visit, and the patient was prepared for Jude's appearance. Which meant that she must have agreed to their meeting. Her behaviour was that of a well-brought-up hostess, offering her visitor tea or coffee. 'The staff are very good at catering for our every need.'

Jude opted for tea, thinking that having a drink might extend the length of her stay. There were a great many things she wanted to ask, but she recognized that she had to be gentle and circumspect in her approach. Beneath Hester's brittle politeness, Jude knew there was a lot of pain, and she did not want to be responsible for aggravating that pain. Given Mike Winstone's unwillingness to have anything potentially unpleasant in his life, having his wife hospitalized (even if it was covered up by the bland lie about 'staying with a friend') must have meant there was something seriously wrong with her.

But in their first few exchanges the woman's mask of middle-class gentility did not crack at all. The only discordant sign was a slight detachment in her manner. Her eyes were not glazed, but they looked distant. She behaved like some skilfully constructed and very correct automaton. Jude presumed this was the effect of her medication.

Their polite surface conversation had almost run out before the welcome interruption of a neatly uniformed woman with tea and biscuits. Hester's expert hostess manner seemed to welcome the rituals of pouring and passing the cup.

Having taken a sip of tea and a bite of biscuit, Jude felt she could risk moving the conversation away from pleasantries. 'All's going well with *The Devil's Disciple*,' she said. 'If they knew I was seeing you today, I'm sure lots of the company would have sent good wishes.'

'That's very nice of them.' Since no actual good wishes had been sent, this comment sounded slightly incongruous.

'And Carole has taken over the job of prompter.'

'Carole?' Hester repeated vaguely.

'My friend Carole. Do you remember? She was with me when we met in the car park. You know, after you'd . . .'

'Yes.' Hester Winstone's face clouded. Perhaps she didn't want to be reminded of her 'cry for help'. 'I'm glad to hear all's going well,' she said with an attempt at insouciance.

'Though Olly Pinto's still having a bit of a problem with the lines . . .' Jude went on. No reaction. '. . . Having had to take over at such short notice . . .' Still nothing. '. . . From Ritchie Good.'

The name did produce a flicker in Hester Winstone's eyes. Quickly followed by a welling up of tears. Sobs were soon shuddering through her body.

Instantly Jude was up and cuddling the woman to her capacious bosom. 'Just lie down on the bed,' she said. Mutely, Hester obeyed. Jude ran her hands up and down the contours of the body, not quite touching, as she concentrated her energy. The sobs subsided.

'What are you doing?' asked Hester drowsily.

'It's a kind of healing technique,' said Jude.

She continued in silence for about twenty minutes, focusing where she felt the greatest tension, on the shoulders and the lower back. During that time Hester dropped into a half-doze, from which she emerged as Jude drew her hands away and collapsed, drained, into her chair.

'God, that feels better,' said Hester. 'Thank you.'

'My pleasure.'

'How do you do it?'

'I honestly don't know. It's just something I found I could do.' Jude looked into her client's hazel eyes. 'How're you feeling now?'

'As I said, better.'

'Is there anything you want to talk about?'

'Like what?'

'What's been bugging you. What's got you into this state.'

'Hm.' There was a long silence. Then, slowly, Hester Winstone began, 'It was Ritchie . . . seeing Ritchie, that's what pushed me over the edge.'

'But what brought you up to the edge – that had been building for some time, hadn't it?'

Hester nodded. 'Most of my life, I sometimes think.' Jude offered no prompt, just let the woman take her own time. 'I think I've always had this sense of inadequacy. This feeling that when it came to the test – any kind of test – I'd be found wanting. And whereas I thought I'd grow out of it, in fact, as I've got older, it's got worse.'

'Was there anything particular that made it get worse – I mean, apart from what's happened the last few weeks?'

'I suppose when my father died, that hit me quite hard.'

'You were very close to him?'

Hester nodded. 'Yes. He probably spoiled me, actually. But he always, kind of, appreciated things I did. I was never particularly brilliant at anything – exams, sport, I was just kind of average. But Daddy seemed quite happy with that. He didn't want me to achieve more – or if he did I was never aware of him putting any pressure on me. So I, kind of, felt secure when Daddy was around.'

'How old were you when he died?'

'Nineteen. In my second year at catering college. My mother was disappointed – she said I ought to have gone to a proper university, but Daddy told me catering college was fine. I've always liked cooking and . . .' For a moment some memory clouded her focus.

'And then your father died . . .' Jude prompted gently.

'Yes, it was very sudden. I had a very bad time then. I couldn't finish my course, I dropped out.'

'Was it some kind of breakdown?'

'I suppose, in retrospect, that's what it was.'

'Did you have any treatment then?'

'No. Perhaps I should have done. I went back home and lived with my mother. And that wasn't good. Because she was in a pretty bad place too, and . . . It was almost as if she was jealous of me.'

'Why?'

'I suppose because my father had found me easier to love than he had her.'

Hester looked shocked by her words, as though it was a thought that she'd had for a long time, but never before articulated.

'Anyway, then my mother remarried.'

'Did you get on with her new husband?'

'Yes, no worries there. He was fine. And I was quite grateful to him, actually. Because he kind of took my mother's focus away from me. And I got better and . . . well, to say I blossomed might be overstating things, but I was OK. And then I did a course in sports marketing – not a university course, just a one-year diploma, but it was good. It was out of that I got a job with a company that was trying to raise the profile of cricket as a participant sport. They don't exist now, but it was quite fun back then. I mean, I'd only got a secretarial job, but the people I was working with were quite jolly.'

'And was it through your work there that you met Mike?'

'Yes. We went out a few times and I thought it was just for laughs, but suddenly he's asking me to marry him.'

Classic syndrome, thought Jude. A girl who adored her father tries to replace him with another older man. But of course she didn't say anything.

'So we get married and suddenly we've got the two boys and . . . so it goes.'

'And how have you been since that time?'

'What, you mean mentally?'

'Yes.'

'Fine. Quite honestly, bringing up two boys, you don't exactly have time to think about your own state of mind . . . or anything else much.'

'So your feelings of inadequacy . . . you didn't have any time for those?'

Hester grinned wryly. 'Oh no, they were still there. I think they were born with me, part of my DNA . . . like red hair.' By instinct her hand found the hair at her temple before she said tellingly, 'And Mike does have very high standards.'

TWENTY-TWO

'You mean,' asked Jude, 'you feel under pressure to keep up with those standards?'

'I suppose so, yes. Mike likes things done a certain way. Not unreasonably,' she hastened to add, lest her words might sound like criticism. 'But he and the boys, well . . . they're a lot more efficient and organized about things than I am.'

Her words confirmed the impression of the Winstones' marriage that had been forming for some time in Jude's mind: Hester cast in the role of the slightly daffy woman in a chauvinist household of practical men, her fragile confidence being worn away by the constant drip-drip of implied criticism. But again Jude didn't say anything about that.

'You once told me that you joined the SADOS because you had time on your hands.'

'Yes, well, with the boys both boarding at Charterhouse, there was so much less ferrying around to be done. I seem to have spent most of the last twelve years driving them some-where or other, so yes, it did feel as if I had time on my hands.'

'And also it was doing something for you, rather than for somebody else,' Jude observed shrewdly.

'I suppose that was part of the attraction.'

'And was Mike positively against the idea?'

'No, he wouldn't come out strongly against something like that. Not his style. But he'd sort of dismiss it as something silly that women do.'

And so the process of undermining would continue.

Jude wondered whether she should ask whether Hester minded the kind of gentle interrogation she was undergoing, but thought that might be unwise. The healing had created an intimacy between the two women that was too precious to break.

'And helping out with front of house on the pantomime was the first thing you'd done for SADOS?'

'Yes. I got in touch when Mike went off to New Zealand. In a rather pathetic fit of pique, I suppose.'

'Sounds to me like a fairly justifiable fit of pique.'

'I don't know about that. Anyway, I said I'd help out with the panto.'

'Did you actually become a member of SADOS?'

'You bet. I had Mimi Lassiter on to me straight away, demanding a subscription. She's like a terrier about ensuring everyone in SADOS is fully paid up. I think she regards it as her mission in life.'

Jude smiled. 'And it was then that you met Ritchie Good . . .?' She spoke the name gently, worried that it might once again set off the hysterics.

But Hester was calmer this time. The healing had done its work. 'Yes,' she replied.

'And you got the full chat-up routine from him?' She nodded. 'And were flattered by the attention?' Another slightly shamefaced nod. 'How far did he go?'

'What, in terms of what he wanted us to do?'

'Yes.'

'Well, he . . .' This was embarrassing too. 'He sort of implied he wanted us to go to bed together.'

'And were you shocked by that, or what?'

'Well, I was . . . I don't know. I suppose I was attracted by the idea . . . a bit. I mean, I was in a strange state, sort of vulnerable and . . . And then Mike had just gone off to New Zealand – virtually without saying goodbye to me and . . . I don't know,' she said again.

'And when Ritchie had virtually got you to agree to go to bed with him, he then went cold on the idea, saying that he couldn't cheat on his wife?'

Hester Winstone's eyes widened. 'Jude, how on earth do you know that? You weren't there in the Cricketers, were you?'

'No. Let's just say there seems to be a pattern in Ritchie Good's chatting-up technique.'

'Oh.' Hester still looked bewildered.

'And I dare say that left you feeling pretty bad?'

'Well, yes. I mean, the fact that I'd even gone along with the idea, that I'd even contemplated betraying Mike, it was . . . It made me feel even worse about myself. It made me feel stupid and unattractive.'

'And weak when Neville Prideaux came on to you?'

'Yes.' Hester looked vague again. 'I told you about that, did I?' Jude nodded. 'Yes, Neville was much more practical about the whole business than Ritchie.'

'He really wanted you to succumb to his charms?'

'Mm.' She spoke with slight distaste. 'Though I don't know whether it was me he wanted, or just a woman. A conquest.'

'But you allowed him to . . . conquer you?'

A quick nod. 'Really, once I'd agreed to go back to his flat . . . well, he seemed to take it for granted that I'd agreed to everything else. And he kept saying he'd really fallen for me, and that I was beautiful and . . . I suppose I behaved like a classic inexperienced teenager.'

'And Neville behaved like a classic experienced seducer?'

'Yes. I felt terrible afterwards. I mean, while I could convince myself there was some love involved, well, it was . . . sort of all right. But when it had happened, and I realized he'd just taken advantage of me, and I'd done God knows how much harm to my marriage and . . . Neville didn't want to see me again. He didn't want to have any more to do with me, and at the read-through for *The Devil's Disciple* he behaved like nothing had happened between us.'

'And that's what made you feel so miserable that, in the car park, you took the nail scissors out of your bag and . . .?'

Hester nodded again. She looked very crumpled, very downcast. Jude let the silence last. Then she said, 'Can we talk now about the Sunday rehearsal when Gordon Blaine and Ritchie Good demonstrated the gallows?'

A shudder ran through the woman's body. 'That . . . I don't . . . That was what pushed me over the edge. I can't talk about it.'

'Don't you think talking about it might help?'

'No, it could only make things worse.'

'You must have talked to the police about it, Hester.'

'What makes you say that?'

'The fact that they released you.'

'How do you mean?'

'When I saw you that afternoon, you said that it was your fault, that you were the reason he was dead. By the way, I didn't tell the police you'd said that.'

'Why not?'

'Because, heard by the wrong people, it could sound as though you were confessing to having killed him.'

'What do you mean by "the wrong people"?'

'I mean people who thought Ritchie had been murdered, And, at least at first, the police must be included in that number. But you must have told them something which stopped them being suspicious of you, something that let you off the hook.'

'Yes, I suppose I did.'

'Are you happy to tell me what you told the police?'

There was a long silence. Then Hester said, 'I've tried to blank it out of my mind.'

'I'm sure you have.'

'I don't like going back there.'

'But you must know that your mind's going to have to come to terms with it at some point.'

'Mm.'

'And I think you'll feel better when you face it, face what actually happened.'

'Maybe.' But she didn't sound convinced.

Jude waited. She sensed that to push further at this point might break the confidential atmosphere between them.

The silence became threateningly long. Jude was just reconciling herself to having reached the end of any revelations she was going to get, when Hester said, in a thin, distracted voice, 'What I said to you was true. I was the reason why Ritchie was dead.'

'In what way?'

'If I hadn't been there, he still would have been alive.' Jude didn't prompt, just waited. 'I wasn't in the hall when Gordon and Ritchie did their demonstration of the gallows for everyone. I'd gone to the loo. I was finding it increasingly awkward just hanging out with people during rehearsals. Because of Neville. He seemed so cold and unaffected by what had happened between us . . . and also by then he seemed to be coming on to Janie Trotman. It was painful for me. So, as soon as the rehearsals finished, I tended to rush off to the loo, to avoid socializing. And I stopped going on to the Cricketers.

'But that Sunday afternoon I stayed in the loo until I thought everyone would have gone, but when I came out I found Ritchie was still there in the hall. And I was, kind of, a bit awkward with him – not as bad as with Neville – but not relaxed, anyway.

'He asked me what I'd thought of his escaping death by inches on the gallows. I had to confess that I hadn't seen the demonstration, and so he insisted that I must have a private showing of it. Ritchie was just a show-off, really. Like a little boy who won't allow anyone to miss the new conjuring trick he's just learnt.

'I thought it was a bit silly, but it couldn't do any harm to humour him. So Ritchie got himself up on stage and climbed on to the wooden cart underneath the gallows. And he put the noose round his neck – and told me to pull the cart away.

'He was being all silly and melodramatic, saying, "You can be the one, Hester! You can be the person who sends me to my death!" But I'm sure he didn't mean it, he was just joking, just playing the scene for all it was worth, "showing off" again, I suppose I mean.

'So, anyway, I did as he told me to – I pulled away the cart. And there was quite a thump as he fell and the noose tightened around his neck. He was kicking out and gasping – and I thought that was just Ritchie playing up the drama and about to free himself. And his hands were up at his neck, trying to get a purchase on the rope, but it was too tight.

'Then finally I realized he wasn't play-acting, that he was being strangled for real. And I put the cart back and tried to get his feet on to it, but they were just hanging loose, with no strength in them. And I got up on the cart and tried to loosen the noose around his neck. But I couldn't, it was too tight.

'And then I realized that Ritchie was dead.'

TWENTY-THREE

'And what the hell are you doing here?'

Neither of them had noticed the door open, but they both looked up at the sound of Mike Winstone's voice. He was standing in the doorway, blazered and more red-faced than ever.

'I just came to visit Hester,' replied Jude, sounding cooler than she felt as she rose from her chair.

'Oh yes? And aren't you aware that she's meant to be having a course of rest and recuperation?'

'I don't think my presence will have delayed either her rest or her recuperation.'

'I'll have a strong word with the people downstairs. They shouldn't just let anyone wander in to a place like this.'

'I spoke to the Director. I'm here with his blessing.'

'Well, you're not here with my blessing.' As he spoke Mike Winstone's face grew redder still. He sat himself down with a proprietorial manner in the chair that Jude had just vacated.

'I'll be leaving shortly,' Jude said.

'I'm glad to hear it. And you're involved with that "Saddoes" lot, are you?' He deliberately used the diminishing mispronunciation.

'Yes.'

'Well, if you value your life, don't you dare mention to any of them that Hester's in here, will you?'

'I had no plans to mention it.'

'Keep it that way.'

'So officially she's still "staying with a friend", is she?'

'Yes. And it's bloody inconvenient having her away from the house. There are only so many takeaways and pub meals I can put up with.'

'I'm sorry, Mike.' It was the first time Hester had spoken since his arrival.

'So you bloody should be. Have the quacks here given any indication of when they're going to let you out?'

'I'm afraid not.' Hester sounded very down. 'The psychiatrist says he can definitely see some improvement.' She offered this tentatively, a sop to her husband's anger.

He rolled his eyes in exasperation. 'Huh, it's all so bloody vague, isn't it? The whole business of "mental illness". Because ultimately, at some point the patient has to make the effort themselves. You know, snap out of it, stand on their own two feet, start to take responsibility for their life again.'

'I am trying to get better, Mike. Really.'

Hester sounded so reduced that Jude was tempted to say something in her defence, but it wasn't the moment to step in between husband and wife. Though she couldn't envisage much improvement in Hester's condition until Mike acknowledged that she was genuinely ill.

'Well, I hope you get sorted by the end of next week. The boys have got an exeat from school, and subjecting them to a whole weekend of my cooking comes under the definition of child abuse.'

'I'll do my best,' said Hester in a very thin voice.

'None of this would have happened,' Mike grumbled, 'if you hadn't got involved with that bunch of "Saddoes". God, what a load of posturing toss-pots they are. When I saw that idiot showing off his hanging on that gallows contraption . . .'

'Were you actually in Saint Mary's Hall for the demonstration?' asked Jude.

'Yes, came in to hurry Hest along a bit. She said the rehearsal finished at six, and it was easily ten past before—'

'And,' Jude interrupted, 'you knew that Ritchie Good was later strangled by the apparatus?'

'Oh certainly, I heard. Serve the bugger right, I thought. So end all show-offs, if I had my way. Good riddance. As I say, except for his bloody stupidity, my wife wouldn't have been traumatized – or whatever other fancy word the shrinks use for it – and she wouldn't be locked up here in a loony bin.' Clearly Mike Winstone was never going to score any points for political correctness. His bluff cricketing bonhomie had completely evaporated.

Jude didn't think there was a lot more she could do. She didn't want to create any further cause of discord between Hester and her husband. Sorting out what was already wrong with their relationship would involve going back many years into the past – and might only serve to make things worse – so she said she'd better be on her way. 'But I've got your mobile number, Hester, so I'll give you a call when—'

'My wife doesn't have her mobile phone with her,' Mike Winstone announced.

'Oh? Don't the authorities here at Casements allow clients to—'

'I don't allow it. Hest is here for rest and recuperation, not for chattering endlessly to all her women friends.'

'But surely talking to her friends—'

'Will you allow me to know what is right for my own wife!' The words were almost shouted.

Jude left. In spite of Mike Winstone's clear disapproval, she gave Hester a hug and a kiss. Then she went downstairs to Rob's office. He was interested to hear that Jude had done some healing on the patient, and wanted to know how it had gone. 'Maybe you could try some more with her?' he suggested.

Jude grimaced. 'I don't think I'd better until it's been cleared with her husband.'

'Ah yes. I saw him coming in. Apparently he was just passing. Maybe I should try to persuade him of the efficacy of another healing session?'

'Good luck,' said Jude.

'Well, we have made one big advance,' said Carole when Jude had finished reporting her encounter with Hester Winstone.

'Hm?'

'Assuming that Hester was telling the truth – and there doesn't seem to be any reason why she shouldn't be – we know that Ritchie Good caused his own death. He just wanted to show off the gallows to her.'

'Yes.'

'Which is quite a relief, in a way.'

'In what way?'

'Well, trying to create a scenario in which someone actually persuaded him to put the noose round his neck, or manhandled him into doing it or made him do it at gunpoint . . . well, none of those ever sounded very convincing, did they? But the idea that he put his head in the noose of his own volition, that makes a lot more sense.'

Jude nodded. 'And then there's only one thing we have to find out. Who switched the Velcroed noose for the real one.'

'Exactly.'

'And why they did it.'

TWENTY-FOUR

I t was clear to Carole and Jude the moment they were admitted by Elizaveta Dalrymple on the Saturday evening that the seafront house in Smalting was a shrine to her late husband Freddie. The hall was dominated by a top-lit large portrait of him in the purple velvet doublet of some (undoubtedly Shakespearean) character. The pearl earring and the pointed goatee beard were presumably period props.

Except, as Elizaveta led them up a staircase lined with photographs of Freddie, it became clear that the beard at least was a permanent fixture. Whatever part he was playing, the presence of the goatee was a non-negotiable.

His wife's hair was the same. Jude remembered the scene reported by Storm Lavelle of Elizaveta not wanting to have her head covered by a shawl when she was still going to play Mrs Dudgeon. In some of the earlier photographs on the wall, before she'd needed recourse to dying, her natural hair did look wonderful, though not always of the same period as the costume that she was wearing. The flamenco dancer look was fine for proud Iberian peasants, but it didn't look quite so good with Regency dresses or crinolines.

But clearly that was another unwritten law of SADOS. Freddie and Elizaveta Dalrymple had set up the society, so it was as if everyone else was playing with their ball. Whatever the play, Freddie and Elizaveta would play the leads, he with his pointed goatee and she with her long black hair.

There was further proof of this at the top of the stairs, in one of those large framed photographs which are textured to look like paintings on canvas. Their crowns, Freddie's dagger and the tartan scarf fixed by a brooch across Elizaveta's substantial bosom, left no doubt they were playing Macbeth and Lady Macbeth. With, of course, the goatee and the long black hair.

The space into which Carole and Jude were led showed exactly why the house's sitting room was on the first floor. It was still light that April evening and the floor-to-ceiling windows commanded a wonderful view over Smalting Beach to the far horizon of the sea.

The sitting room demonstrated the same decorative motif as the hall and stairs. Every surface, except for the wall with the windows in it, bore yet more stills from SADOS productions, again with the goatee and the black hair much in evidence. Presumably the plays in which Freddie and Elizaveta Dalrymple took part featured other actors in minor roles, but you'd never have known it from the photographs.

'Welcome,' Elizaveta said lavishly as she ushered Carole and Jude into the sitting room, 'to your first – but I hope not your last – visit to one of my "drinkies things". Now I'm sure you know everyone here . . .'

They did know everyone, except for a couple of elderly ladies who had 'retired from the stage, but as founder members were still massive supporters of SADOS'. Otherwise Carole and Jude greeted Olly Pinto, Storm Lavelle, Gordon Blaine and Mimi Lassiter. All had glasses of champagne in their hands. Storm's hair was now black and shoulder-length (hair extensions at work – there was no way it had had time to grow naturally to that length).

'Now,' said Elizaveta. 'Olly's in charge of drinks this evening, so you just tell him what you'd like.' On the wall facing the sea, space had been made among the encroaching photographs for a well-stocked bar. Olly apologized that there was no Chilean Chardonnay – he knew their tastes from the Cricketers – but wondered if they could force themselves to drink champagne. They could.

A lot of glass-raising and clinking went on, then Elizaveta said, 'Now, Carole and Jude, the agenda we have for my "drinkies things" is that we have no agenda. We're just a group of friends who talk about whatever we want to talk about . . . though more often than not we do end up talking about the theatre.'

'In fact just before you arrived,' volunteered Olly Pinto, 'we were discussing the wonderful *Private Lives* the SADOS did a few years back, with Freddie and Elizaveta in the leads.'

'Oh, we're talking a horribly long time ago,' said Elizaveta coyly.

'Sadly I never saw it,' said Olly, 'but I did hear your Amanda was marvellous.'

'One did one's best.' This line was accompanied by an insouciant shrug. 'And of course I was so well supported by Freddie. So sad that Noel Coward was never able to see the SADOS production. He would have seen the absolutely perfect Elyot. The part could have been written for Freddie.'

'I think it was actually written for Noel Coward,' Carole ventured to point out. The information was something that had come up in a *Times* crossword clue. 'He played the part himself.'

Elizaveta Dalrymple was only a little put out by this. 'Yes, but Noel Coward was always so mannered. I'm sure Freddie brought more nuance to the role.'

Not to mention a goatee beard, thought Jude. And a barrel-load of impregnable self-esteem.

'It was a very fine performance,' said Gordon Blaine, as if he wanted to gain a few brownie points. 'And of course your Amanda was stunning.'

'Thank you, kind sir,' said Elizaveta with a little curtsy. 'Freddie always had such a touch as a director too. Very subtle, he was. Not one of those bossy egotists. He let a play have space, let it evolve with the help of the actors. "A gentle hand on the tiller" – that's how Freddie described the business of directing.'

'Did he always direct the plays he was in?' asked Jude.

'Invariably. Freddie was always very diffident about it, said he'd be very happy for someone better to take on the role. But there never was anyone better, so yes, he directed all the shows we did together.'

Carole and Jude exchanged the most imperceptible of looks. Both of them were realizing to what extent the SADOS was the Dalrymples' private train set. Other children were allowed to play with it, but only under the owners' strict supervision. They also realized how painful relinquishing total control of the society must have been for Elizaveta.

'Freddie often designed the shows too,' Gordon chipped in. 'I mean, he didn't do elaborate drawings of what he wanted, but his ideas were very clear. I was more involved in building the sets when Freddie was around.' This was said in a slightly accusatory tone, as though there might be someone present who had caused the limiting of his involvement. 'And Freddie would always say to me, "I have this image in my mind, Gordon, and I'm sure you can turn that image into reality."'

'And did you build lots of stage machinery, special effects, that kind of thing?' asked Carole. 'Like the gallows for *The Devil's Disciple*?'

'Oh yes, that sort of thing was always my responsibility. Freddie would come up to me and he'd say, "Now I may be asking the impossible, Gordon, but it seems to me that the impossible has always rather appealed to you." And then he'd say what his latest fancy was. Do you remember, Elizaveta, when we were doing *As You Like It*, and Freddie asked me if I could make those thrones for the palace which were trees when they were turned round?'

'Oh, goodness me, yes, Gordon! Such a coup de théâtre they were. Suddenly, with just the turning of a few chairs, we were right there in the Forest of Arden. It got a round of applause every night. Wonderful, Gordon, wasn't it?'

He positively glowed beneath his ginger beard. 'All my own work. Yes, though I say it myself.'

But, from Elizaveta Dalrymple's point of view, Gordon was now taking too much credit on himself. 'Though, of course, it was Freddie's concept,' she said quite sharply.

'Oh yes,' a chastened Gordon Blaine agreed. 'It was very definitely Freddie's concept.'

'And the *Fethering Observer* gave a real rave of a review for my Rosalind. Which was rather one in the eye for those SADOS members who suggested I might be a bit old for the part.'

'I remember,' Mimi Lassiter chimed in. 'The *Fethering Observer* actually talked about you moving "with the coltish grace of a teenage girl".'

'But that's what acting's about,' Elizaveta enthused. 'You think yourself into the character you are playing, you become that person. Considerations like age and size and shape become totally irrelevant once you're caught up in the magic of the theatre. And, Gordon,' she said, feeling that the technician should now be thrown some kind of magnanimous sop, 'your chairs that turned into trees were part of the magic of that *As You Like It*.'

He grinned, his good humour instantly restored.

'Anyway, Gordon,' said Carole, eager to steer the conversation round to Ritchie Good's death, 'you've also done a splendid job on those gallows for *The Devil's Disciple*.'

'Oh, relatively straightforward, those were.' He started to laugh. 'Certainly compared to the palaver I had with that balcony on wheels Freddie wanted for *Romeo & Juliet*!'

Elizaveta Dalrymple laughed theatrically at the recollection, while Jude winced inwardly, visualizing a Juliet with flamenco hair and a Romeo with a pointed goatee beard.

'But the gallows,' Carole insisted. 'They seem to work very well. Possibly even *too* well,' she dared to add.

Her words did actually prompt a brief silence. Then Gordon said, rather defensively, 'I created a set of gallows that were completely safe. Everyone saw that. If they'd been used properly, Ritchie Good'd be alive today. I can't be held responsible if people mess around with the equipment I've made.'

'By "messing around" you mean changing the doctored noose for the solid one?' suggested Carole.

'Exactly.'

'Can I ask something?' said Jude innocently. 'Why did you have a solid noose when the one that was going to be used would always be the one with Velcro?'

Gordon appeared pleased to have been asked the question,

as it gave him an opportunity to provide a technical explanation. 'I was determined to make the gallows look real, so I needed to see what it would look like with a proper noose attached. Then I'd know what the doctored one had to look like.'

'But why did you bring it with you to St Mary's Hall that Sunday when you were demonstrating it?'

'Ah well.' He coloured slightly. 'The fact is, I had planned to have the stage curtains open during the rehearsal, with the gallows there with a proper noose. Then anyone in the company who had a look at it would see a real, businesslike noose there, and they'd be even more surprised when Ritchie appeared to have it round his neck.'

'What, and you would have switched the two nooses just before the demonstration?'

'Yes. We'd have drawn the curtains for a moment and done it. I thought that'd be more dramatic. But Ritchie didn't. He said we'd get the maximum effect if the curtains were closed right through the rehearsal, and then when we opened them we'd get a real coo . . . what was that thing you said, Elizaveta?'

'Coup de théâtre,' she supplied.

'Exactly. One of those.' Gordon looked grumpy. 'I still think my way would have been better.'

'Well, it was quite dramatic,' said Jude. 'Of course, you weren't there, were you, Carole?'

'No, but you told me about it. So after the demonstration, Gordon, someone must have switched the two nooses round.'

'Yes.'

'But you don't know who?'

'I know it wasn't me,' he said huffily.

'I wasn't suggesting—'

'Mind you, I can think of one or two people in SADOS who might have—'

'I'm not sure,' Elizaveta Dalrymple interrupted magisterially, 'that I want my entire "drinkies thing" taken up with talk about that ill-mannered boor Ritchie Good.'

'I'm sorry,' said Jude meekly.

'But I've spent a lot of time,' Gordon continued, 'thinking how the two nooses got switched, and I've come to the conclusion that—'

'Nor,' Elizaveta steamrollered on, 'do we want to spend the whole time talking about your wretched gallows – particularly since you've already spent one entire evening telling us all about them.'

'Have I?' asked Gordon, puzzled.

'Yes,' said Olly Pinto. 'It was three weeks ago, the day before you were going to do the demonstration. We were all here for Elizaveta's "drinkies thing" and you couldn't talk about anything else. Goodness, by the time you'd finished we all knew enough about your gallows to have built a replica ourselves.'

Carole and Jude exchanged a quick look before the SADOS Mr Fixit said abjectly, 'Oh, I'm sorry. Was I a bore?'

'Yes, I'm afraid you were, Gordon darling,' Elizaveta replied. 'Let's just say that by the time the evening finished the gallows was a subject on which you had "delighted us long enough".'

Her coterie sniggered at the line, unaware that Elizaveta had filched it from Jane Austen. Then the star of the show vouchsafed a gracious smile to Carole and Jude. 'Now do tell me, you two, what's *The Devil's Disciple* going to be *like*?'

'I think it's coming together,' Jude replied cautiously.

'And is Olly keeping you busy as prompter?'

'Still a little ragged on the lines,' Carole was forced to admit.

Elizaveta smiled indulgently on the young man under discussion. 'Yes, you always go for the approximate approach, don't you, Olly? I remember you were all over the place as Lysander in Freddie's *Dream*.'

'It didn't matter,' said Olly gallantly. 'No one in the audience had eyes for anyone except your Titania.'

'And Freddie's Oberon,' said Elizaveta in gentle reproof.

'Oh yes, of course.'

'And our doubling, me also playing Hippolyta and Freddie giving his Theseus.'

'Yes, they were all splendid,' said Olly.

'There was a very good production of *A Midsummer Night's Dream* at the RSC last season,' Jude volunteered.

'Really?' Elizaveta Dalrymple dismissed the idea. For her theatre began and ended with the SADOS. No stage other than St Mary's Hall was of any significance. 'Anyway,' she went on, 'it doesn't matter so much, I suppose, if Olly's paraphrasing George Bernard Shaw's lines. They are at least in prose. But with Shakespeare's blank verse it was a complete disaster.'

Olly grinned winsomely, as if already enjoying the chastisement he was about to receive.

'"Doesn't the boy have any sense of rhythm?" Freddie kept asking. "How can anyone have such a tin ear for the beauties of blank verse?"' Elizaveta laughed and the others joined in, Olly as heartily as anyone. 'He did try to help you, didn't he?'

'Oh yes,' Olly agreed. 'Freddie was always so generous with his time and his talent.'

'He was.' Elizaveta let out a nostalgic sigh. 'And of course Freddie was a wonderful verse speaker.' Everyone mumbled endorsements of this self-evident truth, as she focused a beady eye on Olly. 'So, will you know your *Devil's Disciple* lines by the first night?'

'Of course I will. Sheer terror will keep me going.'

'Oh yes. When a man knows he is to be hanged in a fortnight, it concentrates his mind wonderfully.'

The coterie greeted Elizaveta's latest bon mot with more laughter, unaware that she was quoting Dr Johnson. Then she turned sharply to Jude and asked, 'How's Davina doing?'

'Doing in what way?'

'As a director, of course.'

'Well, she seems to be . . . fine.' Jude wasn't sure what kind of answer was expected. 'I mean, obviously her plans were all disrupted by what happened to Ritchie, but she seems to have managed to regroup and . . . As I say, everything's fine.'

'Hm.' Elizaveta Dalrymple managed to invest the monosyllable with a great deal of doubt and suspicion. 'Of course, Freddie and I taught her everything she knows.'

'In the theatre?'

'Oh yes. Hadn't an idea in her head when she started in amdram. Freddie sort of took her under his wing. And she's developed into quite a nice little director. But I'm not sure how this *Devil's Disciple* is going to go.'

'As I said, I think it'll be fine.'

Another loaded 'Hm.' Elizaveta looked across to where Olly Pinto was deep in flirtatious chatter with Mimi Lassiter and the two old ladies. Then she moved closer to Jude and started to whisper.

Carole felt awkward. She wasn't quite near enough to hear and she didn't know whether she was meant to be included in the conversation. Rather than moving closer, she shifted nearer the window, as if suddenly fascinated by the movement of shipping beyond Smalting Beach.

'At least,' Elizaveta whispered fiercely at Jude, 'from Davina's point of view, she'll be better off with Olly as Dick Dudgeon than she would have been with Ritchie.'

'Oh?'

'Bit of bad blood between her and Ritchie. She thought he was keen on her, which he certainly appeared to be. But when she suggested taking the relationship further, he dropped her like a brick.'

Par for the course with Ritchie Good, thought Jude.

'And Davina didn't like that at all. Hell hath no fury . . . you know the quote. No, Davina would have done anything to remove Ritchie from her production of *The Devil's Disciple.*'

TWENTY-FIVE

As they walked to the Renault from Elizaveta Dalrymple's front door, Jude quickly told her neighbour what their hostess had whispered to her.

'Strange,' Carole observed. 'That's two people who've pointed the finger at Davina.'

'Two?'

'Come on, Jude. Neville Prideaux. I told you what he said.'

'Oh yes.'

It was after eight and still just about light. They were suddenly aware of the spluttering sound of a car engine failing to fire.

Then the slam of a door, a muttered curse and a bonnet being opened. They found themselves facing a very cross-looking Gordon Blaine in front of his ancient Land Rover.

'Trouble?' asked Jude.

'Bloody thing. It's got a new engine and . . . not a sign of life.'

'Oh well, if it's a new engine,' said Carole, 'at least you can bawl out whoever put it in for you.'

'I put it in,' said Gordon Blaine lugubriously.

'Ah. Oh. Well . . .'

'Bloody useless!' He slammed the bonnet down, disturbing the genteel Saturday evening quiet of Smalting, and looked around in frustration. 'Where the hell do you get a bloody cab in this place?'

'Can I give you a lift somewhere?' asked Carole. 'Where do you live?'

'Fethering,' came the grumpy response.

'What serendipity,' said Jude.

Gordon Blaine's house was a semi with a garage on the northern outskirts of the village. A couple of streets further along and he'd have been in Downside, regarded by people like Carole as the 'common' part of Fethering.

She had insisted he sat in the front seat of the Renault, 'because you've got longer legs than Jude'. As he got out he said, 'Can I invite you two ladies in for a drink?'

Anticipating Carole's refusal on the grounds that they'd already had plenty, Jude said quickly that it was very kind of him, they'd love that. Reflected in the rear-view mirror, she could see the tug of annoyance at her neighbour's mouth.

The interior of the house was strangely cramped, a tiny sitting room with an even tinier kitchen en suite. The furniture was old and dark and the décor gave the impression that the owner didn't notice his surroundings. There seemed no evidence that Gordon cohabited with anyone. Nor did their host give the impression that he was much used to having guests.

'Now, drinks . . .' he said rather helplessly. 'You were drinking champagne at Elizaveta's, weren't you? I'm afraid I

don't have any of that. Or white wine, actually. I think I've
got some red . . . certainly beer. I'm going for the Scotch
myself.'

'That would suit me perfectly,' said Jude.

'I'll just have water, because I'm driving.'

'It'll have to be from the tap,' Gordon apologized. 'I don't
have any of that sparkling mineral stuff.'

'Tap is fine.'

The ease with which he found the bottle of Teacher's and
the size of the measures he poured suggested that he might
have quite a taste for the whisky, though he probably rarely
had company to share it with. He raised his glass. 'Well, thanks
very much for rescuing me.'

'No problem at all,' said Carole.

He sat down, shook his head and said, 'It doesn't seem
right, Elizaveta not being involved in this *Devil's Disciple*
production.'

'Really?'

'Well, you wouldn't know, Jude. Nor you, Carole, only just
having joined the society.'

'And having paid my subscription, after what almost
amounted to harassment from Mimi Lassiter.'

'Oh yes.' Gordon chuckled. 'She does take her job a bit
seriously. No, but what I was saying, you wouldn't know
because you're new, but SADOS without the Dalrymples just
doesn't seem right. I mean, it was bad enough when Freddie
passed away, but now with Elizaveta not being involved . . .
well, it doesn't seem right.' He couldn't think of another way
of saying it.

'I heard from Storm Lavelle,' said Jude, 'that Elizaveta
walked out of *The Devil's Disciple* because Ritchie Good was
so rude to her.'

'Well, I think that was part of it . . .'

'You mean there was something else?' demanded Carole,
instantly alert. She had now caught on to Jude's reasons for
agreeing to come in for a drink. It was an investigation
opportunity.

'Well, she didn't seem to be getting on so well with Davina.'

'Oh?'

'They'd always seemed to be great mates. You know, Freddie took quite a shine to Davina when she first joined SADOS. He thought she had potential as a director, so he was very helpful to her, and gave her opportunities to get the directing going.'

'You don't mean,' asked Carole, 'that he "took a shine" to her in any other way?'

Gordon looked puzzled for a moment before he understood what she meant. 'Oh, good heavens, no! There was never anything like that with Freddie. He and Elizaveta were always the most devoted couple. A lot of the younger actresses in the society kind of hero-worshipped him, but he was never the type to take advantage.'

He shook his head again. 'No, but something really seemed to have gone wrong between Elizaveta and Davina. I think that may have been the real reason Elizaveta wanted out of the production. Ritchie's rudeness just gave her a good excuse.'

'But you've no idea what the problem was?'

'No. Here, Jude, let me top you up.' She didn't need more, but he was drinking faster than her and wanted to justify refilling his own glass.

Gordon sat back down again and said gloomily, 'A rift like that could spell the end of SADOS.'

'Do you really think so?'

'Yes. Now Freddie's gone, Elizaveta is so much the dynamo of the society. Without her, it would be . . .' The prospect seemed too dreadful for him to put into words.

'You've been with SADOS for a long time, have you?' asked Jude gently.

He nodded. 'Since my mother died. Elizaveta and Freddie sort of took me in. They needed someone with engineering skills and, though I'd never had anything to do with the theatre, I have got quite a practical mind. Till I retired I worked for a firm that fitted kitchen cupboards, so I was quite used to building stuff and . . .' He looked very forlorn. 'If I hadn't got the SADOS, I don't know how I'd fill the time.'

'I was interested,' said Carole, moving the conversation along, 'in what you were saying at Elizaveta's about the two nooses on your gallows . . .'

'Oh yes?'

'. . . and how they got mixed up.'

There was a new caution in his expression as he said, 'What about it?'

'You said you had some thoughts of people who might have switched them round, but then Elizaveta interrupted you.'

Gordon Blaine was silent. He looked from one woman to the other. 'Are you thinking that what happened to Ritchie might not be an accident?'

'The thought had occurred to us, yes.'

'Hm. The police were very interested in that possibility when they talked to me.'

'But presumably they did come down on the side of accidental death?'

'What makes you say that?'

'Well, they've ended their investigation.'

'How do you know?'

'I've just assumed it,' said Carole. 'Jude told me there've been no more enquiries. And they released Ritchie's body for his funeral.'

'That's true.' Gordon spoke as if he hadn't thought of it before.

'You sound relieved.'

'Well, I suppose I am in a way.'

'Why?'

'Because the gallows are my work. I built them. If there was anything unsafe about the design, it'd be my fault. And I've been worried about the police coming back to me at some point. So if their investigation is really over, that's quite a relief.'

'I don't think you need worry any more,' said Jude. Gordon looked pathetically grateful. Clearly the anxiety had been weighing on him. 'Where are the gallows now?' she asked.

'People seemed a bit spooked by having them still there in St Mary's Hall. So I brought them back to my workshop – that was in the brief period when my bloody Land Rover was working. I've been doing a bit of fine tuning on them.'

'Where is your workshop?' asked Carole.

'Would you like to see it?' The excitement in his voice showed that he very much hoped they would.

And indeed, when they assented, there was a trace of schoolboy glee in the way he led them through to the back of his tiny kitchen. And once through the door they could understand why the front two rooms of the house seemed so cramped. The house must originally have had a sitting room at the front with an equally large dining room and kitchen behind it. But this space had been opened out and the wall to the garage taken down to create an extended working area. The slightly makeshift black-painted plasterboard walls suggested that Gordon had done the conversion himself.

The bright overhead lights revealed something on the lines of a mad professor's lab. There had clearly been attempts to impose order on the chaos. On the walls were rows of neat racks, but the tools that should have been stowed there lay on the floor or on work benches, along with paint pots, piping, rolls of wire netting, offcuts of wood and plastic. There was a musty smell of sawdust, oil and paint.

The *Devil's Disciple* gallows were there, but in the midst of a huge selection of other stage props. Papier mâché rat masks had perhaps featured in a SADOS pantomime, plywood battlements adorned a Shakespeare production. And the chairs with cut-out trees on the back were probably the famous ones designed for *As You Like It*.

Also on the floor were car tyres, jacks and other automobile impedimenta. Clearly this was where Gordon had replaced the engine of his Land Rover. A procedure which, as Carole and Jude had cause to know, hadn't worked properly. There hung about the workshop the aura of a great many things that hadn't worked properly.

'Wow,' said Jude as they looked around the space. 'So this is where you work your magic.'

The beam on Gordon Blaine's face showed that it had been exactly the right thing to say. Carole recognized rather wistfully that it was the kind of thing she'd never have thought of saying in a million years.

'Would you mind showing us,' Jude went on, 'how the noose gets changed on the gallows?'

'It's very easy,' said Gordon, more confident in his own environment. 'Simple design. I always go for simple, no point in faffing around with stuff that's more complicated than it needs to be.'

He picked up a noose from a workbench, clattered a pair of metal stepladders over the floor to the side of the gallows and climbed up. There was already a noose in position hanging from the beam. 'This is the doctored one,' said Gordon, slicing down on to the loop with his hand and causing the Velcro joint to swing apart. 'You see, as soon as that takes any weight, it gives way . . . greatly to the delight of the Health and Safety boyos.

'But what holds it up, you see,' he said, reaching to the top of the beam, 'is this hook . . . from which the doctored noose can be simply removed –' he matched his actions to his words – 'and the real one hooked on . . . threaded through . . . and left to dangle . . . ready for its next victim.'

'So the whole process,' said Carole, 'takes less than thirty seconds.'

'Yes,' Gordon agreed, as though accepting a compliment.

'And anyone could work out how to do it?'

'I would think so. Certainly anyone who'd watched me do the switch.'

'Or someone who'd heard you describe how to do the switch,' said Jude.

'Sorry?' He looked down in puzzlement from the ladder. 'Don't know what you mean?'

'Well, we just heard, earlier this evening at Elizaveta's, how you described the working of your gallows in meticulous detail at another of her "drinkies things".'

'Oh yes, I remember that. Elizaveta seemed very interested in it. Which was unusual. Usually she shut me up when I got on to the details of the technical stuff. "Gordon darling," she'd say, "I'm an actress. I deal with the emotional side of putting on a play. I can't be expected to understand the nuts and bolts of the business."'

'And that particular "drinkies thing",' said Jude, 'was three weeks ago.'

'Was it really? I can't remember.'

'Three weeks to the day.'

'The day before Ritchie Good got strangled,' said Carole.

TWENTY-SIX

'Who is this speaking?' asked the elocuted voice at the other end of the line.

'Jude.'

'Jude? Oh yes, Jude!' said Elizaveta Dalrymple.

'I was just ringing to say thank you so much for the party last night.'

'Oh, hardly a party, Jude darling. Just one of my little "drinkies things".'

'Well, it was much appreciated, anyway. I really enjoyed it. And I'm sure Carole will be in touch soon to say thank you too.' Though, actually, knowing Carole, she was much more likely to post a graceful note of thanks than use the telephone.

'It was a pleasure to see you both. I do like to keep up with the new members of SADOS . . . even though I'm not involved in the current production.'

'But presumably you'll be back for others,' suggested Jude, 'now that Ritchie Good's no longer around to insult you?'

'Oh, I don't know, darling. I'm not as young as I was.'

'You're still looking very good,' said Jude, shamelessly ingratiating.

'Yes, well, of course I am lucky to have the bone structure. If you have the bone structure, the ravages of time are not quite so devastating. But,' she concluded smugly, 'so few people do have the bone structure.'

Jude, whose face was too chubby for much bone structure to be discernible, made polite noises of agreement. Then she said, 'Carole and I took Gordon Blaine back to his place yesterday.'

'Really?' Elizaveta sounded affronted. She didn't like people in her coterie doing things she didn't know about. 'Why was that?'

'His Land Rover had broken down.'

'No surprise there. I must say, for someone who's supposed to have engineering skills, dear Gordon is astonishingly inept.'

'He showed us his workshop.'

'Oh, that glory hole. He used to keep dragging Freddie down there to show him the development of his latest bit of stage wizardry – frequently rather less than wizard, I'm afraid. At times Gordon has qualities of an overeager schoolboy.'

'Maybe. When he was talking yesterday he seemed to be worried about the future of SADOS.'

'Oh?'

'Well, if you were not involved, he thought there was a danger the whole thing might pack up.'

'Really? I hope not.' But Elizaveta's voice betrayed her attraction to the idea. 'SADOS is more than one person, just as it was more than two people while Freddie was still alive. I owe it to his memory to keep the society going.'

'Gordon seemed worried that, with you having walked out of *The Devil's Disciple*, there might be—'

'I did not *walk out* of *The Devil's Disciple*. Ritchie Good's behaviour put me in a position where I could no longer stay as part of the production.'

'Well, however you put it, Gordon seemed worried that you might be so angry that you wouldn't come back for another show.'

'Oh, he shouldn't have thought that. Of the many things I may be, Jude, vindictive is not one,' Elizaveta lied. 'If the right part comes up, and if I'm lucky enough to pass the audition, then I'm sure I'll be back for the next production.'

'And what is that? I haven't heard yet.'

'The autumn show's going to be *I Am A Camera*.'

'Isn't that the play on which the musical *Cabaret* is based?'

'I believe so.'

'Based on the book by Christopher Isherwood.'

'I've no idea who wrote it. I just know it wouldn't have been my choice, but now Neville Prideaux's on the Play Selection Committee all kinds of weird stuff's getting through. If there really is a threat to the future of SADOS, it's much more likely to be Neville Prideaux's choice of plays driving the audiences away.'

'But you will audition for it, Elizaveta?'

'Oh, I suppose I'll have to. I mean, Sally Bowles is meant to be quite a mature character.'

Jude only just stopped herself from voicing her disbelief and saying, Oh, for heaven's sake, there's *mature* and there's *far too old for the part*. But she didn't want to break the confidential mood between them.

'Last night Gordon was talking about his gallows and what had gone wrong with them.'

'Oh, I'm sure he was. Gordon can be a very tedious little man.'

'We were discussing how the two nooses might have got switched.'

'Incompetence on his part, I would imagine.'

'I wonder . . .'

'What do you mean by that, Jude?'

'Well . . .'

'Are you suggesting the nooses might have been switched deliberately?'

'It's a thought, isn't it? Which would have meant someone in the *Devil's Disciple* company really had it in for Ritchie Good.'

There was a silence. Jude could sense Elizaveta assessing her response. Then the older woman said, 'Well, if you're looking for that person, Jude, you might do a lot worse than remember what I said to you last night.'

'Davina?'

'You said it.'

Both Carole and Jude were required for the rehearsal that Sunday afternoon. Rather boldly, the director had announced that they were going to do the whole play for the first time, 'which, given the fact that we open in a month's time, should put the fear of God into all of you.'

If that was the sole aim of the exercise, it certainly worked. The unreadiness of the entire company was made manifest, and no one seemed less ready than Olly Pinto. His lines were still all over the place, and Carole as prompter had one of the busiest afternoons of her life.

Olly's incompetence seemed to infect the others like some quick-spreading plague. Even Jude, who'd always been rock solid on her lines, found herself stumbling and mumbling. And she was by no means the worst. By the time they got to the end of the play, the whole thing was a complete shambles. The final scene, the near-hanging of Dick Dudgeon, had never been rehearsed properly with all of the extras who were meant to populate the town square, and they milled around like sheep in search of a shepherd.

As Davina's mood grew increasingly frayed, Carole and Jude found themselves watching the director closely and trying to reconcile her with the suspicions raised by both Elizaveta Dalrymple and Neville Prideaux. What he had said did make a kind of sense. Until that Sunday afternoon Davina had been more relaxed in rehearsal without the presence of Ritchie Good. In Olly Pinto she'd got a much less convincing Dick Dudgeon, but a considerably more biddable actor. She seemed to revel in bawling him out, in a way she never would have done with Ritchie.

Davina was dressed that day in jeans and a bright coral jumper with a high collar. Jude observed that she always seemed to wear high collars. She wondered whether this was a vanity thing, disguising the age-induced stringiness of her neck.

And Jude tried, without success, to think of Davina Vere Smith as a murderer. It just didn't fit, didn't seem right.

When the last line of the play had finally been spoken, at just before six o'clock, the director indulged herself in a major tantrum. This was all the more effective for being unexpected. Up until then in rehearsal, except for her regular verbal assaults on Olly Pinto, Davina had been conciliatory and friendly to the rest of the cast. So they all looked shocked to hear her finally losing her rag.

'The whole thing was complete rubbish! I don't know why I've been wasting my time with you lot for the last three months! This afternoon was an example of absolutely no one showing any concentration at all! OK, this is just an amateur production, and if you've come along for the ride and don't care about the quality of the show and just want to have a giggle at rehearsals, then fair enough. I think you should leave now. We can very happily manage without you.

'But I have certain standards I want to maintain. SADOS has certain standards it wants to maintain, and on the evidence of what I've seen this afternoon, we aren't achieving any of them. But for the fact that the box office is already open and tickets have already been bought for *The Devil's Disciple*, I would pull the plugs on the whole production now!

'So . . .' Davina paused for a moment to gather her breath and her thoughts. The *Devil's Disciple* company were too shocked to say anything, as she continued, 'I know it's six o'clock and you're all gasping to go to the Cricketers, but I'm afraid I'm not going to let anyone go until we've had another look at the blocking of that last scene. It's a complete dog's dinner and we need to do a bit of basic work on it.

'So those of you who aren't involved can go. Jude, obviously, since Mrs Dudgeon is long dead. And Carole, you can go. I'll be concentrating on the movements not the words for this bit. But the rest of you . . . will you please all pull your bloody socks up and concentrate for the next half-hour!'

It was a measure of the effect Davina's unwonted outburst had had that nobody moaned about being kept from their liquid refreshment in the Cricketers. All of the company looked very chastened as Carole and Jude slipped out to the pub.

'I was idly thinking about Davina's neck,' said Jude, as they settled down with their large Chilean Chardonnays. The pub was virtually empty, just Len behind the bar reading the *Mail on Sunday*. Again she wondered how the Cricketers would keep going without the regular custom of SADOS members.

'Davina's neck? What on earth do you mean?' asked Carole.

'Well, every time I see her at rehearsal she's wearing these high collars. I assume it's because – as happens at our age – her neck is getting a bit stringy and her cleavage a bit wrinkled.'

'What do you mean – "as happens at our age"?' Carole was quite put out. 'I don't believe I'm getting either stringy or wrinkled.'

'No, but you're so thin no wrinkle would dare to sully your skin.'

Carole looked beadily at her neighbour, unsure whether she was being sent up or not. Eventually she decided that what she'd just heard was probably a compliment. 'As a matter of fact,' she said, 'Davina's cleavage is in very good condition.'

'Oh? When have you seen it?'

'First time I met her. First time I met her properly, that is. In the Crown and Anchor, when she tried to persuade me to take over as prompter.'

'She not only *tried* to persuade you. She *succeeded* in persuading you.'

'Well, all right. Anyway, on that occasion she was wearing a purple cardigan, unbuttoned to show quite a lot of cleavage. And, as I say, the cleavage in question was in very good condition.'

'I'm glad to hear it. Then I wonder why she always wears high collars at rehearsal?'

'Up to her, I would have thought.'

'Sure.'

'Incidentally, I don't want you to get the impression that I make a habit of staring at other women's cleavages.'

When Carole made remarks like that, Jude could never be quite sure whether she was serious or not. Deciding on this occasion she probably was, Jude said, 'Thought never occurred to me.'

'The reason I noticed it on that occasion was that Davina was wearing a rather distinctive pendant.'

'Oh?'

'Silver. Shaped like a star.'

This prompted a much less casual 'Oh.' Jude's brown eyes sparkled with excitement as she asked, 'Was it like the one Elizaveta wears?'

'I've never noticed Elizaveta wearing any particular jewellery.'

'But she showed it that first evening in here. After we'd delivered the chaise longue.'

'What? I've no idea what you're talking about, Jude.'

'Oh, of course you weren't in the group with Elizaveta, were you? You were being bored to death by Gordon Blaine.'

'I still don't understand a word you're saying. I just . . .'

But Jude was already out of her seat, crossing to the bar and snatching the landlord's attention away from his *Mail on Sunday*. 'Len, do you remember the silver pendant that got left here after a pantomime rehearsal?'

'Oh yes. What about it?'

'I remember, first time I ever came in here you asked Elizaveta Dalrymple if it was hers. And when she said it wasn't, you said you'd keep it behind the bar until someone claimed it.'

'Uh-huh,' he agreed.

'Well, did anyone ever claim it?'

'Yes. Only a few days later. I can't remember whether it was the Tuesday or the Thursday, but she came in early for rehearsal and said it was hers.'

'Who did?'

'Davina.'

'Are you sure?'

'Yes. I remember particularly because she was the only person in the pub, and she very specifically asked me not to tell Elizaveta that she'd claimed it.'

'And so you didn't tell her?'

'No. Mind you, the wife might have done.'

'Why did your wife know about it?'

'Because I mentioned the engraving on the back of the pendant to her.'

'Engraving? What did it say?'

'"YOU'RE A STAR – WITH LOVE FROM FREDDIE".'

TWENTY-SEVEN

The members of the *Devil's Disciple* company who trickled over to the Cricketers round half past six looked very subdued. They were not used to Davina Vere Smith bawling them out and the rarity of such behaviour had had a powerful effect. As they bought their drinks and formed into little groups, the laughter was nervous rather than convivial. Facing the reality of *The Devil's Disciple*'s unpreparedness had wiped smiles off quite a few faces.

Davina herself stalked in last of all and there was a silence, not of unfriendliness but rather of trepidation. None of the cast dared to speak to her, afraid that they might again get their heads bitten off. She ordered 'a large G and T' from Len and stalked across the bar to sit at a table, studiedly alone. The actors shuffled around, talking in low voices, as though there was an unexploded bomb in the room.

This in fact suited Carole and Jude rather well. Since neither of them was involved in the play's final scene, they alone had not felt the wrath of Davina Vere Smith. They felt rather like the class goody-goodies as they picked up their glasses and went across to join the director at her solitary table.

'How was the second run of the last scene?' asked Jude tentatively.

'Terrible,' Davina replied. 'I didn't think anything could be worse than the first run at it, but that lot proved it was possible.' She didn't seem upset. The outburst seemed to have given her increased confidence. There was even a slight twinkle in her eye.

Catching this, Jude said, 'Did you stage it?'

'My tantrum? Yes, of course I did.' The twinkle had now become a grin, which Davina was having hard work suppressing. She didn't want her secret to be known to the rest of the company.

'It's a very effective tactic,' she went on. 'I know enough about acting to control when I do it. And because I'm normally sweet and chummy to everyone, the effect is devastating.'

'So you don't do it often?' said Carole.

'Ooh no. It wouldn't work if I did it often. I ration myself to one tantrum per production – sometimes not even one. The longer I go without throwing my toys out of the pram, the more effective it is when I do. And everyone in *The Devil's Disciple* really did need a kick up the arse. They're all getting very lazy and lackadaisical.'

'I suppose that's the effect of the long rehearsal period,' suggested Jude.

Davina nodded. 'Yes, it can seem to drift on forever. Then suddenly you're within days of the Dress Rehearsal and it all gets very scary.'

'Yes,' said Carole, wanting to move the conversation into investigative mode. 'Do you think the production would have been in as bad a state if you still had Ritchie Good playing Dick Dudgeon?'

The director shrugged. 'We might not have to stop as often as we do when Olly cocks up another line, but I don't think it'd make a great difference. There's a kind of rhythm to a production, you know. About a month before the show actually opens, rehearsals always tend to get a bit ragged and chaotic. But the thing with Olly and his words, that is quite serious. I was wondering, Carole, if you wouldn't mind doing a bit of "one-on-one" with him.'

'I'm sorry?' said Carole stiffly. 'I don't know what you mean by "one-on-one".'

'Just line-bashing.'

'What?'

'A sort of extension of your job as prompter. If you could spend an evening with Olly, one night when we're not rehearsing, just going through the text line by line. That might make some of them stick to the Teflon interior of his brain.'

'Oh. Well, I'd be prepared to have a go, I suppose . . . if you think it might help.'

'I can guarantee it would help. I'll tell him to have a word with you. See if you can sort something out.'

'Very well.'

Jude, also keen to move on to what they really wanted to talk about, said, 'By the way, Carole and I were honoured yesterday.'

'Oh yes?'

'We got invited to one of Elizaveta's "drinkies things".'

'Did you? Maybe she's trying to keep up the numbers.'

'What do you mean?'

'You may have been invited to replace me.'

'Oh?'

'Yes, I used to be a regular at those, certainly always went when Freddie was alive. But recently I've become persona non grata, so far as Elizaveta's concerned.'

'Do you have any idea why?' asked Jude.

Davina grinned enigmatically. 'I have a few thoughts on the subject.'

Carole went for the bald and bold approach, asking, 'Do any of them have anything to do with the star pendant that Freddie Dalrymple gave you?'

There was a silence. Davina looked calculatingly from one woman to the other. 'What do you know about that?'

'You were wearing it when I met you in the Crown and Anchor.'

'Ah yes. So I was. Normally, if I'm doing anything to do with SADOS, I keep it covered.'

Jude chipped in, 'Len here told us what was engraved on the back of it.'

'Hm.'

'Just like, presumably, what is engraved on the back of the one he gave to Elizaveta?'

'Yes. And to who knows how many other of Freddie's "little friends".' Davina looked rueful, but she made no attempt to deny anything. 'Freddie Dalrymple was basically rather a dirty old man.'

'Was he?'

'He had a flat in Worthing, on the seafront. That was where he used to go, as he used to tell Elizaveta, to "plan his productions".'

'So she never went there?'

'No. Which was probably just as well.'

'But you did go there?'

Davina nodded. 'I, and, as I say, who knows how many others.'

'Elizaveta told us that, as a director, Freddie took you "under his wing".'

'Yes. Not just his wing. Also his duvet.'

'Oh.'

'I did love him.'

'Right.'

'My father died when I was in my early teens. I think the older man always . . .'

Just like Hester Winstone, thought Jude, a pattern of going for the older man.

'Presumably,' said Carole, 'Elizaveta had no idea anything was going on?'

'No, I really think she didn't. She was wedded, not only to Freddie, but to the image of the perfect marriage that she and Freddie shared. I think it suited her not to know what Freddie got up to in Worthing.'

'But when she saw your pendant . . .' said Jude.

'Yes. I realized I'd lost it, but I didn't know where. The clasp's loose – or it was, I've had it repaired. It must have slipped off in here during the post-pantomime cast party. And then when Len showed it to Elizaveta after the *Devil's Disciple* read-through . . .'

'I remember. You said you didn't wear that kind of jewellery.'

'Well, I couldn't claim it right then and there, could I? In front of Elizaveta?'

'But you came back a few days later to get it?' Davina nodded. 'And Len told Elizaveta who'd claimed it.'

'I think, Jude, to be fair to Len, it was his wife who told her.'

'And was that why she stormed out of the production?'

'Yes. The flare-up with Ritchie was something she staged. She provoked him into being so rude to her. It gave her an excuse to stomp out. But the real reason was that she couldn't stand being around me once she knew that Freddie and I had . . . it must have hit her quite hard.'

'Do you think,' asked Carole, 'that she hoped her departure – and the departure of all her supporters – would totally screw up your production of *The Devil's Disciple*?'

'That may have been at the back of her mind. She doesn't think that anything can happen in SADOS if she's not involved. And whereas that might have been true while Freddie was still around, I don't think it is any longer. Thanks to you, Jude, for stepping in to play Mrs Dudgeon.'

'But of course,' said Carole stepping deeper into investigative mode, 'Elizaveta's departure wasn't the only disaster that struck your production, was it?'

'What? Oh, you mean what happened to Ritchie?'

'Yes. That was a big setback.'

'By the way,' said Jude, 'did Ritchie ever come on to you?'

'Oh, when we first met, yes, of course. He had a kind of knee-jerk reaction to chat up any woman he met. He didn't get far with me, though. Freddie was still alive, and I was far too caught up with him for anyone else to get a look-in.'

'And what about Ritchie's death?' asked Carole.

'What about it?'

'Did you think it was an accident?'

'Well, of course it was. And entirely typical of Ritchie, the way it happened. Like most actors, he was a total show-off. He'd done his show for everyone at the end of rehearsal, but Hester Winstone hadn't been there, so he had to do a command performance for her. I mean, of course I don't want anyone to die, but it did serve Ritchie bloody right, didn't it?'

Carole saw a potential anomaly in Davina's explanation. 'How did you know he'd done a command performance for Hester Winstone?'

'She told me.'

'Oh? When?'

'A couple of days later. She rang to say that she couldn't continue as prompter, and she told me exactly what had happened.'

'Before she had her breakdown?' asked Jude.

'I didn't know she'd had a breakdown. Though she certainly sounded in a pretty bad way when she rang me.'

'But what about the noose?' Carole insisted. 'Someone had switched the noose between the first and second times Ritchie had done the routine.'

'Oh, I assumed Gordon had done that.'

'Why?'

Davina shrugged. 'Just so's his precious gallows would look good. Or because he was making some adjustment to them, I don't know.'

'I detect you aren't part of the group within the company who believes Ritchie was murdered?'

'Good God, no, Carole. I know there are lots of feuds and back-stabbings in amdrams, but I don't think anyone takes it that far.' Davina let out a healthy chuckle and both Carole and Jude were struck by how *normal* she seemed. In fact, amidst all the posturing of the SADOS crowd, she was a veritable rock of sanity.

But there was still something that, to Jude's mind, required an explanation. 'Davina, you remember the evening Ritchie Good died . . .?'

'Hardly going to forget it in a hurry, am I?'

'No, nor me. I was just thinking, though . . . I was the first person to find his body – that is, the first person after Hester Winstone, who'd actually witnessed his death. I went back because I'd left my bag in the hall. And then you came in.'

'Yes.'

'And moments before I'd seen you in the Cricketers working your way through a large gin and tonic.'

'Sounds like me, yes.'

'So I was just wondering why you had come back into the hall?'

'Oh, I suddenly remembered a note I'd meant to give one of the actors. Normally I write my notes down, but I hadn't and didn't want to forget it. I looked round, but couldn't see him in the pub, so I thought maybe he might still be in the hall.'

'Who're we talking about, Davina?'

'Olly Pinto.'

TWENTY-EIGHT

'Maybe he'd just gone home early,' suggested Carole in the Renault on the way back to Fethering. 'Decided to forego the session at the Cricketers.'

'It would have been out of character for him if he did. Anyway, I saw him afterwards while everyone was waiting around for the police to arrive.'

'So you're thinking that Olly switched the nooses?'

'It's a possibility, Carole. He very definitely stood to gain from Ritchie's absence.'

'Getting the part of Dick Dudgeon?'

'Exactly.'

'For which he still doesn't know the lines.'

'No, that's true.' An idea came to Jude. 'I think you should set up your "line-bashing" session with Olly as soon as possible.'

Davina Vere Smith's eruption at the Sunday rehearsal had had the desired effect of putting a rocket up at least one of the *Devil's Disciple* cast. When Carole rang Olly Pinto later that evening and suggested he might benefit from a run-through of his lines, he was almost pathetically eager to set up the encounter as soon as possible.

It was agreed that he would come round to High Tor the following day after work (he was employed in one of Fethering's many estate agencies). Carole said she thought it'd help to have Jude there too, so that she could read the other parts. The real reason for this proposal was that, given the way her suspicions were currently veering, Carole didn't want to be alone with Olly Pinto.

She had only just put the phone down after her conversation with Olly when it rang. Her son Stephen. Gaby was laid low with another stomach bug. Could Granny possibly drop everything and come to look after Lily in Fulham for a couple of days?

Carole apologized that she couldn't. She might be able to come up for a couple of hours during the day on the Monday, but time would be tight as she had to be back for a 'line-bashing' session in the early evening. And then of course she had a regular rehearsal on the Tuesday.

Stephen said not to worry, he'd sort out one of Gaby's friends to drop in. But he did sound a bit bewildered by his mother's reaction. Normally, if it was something to do with Lily, Carole in Granny mode would be in the Renault and on her way the minute the phone call had ended.

Carole herself was a bit surprised at her reaction. She didn't love Lily any the less, but she couldn't let SADOS down. It was a measure of how much she had come to embrace amateur dramatics.

Olly Pinto arrived at High Tor about quarter past six on the Monday, not wearing his customary rehearsal garb of jeans and a fleece, but in his work livery of pinstriped suit and something that looked like a club tie but probably wasn't.

Olly accepted Carole's offer of coffee and replied to her polite enquiry as to the state of the housing market, 'Maybe picking up a bit. We usually see an upsurge in enquiries round Easter time. This year's better than last year at the same stage, though we're still way off where we used to be before the financial crash.'

Jude was once again struck by the contrast in the lives of these people, plodding through monochrome jobs by day and transforming into the variegated butterflies of amateur dramatics in the evenings.

The sitting room at the front of High Tor was not actually cold, but the austerity of its furniture always made it feel chilly. The pictures had all been inherited from distant Seddon aunts and put up on the walls out of duty rather than enthusiasm. The only positive colour came from a bright photograph of Carole's beloved granddaughter Lily on the mantelpiece.

Still, the sober appearance of the room seemed to fit the seriousness of the evening's task in hand. Olly Pinto had brought his copy of *The Devil's Disciple* with him, but Carole very soon confiscated that. 'No cribbing,' she said in the voice that had silenced many committees at the Home Office. 'Jude'll give you the cues and I'll prompt you when you get things wrong.' Carole's lack of confidence in the actor's memory was emphasized by her use of the word 'when' rather than 'if'.

'Shall we start at the beginning?' asked Olly hopefully because, allowing for a bit of paraphrase, he knew Act One pretty well.

'No,' Carole replied implacably. 'It was Act Three you were worst on. We'll start there, then go back to the beginning.'

He didn't argue. As Jude patiently fed him the lines, it

occurred to her that, beyond the fact of his working for an estate agent, she knew virtually nothing about Olly Pinto's private life. And maybe for some participants that was the appeal of amateur dramatics, the opportunity to be someone other than your mundane self . Rather like the appeal of acting itself.

The 'line-bashing' was a hard and tedious process, but it did work. The one-to-one concentration – and perhaps the embarrassment of showing himself up in front of the two women – actually improved Olly's grasp of George Bernard Shaw's words. In rehearsal when he cocked up a line he could sometimes get a laugh about his incompetence from his fellow actors; no such levity was allowed in the sitting room of High Tor. The world did actually lose a good dominatrix when Carole Seddon decided to forge a career in the Home Office.

It took them an hour to get through Act Three to the end, and then Carole offered more coffee. 'I'd offer you a proper drink, Olly, but alcohol might affect your concentration. We'll have a proper drink when we've done the whole play.'

When Carole opened the door on her way to the kitchen, her Labrador Gulliver nosed his way in to inspect the visitor. After he'd been hustled out by his mistress, Jude asked Olly whether he had a dog.

'No. Did have. When I was married.'

'Oh?'

'Yes. Divorced – what? – three years ago.'

'Children?'

'Two. I don't see them as much as I should. My wife – ex-wife – is not very cooperative about access.'

'I'm sorry.' And Jude could see the appeal of SADOS as a displacement activity for someone like Olly Pinto.

Carole returned with the coffee pot and recharged their cups. 'Feeling a bit more confident now, are you, Olly?' she asked with surprising gentleness.

'Yes, I am a bit. It makes me realize that, if I really do concentrate, I can drill the lines into my head.'

'Exactly.' When she had refilled the coffee cups, she announced, 'I think we should go back to Act Two now. You were shakier on that than Act One.'

'All right,' said Olly, not exactly welcoming his fate but reconciled to it.

'Then we'll rattle through Act One at the end.'

So Act Two it was. And the build-up of concentration in the one-to-one setting still seemed to be working. Olly got more of the lines right than he had on any previous occasion. And he didn't lose his temper when Carole patiently dragged him back out of the realms of paraphrase.

So there was unaccustomed cheer in the sitting room of High Tor when they'd finished the Act.

'I think,' said Jude, 'you should open a bottle now, Carole. Olly's earned it, and I'm gasping. And he knows Act One pretty well. Lubricated by a glass of wine, he'll rattle through it, no probs.'

Carole looked dubious. Her upbringing had set her resolutely against the idea of bringing forward a promised treat. But she acceded to Jude's suggestion. 'White wine all right for you, Olly?'

'Lovely. Thank you very much.'

While Carole was in the kitchen, Jude said, 'We were very honoured to be included in Elizaveta's "drinkies thing" on Saturday.'

'So you should be. That really puts you in the charmed circle. But I'd be a bit wary.'

'Oh?'

'There's no such thing as a free lunch – or a free drink with Elizaveta Dalrymple. The fact that she invited Carole and you means she wants something from you.'

'What could we possibly have that would be of any use to her?'

'Information, usually. Reports from the front line of *Devil's Disciple* rehearsals.'

'I thought she was getting those from you.'

'Someone like Elizaveta can never have too many sources.'

'Do you think she'll actually come to the production?'

'Come to see *The Devil's Disciple*? Tricky diplomatic one for her. It's a SADOS production and, now Freddie's gone, Elizaveta is the spiritual leader of SADOS. So she should support it. On the other hand, she's had this big bust-up. She stormed out of the show, apparently because of things Ritchie said to her – though in fact it was because she'd fallen out with Davina.'

Jude was surprised Olly was shrewd enough to have worked that out. In fact, she was surprised how much more intelligent and congenial he was that evening than he had ever been at rehearsals. When he wasn't showing off, he was actually rather nice.

'Anyway,' he resumed, 'the one thing Elizaveta wouldn't want to appear is churlish. The thought of a SADOS production going ahead without her seeing it would be anathema to her. Also, she'd want to be there to see how bad the production is.'

'Do you think it's that bad?'

'No, but Elizaveta would as a matter of principle. She'd also be convinced that she would have played Mrs Dudgeon infinitely better than you're playing it.'

Jude grinned. 'She might be right.'

'Well, who knows? All I do know is that Elizaveta will be there – almost definitely on the first night – and afterwards she'll say that the production was absolutely *mahvellous*, and your performance was particularly *mahvellous*.'

'So, what – she'll book a ticket for the first night?'

'Oh no, it won't be as straightforward as that. There'll be some drama involved. Elizaveta will let it be known through her grapevine that she won't be going to the show, that it'd be totally against her principles to go. And then a friend of one of her friends will drop out and she'll be offered the ticket at the last minute and – surprise, surprise – she'll be there. May not be exactly what'll happen, but something along those lines.'

'You seem to have a very good understanding of how Elizaveta Dalrymple works.'

'I've observed her for a long time. And I know she can be a monster, but she's also lively and fun, and if I hadn't got my relationship with Elizaveta and SADOS, I wouldn't have any social life at all.'

The confession was so honest, so potentially sad, that Jude couldn't think of anything to say. She was quite relieved that Carole returned that moment with a bottle of Chilean Chardonnay, three glasses and a bowl of cashew nuts.

'Olly was just telling me about the deviousness of Elizaveta.'

Carole snorted. 'Well, I've only met her the once, at her "drinkies thing" on Saturday. But I don't think anything I heard about her would surprise me. She seems the archetypal Queen Bee.'

Olly nodded. 'That's about right.'

'Or,' suggested Jude, 'while Freddie was still alive, the archetypal Lady Macbeth.'

'Well, of course, she did play the part for SADOS,' said Olly.

'I know. I saw the photo at her house.'

'Of course you did.'

'I was just wondering, though,' Jude went on, 'whether she ever played Lady Macbeth in real life . . .?'

Carole looked across at her neighbour in some confusion. She couldn't understand the new direction in which the conversation was being taken.

Olly also looked a little uncomfortable, but for different reasons. 'Not sure I like this discussion of "The Scottish Play". Bad luck, you know.'

Characteristic of an amateur actor to know all the theatrical superstitions, thought Jude. But what she said was, 'Only bad luck inside a theatre, Olly. Fine everywhere else.'

'Ah.' He looked at his watch. 'Maybe we should get started on Act One.'

But Jude was not to be diverted. 'I was meaning – did Elizaveta ever act like Lady Macbeth, controlling her husband, getting him to do things she wanted done?'

Olly Pinto grinned and nodded. 'All the time. Freddie was nominally in charge of everything at SADOS, but Elizaveta was very definitely "the power behind the throne".'

The tension in Carole relaxed. Now she understood where Jude was going with this, she started to watch with interest.

'And how does she use that power now she hasn't got Freddie to wield it through?'

'You mean how does she get other people to do things for her?'

'Exactly.'

'Oh, she just becomes more Elizaveta than ever, really turns it on. She can be extremely persuasive. I mean, this business about whether or not she attends the *Devil's Disciple* first night, I wouldn't be surprised if I end up somehow being involved in that. I'll get one of Elizaveta's "little phone calls".'

'That's how she organizes things, is it?'

'Oh yes, still the old-fashioned phone. I get quite a few calls from her, though fortunately she's taken on board the fact that she can't ring me at work. God knows what she'd be like if she ever started using email or texts.'

'And has Elizaveta ever asked you to do something you didn't want to do?'

'All the time.' Olly grinned ruefully. 'Mind you, I usually end up doing it. As I said, she can be very persuasive.'

Jude and Carole exchanged a look and there was instant understanding between them. As a result, it was Carole who said, 'We talked to Gordon Blaine after we left after Elizaveta's "drinkies thing" on Saturday.'

'Oh yes?'

'I gave him a lift. His car had broken down.'

'God, not again. I must say, for the engineering genius Gordon always claims himself to be, a surprising number of his projects fail to function.'

'But his gallows functioned,' said Carole. 'Almost too well.'

'Yes,' Olly agreed soberly.

'On Saturday he was talking to us about a previous "drinkies thing" of Elizaveta's. The one the night before Ritchie Good died.'

'Oh?'

'And he said he'd described to everyone exactly how his gallows were going to work.'

'I remember that. Elizaveta was very intrigued – again regretting that she wouldn't be at the next day's rehearsal and so miss the demonstration. She was quite incapable of being "hands off" with anything to do with SADOS.'

'And Gordon described how easily the noose could be switched, did he?'

'Certainly did.'

'So did Elizaveta make any comment on that?'

'Only a joking comment.'

'What?' asked Carole sharply.

'She said, "So if one wanted to get rid of a member of the *Devil's Disciple* company one would have the means readily to hand."'

'And that was a joke?'

'Well, I assumed so at the time,' replied Olly, starting to look a little uncomfortable.

'Did she say anything else?' asked Jude.

'Yes. She said, "I wouldn't be at all upset if someone were to engineer a little accident between Ritchie Good and those gallows."'

'Did she?' said Carole.

'Yes, but I mean, it was a joke. At least, everyone laughed. Elizaveta had been bad-mouthing Ritchie all evening, in her customary very bitchy, funny way. What she said about the gallows just continued in the same vein. Which was why we all laughed.'

'And you don't think anyone took it seriously?' asked Carole.

'Oh God, no.'

'"Who will rid me of this turbulent priest?"' murmured Carole.

'I'm sorry? What on earth are you talking about?'

'It's what King Henry II said about Thomas à Beckett. And some listening knights thought they saw a way of getting into the King's good books, so they went straight down to Canterbury and murdered Beckett.'

'Are you suggesting that's what Elizaveta was doing? She hoped someone would pick up the hint, swap the nooses on the gallows and cause Ritchie's death?'

'It's a possibility, wouldn't you say?'

'It's a possibility in one of those stage thrillers SADOS used to keep doing. I wouldn't have said it was a possibility in real life.'

Carole shrugged. 'Stranger things have happened.'

Olly let out a chuckle which stopped halfway. Then he looked anxiously from one woman to the other. 'You're not suggesting *I* followed through Elizaveta's suggestion, are you?'

'Well, you weren't around in the Cricketers after the

rehearsal ended. Davina went back to St Mary's Hall to find you.'

'Yes, but—'

'And,' Jude chipped in, 'you did benefit quite directly from Ritchie's death. No other way you'd have got the part of Dick Dudgeon, was there?'

Again Olly Pinto looked from one to the other. Then, with considerable dignity, he said, 'Well, I can assure you I did not do what you're suggesting. I've allowed myself over the years to be manipulated in many ways by Elizaveta, and I've been persuaded into doing a good few things that I didn't want to do because of pressure from her, but I would never do anything criminal.'

'But do you think it's possible,' Carole persisted, 'that Elizaveta did plant the idea of switching the nooses, in the hope that someone, wishing to curry favour with her, might act on the suggestion?'

'The thought hadn't occurred to me but, though it seems pretty unlikely, I wouldn't put it past her. Elizaveta likes sort of giving tests to her supporters, always threatening them with the ultimate sanction – the withdrawal of her patronage.'

'So, Olly, who do you think might have wanted to curry favour that much?'

He was silent for a moment, then said, 'I don't think it would be one of the people who's been part of Elizaveta's circle for a long time. We're all fond of her and want to keep in her good books, but we're also quite realistic about her. We know she can be a bit of a monster, so we take quite a lot of what she says with a pinch of salt.'

'So one of the more recent additions to the charmed circle . . .?'

'Perhaps.'

'Who?'

'Well,' Olly replied slowly, 'the newest regular – and indeed the one who seems most eager to please – is Storm Lavelle.'

TWENTY-NINE

J ude rang Storm that evening, but got no reply from either her landline or the mobile. She left a message on each, calming herself so as not to sound alarmist and asking Storm to ring her back.

The reply came the next morning, the Tuesday, just as Jude was washing up her breakfast things. 'Hello?'

'Oh, it's Storm, returning your call. What is it? Have you got transport problems for rehearsal tonight, because I'll happily give you a lift.'

'No, it's not that.' Storm sounded so cheerful, so full of life, that Jude found it really difficult to bring up the subject she wanted to discuss. 'Actually, it's in relation to you and Ritchie Good.'

'Oh?' The caller's tone changed instantly, from open and enthusiastic to crabby and suspicious.

'And it also concerns Elizaveta Dalrymple.'

The call was instantly ended. Jude tried ringing back straight away, but the mobile had been switched off. And calls to the landline switched straight through to the answering machine.

Jude didn't finish tidying up breakfast. She went straight round to High Tor.

The two neighbours quickly agreed that it was time to confront Elizaveta Dalrymple. 'There was no way she could have done it herself,' said Carole, 'but if she set up Storm . . .'

'I'm still finding it difficult to cast Storm in that role.'

'Maybe, but that's just because she's a friend.'

'Yes, I know.'

'And from all the encounters with murderers you've had, you should know by now that appearances are very rarely other than deceptive.'

'I know all that too.'

'Come on,' said Carole brusquely, 'I think you should ring Elizaveta and find out when we can see her.'

'Why me?'

'Because you know her better than I do.'

It was only when she had dialled the number that Jude realized that the two of them had spent almost exactly the same amount of time in Elizaveta Dalrymple's company. Still, there were times when arguing with Carole just wasn't worth the effort.

The late April weather, particularly benign that morning and with a promise of summer, had brought a surprising influx of tourists to Smalting. All the parking on the road facing the sea was taken and Carole was annoyed to have to pay at the small car park at the end of Elizaveta's road.

'Will we be out within the hour?' she asked as she took her change purse out of her neat and nearly empty handbag.

'I'd pay for two,' said Jude. 'Never know how long something like this'll take.'

Huffily Carole paid for the requisite ticket, placed it prominently on the dashboard and locked the car. The two women were both rather tense as they walked along.

'I wonder if she'll be on her own . . .' Jude mused.

'Why shouldn't she be? Did she say there was anyone with her when you rang?'

'No, she didn't. But I'll bet from the moment I put the phone down she's been ringing round all her cronies to tell them about our visit.'

'Do you think so?'

'I'm sure so. Maybe some of them will have rushed round to give her support.'

'You don't think any of them will be armed, do you?' asked Carole.

Jude giggled. 'No, I don't think any of them will be armed.'

The doorbell was answered promptly. Dressed in another ample kaftan, Elizaveta once again led them to the upstairs sitting room. Once again they took in the memorabilia of past SADOS triumphs on the walls. Jude looked particularly at the 'canvas effect' print of the Macbeths.

The beauty of the day meant that the view over Smalting

Beach was better than ever. One of the high windows was raised a little to let in a soft, salty breeze. On the sand they could see parents and grandparents playing with pre-school-age children. Both Carole and Jude found themselves instinctively looking over towards the rows of beach huts and remembering a previous investigation that had focused on one of them.

Elizaveta sat them down. They refused her offer of coffee and so she sat facing them. Her chair had pretensions to being a throne. There was another identical one in the room. Presumably 'His' and 'Hers' when Freddie had been alive. Elizaveta looked as if she expected some major confrontation, and it was a prospect that excited rather than frightened her.

'So,' she said rather grandly, 'to what do I owe the honour of your visit?'

They hadn't planned any particular approach, so Carole decided to open the proceedings. 'We're here to talk about Ritchie Good's death.'

'Are you really?' Elizaveta let out a long-suffering sigh. 'If you were listening when you were here on Saturday, you should have realized I do not particularly wish to talk about Ritchie Good.'

'But I think we have to talk about him.'

'Do you? I must say I think it's a bit rich that I should be being told what to talk about by a mere prompter.'

'The fact is,' said Jude, 'that we are not convinced the Ritchie Good's death was an accident.'

'I imagine that is a subject on which there has been a great deal of fevered conjecture amongst the SADOS members. Now I'm no longer with the society, I cannot obviously—'

'Oh, come on, Elizaveta, you get reports from your personal grapevine about everything that goes on there.'

'Perhaps I do. But I still can't see how the accidental or non-accidental death of Ritchie Good has anything to do with me.'

'You can't deny,' said Carole, 'that his death suited you very well.'

She shrugged. 'Sometimes the fates are generous. No, I can't pretend I shed many tears when I heard of his demise.

Apart from being appallingly rude to me, he showed no respect for anything that Freddie and I had achieved in SADOS.'

'And the death was easily engineered,' Carole continued. 'All that was required was for somebody to change the doctored noose on the gallows to the real one.'

'I'm not quite sure what you're talking about.'

'I think you are. Because Gordon Blaine explained the workings of his gallows in exhaustive detail at your "drinkies thing" the night before Ritchie's death.'

'Goodness me. You have been doing your research, haven't you?'

'Do you deny it?'

'No, of course I don't. One thing I would like to know, though. If either of you think I was responsible for Ritchie's death, I'd love to know how I did it. The hanging – or strangulation – happened, I gather, in St Mary's Hall. Now I have not been in St Mary's Hall since I was forced to leave the production of *The Devil's Disciple*, neither to sabotage a gallows nor for any other reason. I'd be intrigued to know how I am supposed to have engineered this fatal accident.'

'You planned it,' said Jude. 'You got someone else to switch the nooses for you.'

'How remarkably clever of me. What, so I had a private meeting with someone, did I? I took them on one side and said, "I wonder if you'd be kind enough to bump off Ritchie Good for me?" And they said, "Terrific idea, Elizaveta. Regard it as done." Is that how it happened . . . roughly?'

'No, it wasn't as overt as that,' said Carole. 'At that same party –' (she couldn't bring herself to say 'drinkies thing') – 'when Gordon Blaine described the mechanism, you said to everyone how pleased you'd be if Ritchie Good was accidentally hanged.'

'Well, I may have said that, but only as a joke.'

'But did everyone present realize it was a joke?'

'I assumed so, but . . .' She seemed rather attracted to the idea as she articulated it. 'Do you think there really was someone who took what I said seriously enough . . . who cared enough about me to take the hint and do what I'd asked for?'

'I think that was what you were hoping,' said Carole.

'Really?' Elizaveta was still intrigued. 'But who might have done it? A few years ago I would have thought it was Olly Pinto. When he first joined SADOS, he was, I have to say, totally besotted with little *moi*. Then he would have done anything for me. Now . . . I don't know what's happened to him, but whatever he once felt for me has been . . . well, to put it mildly, diluted. Now I think he only comes to see me because he's lonely.'

Jude was surprised to see a tear gleaming in Elizaveta Dalrymple's eye.

'I think that's why most of them stay around me . . .' the old woman went on. 'Because they're lonely. I think with most of them, it was Freddie they were really loyal to, not me. When Freddie was around, our "drinkies things" were legendary. Just had to mention we were having one and people'd be falling over themselves to get here. Now I have to ring round those who are left and virtually beg them to come along.'

The tears were really falling now, streaking mascara down on to Elizaveta's heavily made-up cheeks. 'My life really stopped,' she went on, 'when Freddie died. Oh, I've tried to maintain a front. I've acted hearty, bitchy, thick-skinned. It's been the toughest performance of my life . . . and I don't know how much longer I can keep it up. The effort of preparing to see people, of being a hostess, it just gets harder and harder. And after everyone's gone, I just sink back into total black despair. I just can't go on like this.'

Carole and Jude exchanged looks. Though Elizaveta was, as ever, self-dramatizing, they could both recognize the core of genuine suffering. And both wondered how big a blow it had been to her when she had discovered that Davina Vere Smith had also been given a star-shaped pendant. It must have brought home – probably not for the first time – the knowledge that the much-vaunted marriage to Freddie had not been as perfect as its mythology might suggest.

But Elizaveta's personality was not one to stay down for too long. She perked up with her next thought. 'So you do really think that someone took what I said seriously enough to act on it? To switch the nooses? Somebody actually cared for me enough to do that?'

Without commenting on the woman's strangely skewed sense of values, Carole replied, 'We think it's possible. But nobody said anything to you about having done it?'

'No. Why should they?'

Jude shrugged. 'To report back: Mission Accomplished?'

'No. Nobody has. And I think in a way that's rather splendid. Whoever it is did something purely out of love for me, and then didn't want to crow about it.'

They could see Elizaveta Dalrymple transforming before their eyes. A moment ago she had been the sad, neglected, wronged widow. Now she was moving into the role of charismatic inspirer of others. She was eternally recasting herself, but the scenarios in which she appeared all had one thing in common: Elizaveta Dalrymple was playing the lead in all of them.

'So,' she said, now rather magnificent after her grief, 'who do I have to thank for my revenge on Ritchie Good? What is the name of my guardian angel?'

'We think it was probably Storm Lavelle,' said Jude.

'Oh,' said Elizaveta, basking in glee. 'I always thought that young woman had something about her. She's very talented, too. You know, I can see in little Storm something of myself at the same age.'

THIRTY

'Well, we didn't exactly get confirmation, did we?' said Carole as they left the house. 'We got confirmation that Elizaveta did kind of "issue the challenge". Say she wanted Ritchie Good dead.'

'Which presumably was enough to prompt Storm to take action.'

Jude's full lips wrinkled with scepticism. 'It just seems out of character for her.'

'Again you're only saying that because she's your friend. From what I've seen of her, she's pretty volatile – not to say unstable.'

'I agree. She's passionate. I mean, OK, if Ritchie had done something directly to hurt her, I can see Storm taking revenge on him in a fit of fury. I can't see her in this sort of "one-remove" scenario, exacting vengeance on someone else's behalf. It's not in her nature to be so unspontaneous. I'm sure there's some other explanation.'

'Well, it's not an explanation you're about to hear, if Storm continues refusing to answer your phone calls, is it?'

'No,' Jude agreed limply. Then, suddenly, noticing they were passing a little general store, 'Oh, I've just remembered I haven't got any eggs! Could you pick me up here when you've got the car?'

Carole watched her neighbour rush into the shop with some censure. Her own organized shopping routine would never allow High Tor to run out of eggs. Then she looked at her watch and realized sourly that they had only needed one hour's parking.

Jude got her eggs, then realized she needed soy sauce and noodles too. Which meant she had to buy another 'Bag For Life'. If all the similar ones she'd got in her kitchen were counted up, they'd provide her with more lives than a full cattery.

She stepped out between two parked vehicles and looked towards the car park. The white Renault was coming towards her. She stepped out a bit further, so that Carole could see where she was.

It was only when the car was almost upon her that Jude realized it wasn't going to stop. In fact it was accelerating and aiming straight for her.

She tried to leap backwards, but was too late. She felt a thump that shuddered through her whole body. Then she seemed to be lifted up in the air and smashed down.

Everything went dark.

THIRTY-ONE

When Jude came to, she looked up to find herself surrounded by a circle of curious holidaymakers. Amongst the concerned faces looking down at her was Carole's. A confusion of voices commented on what had happened.

'I think we should phone for an ambulance.'

'There's a doctor's surgery just along the road.'

'Should be the police we call for. That car was going way over the speed limit.'

But it was Carole's voice saying, 'How do you feel?' that cut through the others.

'Not too bad, I think,' said Jude, trying to assess the extent of her injuries. 'Give me a hand and I think I could try standing up.'

Ignoring opinions from the growing crowd that 'she shouldn't be moved until the ambulance is here', Carole's thin arms hooked themselves under Jude's chubby ones and got her, first to a sitting position, then upright on her two rather tottery legs.

'Are you all right?'

'Think so, Carole. Just a quick check for damage.'

There was quite a bit. The wing of the car had turned her escaping body and flung her face down on to the edge of the road. Her arms had taken the brunt of the impact. Though that had protected her face, the encounter with the tarmac had shredded the palms of her hands. Blood was just starting to well from rows of little scrapes there. Her knees were in a similar state. They were the kinds of wounds that were too recent to have started hurting, but would be agony when they began to heal.

'Let go of me, Carole. See if I can stand on my own.'

She could. Just about. Not confident, stable standing. More the wobbly, determined kind.

Another voice from the crowd expressed the opinion that an ambulance should be called.

'No,' said Carole firmly. 'Be quicker if I drive her to the hospital.'

Her Renault had stopped in the middle of the road, with the driver's door open. Carole must have stopped when she saw the crowd around the injured Jude.

Ignoring protests from people who all clearly saw themselves as 'good in a crisis', Carole collected up the 'Bag for Life' (the eggs inside it all sadly smashed). Then she manhandled Jude into the passenger seat of the car, ignoring her insistence that 'I'll bleed all over your upholstery.'

The fact that she said, 'That doesn't matter' was a measure of how seriously Carole viewed her neighbour's predicament. Normally nothing would be allowed to sully the pristine cleanliness of the Renault's interior.

They drove a little way in silence, till they had turned off the seafront road. Then the car drew to a sedate halt in a vacant parking space.

'We're not going to the hospital, are we, Carole?'

'No, of course we're not. We're just going to get you patched up a bit first.'

It was entirely in character the Carole Seddon would have a well-stocked first aid box in her car. And the efficiency with which she mopped up and dressed the grazes on Jude's hands and knees suggested that her Home Office training might at some point have included a course in first aid.

'Right,' she said. 'You'll do. Sure you didn't suffer any blows to the head?'

'No, I was lucky in that respect. Just the hands and knees . . . and the general feeling of a rag doll who's just been thrown against the wall by a particularly belligerent toddler.'

'You'll survive,' was the unsentimental response from Carole.

'Yes, I've no doubt I'll survive. Now, who are we going to get the address from?'

'Elizaveta'd know it.'

'Undoubtedly, but I'm not sure how good our credit is there. What about Davina?'

'Do you have her number?'

'It's in the "Contacts" in my mobile. But you'd better ring her. I don't think I can manage the keyboard with my hands like this.'

Carole got through to Davina and the required information was readily supplied.

'It's in Fethering,' she told Jude.

The house was one of the oldest in the village, in a row of small cottages whose original owners had worked in what was then the only industry, fishing. Once regarded as little more than hovels, they were now highly sought-after second homes for wealthy Londoners. Many of them had been refurbished to within an inch of their lives, but there were still a few that had been passed on within families for generations. On these there were fewer window boxes, hanging baskets and quaint cast-iron nameplates.

The house that matched the address Davina had supplied was one of the untarted-up variety. Carole drew up her white Renault behind the already parked white Renault and looked across at Jude. 'Ready for it?'

Her neighbour nodded and the two women got out of the car with, in Jude's case, some discomfort. Even in the short journey from Smalting, as the shock of the impact wore off her individual injuries were starting to give her a lot of pain.

Carole knocked on the door, which was promptly opened. Mimi Lassiter looked unsurprised to see her visitors, though perhaps a bit disappointed that one of them was Jude.

'I think you know why we've come to see you,' said Carole, very Home Office.

'I think I probably do. Come in.'

The sitting room into which she led them reminded both women of Gordon Blaine's. It was not just the small dimensions – in this case due to the original builder rather than the owner's DIY conversion – but the furniture, the ornaments and the pictures on the walls were all from an earlier era. The house had been decorated in the time of Mimi's parents and she had either not wanted to – or not dared to – change a thing.

It wasn't an occasion for pleasantries or offers of coffee. Mimi Lassiter sat in a cracked leather armchair, set facing the television, and her guests in straight-backed chairs either side of the box.

'Rather rash of you this morning, wasn't it?' said Carole. 'Making a public attack on Jude by driving straight at her? There'd have been lots of witnesses on the seafront at Smalting. I'm sure someone would have taken note of your registration number.'

'I wasn't thinking very straight this morning,' said Mimi, sounding as ever like a rather pernickety maiden aunt. 'I was upset.'

'Do you often get upset?' asked Jude.

'Not very often, but I do. My mother used to look after me when I got upset, but since she's passed, I've had to manage it on my own.'

'And,' said Carole, 'do you regard trying to run someone down in cold blood as "managing it on your own"?'

'It made sense. I couldn't see any other way out. And when I heard from Elizaveta that you two were actually investigating Ritchie Good's death . . . as I say, I wasn't thinking very straight. It probably wasn't the most sensible thing to do.'

To Carole and Jude this seemed like something of an understatement.

'No,' said Mimi. 'I've been very foolish. My mother always used to say, "At times, Mimi, you can be very foolish." And she had ways of stopping me being foolish, but now she's gone . . .'

'How long ago did your mother die?' asked Jude.

'Nine years ago. It was just round the time when I was retiring from work.'

'What did you do when you were working?'

'I trained in Worthing as a shorthand typist. I was very good. I got a diploma. I could have got a job anywhere, even in London. But I didn't want to leave Fethering. Mummy needed help with Daddy. He was virtually bedridden for a long time. So I got a secretarial job at Hadleigh's. Do you know them?'

'No.'

'Big nursery, just between here and Worthing. Lots of glass-houses. Well, they were made of glass when I started there. Now they're mostly that polythene stuff. Still a very big company, though. I did very well at Hadleigh's. They very nearly made me office manager. But I wasn't as good on the computers as I had been on the typewriter, so they appointed someone else. I never really took to computers in the same way I took to the typewriter. So they kept me on at Hadleigh's, but there was never any more chance of promotion. Then they opened up a Farm Shop and they suggested I might work in there. But I didn't like it. Some members of the public can be very rude, you know.'

'So,' Jude recapitulated, 'your mother died around the time you retired. That must have been a very big double blow for you.'

'Oh, it was. Two days before I left Hadleigh's. And it wasn't real retirement. I mean, I hadn't served all the time that . . . They gave me my full pension, but it was really . . .'

'Early retirement,' suggested Carole, whose experience of the same thing still rankled.

Mimi nodded. She looked shaken by the memory. 'I was in a very bad state round then, I remember. I know it's wrong, but at times I did think about ending it all. I just felt so isolated.'

'Are you saying you attempted suicide?'

'No, not quite. But I thought about it. I even started stockpiling paracetamol, but then things got better.'

'In what way?' asked Jude. 'Was it because you'd joined SADOS?'

Mimi nodded enthusiastically. 'Fortunately that happened fairly soon after Mummy passed. That's what really got me out of the terrible state I was in. Elizaveta Dalrymple used to come to the Farm Shop while I was still working there. And she said how the society was always looking for new members and she persuaded me to come along to a social meeting. She can be very persuasive, Elizaveta.'

'Yes,' Carole agreed drily.

'So that's how I started with SADOS. As a very humble new member . . . little knowing that I would one day end up at the dizzy heights of Membership Secretary.' Clearly the appointment was one that meant a great deal to Mimi Lassiter.

'I'd never wanted to act,' she went on. 'I couldn't act to save my life, but they found things for me to do backstage. And occasionally I'm in crowd scenes . . . like I am for *The Devil's Disciple*. Elizaveta always makes me feel part of the company, though, and she even started inviting me to parties at her home.'

'Her "drinkies things"?'

'Yes.'

'Of course. Where we saw you on Saturday.'

'Yes.'

'And what about Freddie? Did you have much to do with him?'

'Oh, Freddie.' An expression of sheer hero-worship took over her face. 'He was wonderful. Did you ever meet him?'

'Didn't have that pleasure,' said Jude.

'Though we've heard so much about him,' said Carole, 'that we *feel* as though we've met him.'

'He was just a wonderful man. So talented. And so kind to everyone, particularly to new members of SADOS.'

A look was exchanged between Carole and Jude. Each knew the other was thinking, 'particularly to new, *young, pretty* members of the SADOS'. Who could benefit so much from Freddie's assistance when working on their parts in his flat in Worthing. Another look between the two also made a silent agreement that they weren't about to ask whether Mimi Lassiter had ever been the recipient of a star-shaped pendant. It just didn't seem likely.

'I gather,' said Carole, 'it was a great upheaval for the society when Freddie Dalrymple died.'

'Oh, it was terrible. For a long time nobody knew what would happen to SADOS. It seemed impossible that the society could continue without Freddie. But that's when Elizaveta really came into her own. She's such a strong woman, you know.'

Neither Carole nor Jude was about to argue with that.

'Could we come back to this morning?' Carole's question was not one that would have brooked the answer no.

'All right,' said Mimi, instantly subdued.

'And your attempt to kill Jude.' Mimi did not argue with the phrasing. 'You've told us you were in a bad state this morning, that you weren't thinking straight, but you haven't told us *why* you wanted Jude dead.'

'I wanted both of you dead,' said Mimi with refreshing honesty. 'I still do.'

An anxious look passed between the two women. Was their unwilling hostess about to produce a gun?

'But Elizaveta told me that's not the right way to proceed.'

'I'd go along with that,' Carole agreed. 'But when did Elizaveta say this?'

'Just now. The phone was ringing when I got back from Smalting.'

'And had she rung you earlier in the morning as well?'

'Yes. She told me you were both coming round. And she said you were coming because you thought Ritchie Good's death might not be an accident.'

'Which is why you were waiting for us in your Renault? To run us down?'

'Yes,' Mimi replied quietly.

Jude took over. 'Elizaveta said just now on the phone that what you'd done wasn't the right way to proceed. Did she tell you what *would* have been the right way?'

'Elizaveta had seen what had happened in the street outside her house. She knew that I had tried to kill you, and she said that I shouldn't try to do things like that ever again.' She made it sound like a child being chastised by a parent for not making her bed. And Jude was struck by the fact that Mimi Lassiter was childlike. There was something emotionally undeveloped about her, the little girl who could not make her own decisions, who had to be directed by a stronger woman. Like her mother . . . or Elizaveta Dalrymple.

'Tell us about Ritchie Good's death,' said Jude gently.

'What about it?'

'You switched the real noose for the doctored one, didn't you?'

'Yes.' Once again there was pride in her voice.

'And had you planned to do that,' asked Carole, 'after you'd heard Gordon Blaine describe the mechanism the previous day?'

'That planted the idea in my head, yes.'

'So what actually happened after the rehearsal that Sunday afternoon?'

'Well, it was very lucky, actually.' Mimi was now talking with enthusiasm, and clearly not a vestige of guilt. 'Most people had left St Mary's Hall, but I was gathering my bits together, my bag and what-have-you. I'd left them in the Green Room, so I was near the stage, and I heard some people come in, and I recognized Ritchie Good's voice, and Hester Winstone's. And he was saying how she'd missed a really good show when he used the gallows and she must have what he called "a command performance". Well, Hester didn't sound very interested, and Ritchie was trying to persuade her, and I thought, "I'm never going to get a better opportunity than this." So I went onstage, and the curtains were drawn and it was easy to get on to the cart and switch the two nooses around. And then I slipped out of the hall without them seeing me, and I went to the Cricketers.' She smiled beatifically. 'It all worked remarkably well, didn't it?'

There was a silence. Then Carole asked, 'And did you do it because the night before you heard Elizaveta say that she wanted Ritchie dead?'

Mimi looked at her curiously. 'No, it was nothing to do with Elizaveta.'

'Then why did you do it?' asked Jude.

'Well, obviously . . . because Ritchie Good was in a SADOS production while not being a member of SADOS. He hadn't paid his subscription.'

THIRTY-TWO

'What do you think we do about her?' asked Carole, as she drove her white Renault the short distance back to High Tor.

'Do you mean, do we shop her to the police?'

'Yes, I suppose I do.' Her voice took on its Home Office tone. 'It would be the proper thing to do.'

Jude grimaced sceptically. 'Pretty difficult case for them to bring to court and secure a conviction. Also, what I always think in situations like this is: does a person like Mimi represent a danger to anyone else?'

'Might I remind you, Jude, that we're talking about someone who only this morning tried to kill you by running you over?'

'Yes, I know. I really do think she's got all that out of her system, though. She virtually said as much.'

'But do you believe her?'

'Yes, I do actually. What about you?'

Carole was forced unwillingly to admit that she couldn't see Mimi Lassiter as a public danger either.

'I'm more worried,' said Jude, 'about the threat she might pose to herself.'

'Oh?'

'She told us she'd got near to suicide when her mother died – or "passed", as she insisted on saying.'

'Well, this morning she seemed far from suicidal. Positively gleeful at having got away with killing Ritchie Good.'

'Mm.'

'And, Jude, you made her fix that appointment with her GP to talk about her issues with depression.' Jude nodded. 'In the circumstances I don't think there was a lot more you could have done.'

Over the next few months Carole's words came back to haunt Jude. She felt an ugly tug of guilt. Perhaps there was a lot more she could have done. But during the run of *The Devil's Disciple* both she and Carole had kept a cautious eye on Mimi Lassiter, and neither had seen anything untoward.

They didn't think there was anything significant about her absence from the last night cast party. In fact, to be honest, in such a raucous scrum of posing thespians they didn't notice she wasn't there.

Every night during the run of *The Devil's Disciple,* Mimi had dutifully done her (again unnoticed) performances in the Westerfield crowd at the near-hanging of Dick Dudgeon. That duty discharged, on the Saturday night she had packed up her belongings in St Mary's Hall and driven in her white Renault back to her parents' house (it still felt like her parents' house) in Fethering. Once there she had run a hot bath, got into it, swallowed down about thirty paracetamol from the store she had stockpiled when previously feeling suicidal, and slit her wrists with her father's old cut-throat razor.

The reason she had killed herself had nothing to do with guilt about causing the death of Ritchie Good. That event, she thought, had been very just and appropriate. Mimi had almost as strong an aversion to 'showing-off' as Carole Seddon. Ritchie Good had always been a 'show-off' and it was 'showing-off' that had brought about his demise. Besides, he'd never paid his subscription to be a member of SADOS.

But what had really made Mimi suicidal was the suspension of patronage by Elizaveta Dalrymple. After the attempt to run over Jude, the grande dame of SADOS had decided that perhaps Mimi was no longer the sort of person she wished to have attending her 'drinkies things'. By long tradition Elizaveta issued her invitations to her regulars on the Friday for the Saturday eight days away. By the end of the Friday which saw the penultimate performance of *The Devil's Disciple,* Mimi Lassiter had received no such summons. And by the end of the Saturday she realized she wasn't going to receive one. Mimi had been cast into the outer darkness. She would never get another invitation to one of Elizaveta's 'drinkies things'.

Without her idol's support, patronage and validation Mimi Lassiter crumpled like a rag doll. To her mind suicide was the only available option for her.

Of course, at the cast party nobody knew of the gruesome event taking place in Fethering. It was afterwards they heard the news which caused Jude such disquiet.

But at the party itself there was a high level of good cheer. This was because people in amdrams always like to let their hair down at the end of a production, rather than because *The Devil's Disciple* had been a huge success. Neville Prideaux's conviction that a wordy minor work by George Bernard Shaw was what the good burghers of Smalting were craving for had been proved completely wrong. They had stayed away in droves, and those who had attended had been unimpressed. In spite of all Carole Seddon's assiduous one-to-one 'line-bashing' sessions, when faced by a live audience Olly Pinto's memory appeared to have been wiped completely. He had ensured that Carole, in her role as prompter, had had a very busy week. And the people in the front row of St Mary's Hall had heard more from her than they had from some of the actors.

Storm Lavelle, on the other hand, had really built her performance throughout the run. She did have genuine talent and Jude wondered whether her butterfly brain would allow her to concentrate sufficiently on trying to get work in the professional theatre. Secretly, Jude rather doubted it. Like many aspiring actors, her friend had the talent, but lacked the tenacity required to make a go of it.

Storm had had her hair done on the morning of *The Devil's Disciple*'s final performance and, on removing Judith Anderson's wig, revealed a fuschia-pink crop with a long jagged fringe. For the cast party she wore a diamanté top over silver leggings. She looked terrific, her sparkle increased by the knowledge of how well she had acted in the show.

Storm seemed in such a relaxed mood that Jude thought she could ask about the strange moment when her friend had put the phone down on her. 'Do you remember, I said it was something about Ritchie Good and Elizaveta . . .?'

Storm looked embarrassed. 'The fact is, I had a bit of history with Ritchie which I didn't want anyone to hear about. And when you said it concerned that old cow Elizaveta too, I thought she might spread the news around SADOS.'

'And what was this "history" you had with Ritchie? An affair?'

'No, it didn't quite get that far, but it still left me feeling pretty stupid.'

'May I put forward a theory of what might have happened?'

Storm looked puzzled, but shrugged and said, 'If you want to.'

'I suggest that Ritchie Good came on to you quite heavily, got you keen and interested, got you to the point where you'd agreed to go to bed with him, and then said he couldn't go through with it because of his loyalty to his wife.'

A thunderstruck expression took over Storm's face. 'How on earth did you know that?'

'Let's just say there was a pattern to Ritchie's behaviour.'

'Oh. Well, the thing that worried me was that, I suppose trying to curry favour with the old bat, I told Elizaveta what had happened. Which was very stupid, because it was a sure way of guaranteeing that everyone in SADOS would soon know. And there was one person I really didn't want to know I'd had any kind of relationship with Ritchie Good.'

'And who was that?'

Jude's question was immediately answered by the wide smile that came to Storm's lips as she saw someone approaching them. It was Olly Pinto, grinning broadly.

His disastrous showing as Dick Dudgeon during the week seemed not to have affected him one bit. Jude had noticed him earlier at the cast party, in extremely high spirits, downing beer after beer.

And now she realized from the way he was looking at Storm Lavelle that there was another cause for his good cheer. Jude felt a bit silly for not having seen anything developing between the two of them earlier, because it was now clear that Olly Pinto was destined to be the next man to feel the full force of Storm's adoration. Jude didn't think it would do either of them any harm, and might in fact do them some good.

As a result of *The Devil's Disciple*'s failure to bring in the audiences, there was now a move among the younger members of the society to oust Neville Prideaux from the Play Selection Committee. His star had waned considerably. And some of this younger group at the party were arguing quite loudly that it wasn't too late to change the SADOS's next production from *I Am A Camera* to three episodes of *Fawlty Towers*. The mention of this led to a lot of the men going into comedy goose-stepping, as if auditioning for the part of Basil Fawlty.

Elizaveta Dalrymple, who had somehow got entangled with this group, proved not to be as averse to the idea of doing the three television episodes as some might have expected. The reason was, of course, that she didn't really think she was too old to play Basil's wife Sibyl.

Inevitably, Elizaveta had come back into the SADOS fold. As Olly Pinto had predicted, she had been at the first night ('someone dropped out at the last minute') and had met so many people there who were delighted to see her and urged her to attend the cast party on the Saturday night, that she couldn't really disappoint them. This suited her very well, because she had really wanted to get back in ever since Ritchie Good's death. With the man who'd insulted her removed, there was no reason for her not to reclaim her rightful place, the spider at the centre of the SADOS web.

Her rift with Davina Vere Smith also seemed somehow to have been healed. Jude did not know how this had been achieved, but suspected some telephonic machinations on Elizaveta's part, some agreement whereby Davina would never mention her involvement with Freddie and would always wear high collars at SADOS rehearsals.

Of course, Hester Winstone was not at the cast party. Jude had been in touch with Rob at Casements about future healing work and heard that Hester had left the convalescent home. Where to, Rob couldn't be sure, but he thought she had returned to her family. Jude didn't envy Hester her reunion with Mike because, in her experience, cricketers remained the most misogynist of sportsmen. Maybe she'd try to give Hester a call to offer help, but she very much suspected that the carapace of middle-class respectability would once again have closed over, and the need for any assistance would be denied. Hester would assure her that 'We are all right as we are.' It was frustrating, but there was nothing Jude could do about it. She did definitely plan to do more work at Casements, though.

The wine was flowing and some people were dancing. To provide the music, one of the younger members had produced a portable CD player. (Gordon Blaine had earlier set up a huge system of amplifiers and speakers in one corner of the room, but unfortunately it didn't work.)

Jude didn't feel like dancing. Apart from anything else, her body was still wincing from the bruises caused by her encounter with Mimi Lassiter's Renault. And her body language must have indicated her unwillingness to dance, because nobody asked her. Had Carole been thus neglected, although she 'didn't like dancing', she would have taken it very personally indeed.

Jude didn't mind at all. She just wanted to go home.

But it would be a while yet. Her transport, Carole, who 'didn't like dancing', was in vigorous motion on the dance floor, mirroring the movements of the Heil-Hitlering young man in front of her (yes, it was a continuation of his Basil Fawlty impression).

Her neighbour, Jude concluded with an inward giggle, was actually a little bit pissed. Tired after the evening's concentration on trying to get Olly Pinto to deliver at least a few lines of genuine George Bernard Shaw, Carole had gulped down the first two glasses of wine quicker than she normally would. And now Jude found herself witnessing something she had longed for but never expected to see – Carole Seddon casting off at least some of her inhibitions.

Jude didn't want any more to drink, and wondered mischievously how an offer that she, being the more sober, should drive the Renault back to Fethering would go down with her neighbour. No, probably not a good idea.

She looked around St Mary's Hall. The main sets of *The Devil's Disciple* had been dismantled with surprising speed. Jude could not keep out of her head Lysander's line from *A Midsummer Night's Dream*: 'So quick bright things come to confusion.' There was always a pleasing melancholy about the ending of a theatrical production. The stage crew, encouraged by copious draughts of beer, were still stripping away flats and props. Gordon Blaine was at the centre of the operation, clearly happier doing something useful than trying to be sociable.

And, moved from the wings to the body of the hall, stood the chaise longue. Almost unnoticed by audience and critics alike, it had delivered another sterling performance. Jude didn't think she'd suggest taking it home in the Renault that evening. Carole seemed to be enjoying herself too much for that. They could pick it up another day and take it back to Woodside Cottage. Where it could wait, draped with throws and cushions, till it received its next summons to become part of the magic of the theatre.

Eventually it was clear that Carole's programme of dancing had come to an end. When they stopped, the young man of the Basil Fawlty impressions wrapped her in a bear-hug and it was a rather flushed Carole Seddon who came across to join Jude.

'Promise me I'll see you on the next production, Carole!' the young man called after her.

'Oh well,' she said with a little giggle. 'Never say never.'

Carole had driven with intense concentration from St Mary's Hall back to Fethering. She had not infringed any speed limits or deviated from a line exactly parallel to the kerb of the road. But she had driven rather slowly.

And outside Woodside Cottage she had kissed and hugged Jude rather more effusively than she sometimes might have done. But it was only when she fumbled with the keys of High Tor and had difficulty getting the relevant one into the lock that it occurred to her she might be a little bit drunk.

'Cold water,' she thought. 'Drink lots of cold water.'

As she moved towards the kitchen, Gulliver rose from his favourite position beside the Aga to greet her. As the dog looked up, she wondered if she was being fanciful to see reproach in his large, melancholy eyes.

Then she noticed the single red digit on the answering machine. She fumbled for the playback button and pressed it.

'Mother,' said the rather formal voice of her son Stephen, 'I thought you might like to have some explanation of these stomach upsets Gaby's been getting. Well, we've had the twelve-week scan today and it's confirmed. We thought you'd like to know . . . you're going to be a grandmother again.'